PERFORMANCE, MOVEMENT AND

Theatre and Performance Practices

General Editors: Graham Ley and Jane Milling

Published

Theatre and Performance Practices explores key performance practices encountered in the study of modern and contemporary theatre. Each book in the series charts the critical and historical development of a mode of performance practice and assesses its contemporary significance. Designed to inspire students, scholars and practitioners, the series asks, what are the choices and responsibilities facing performance-makers today?

Performance, Movement and the Body

MARK EVANS

macmillan
international
HIGHER EDUCATION

RED GLOBE
PRESS

First published 2019 by
RED GLOBE PRESS

Red Globe Press in the UK is an imprint of Springer Nature Limited, registered in England, company number 785998, of 4 Crinan Street, London, N1 9XW.

Red Globe Press® is a registered trademark in the United States, the United Kingdom, Europe and other countries.

ISBN 978–0–230–39253–3 hardback
ISBN 978–0–230–39251–9 paperback

This book is printed on paper suitable for recycling and made from fully managed and sustained forest sources. Logging, pulping and manufacturing processes are expected to conform to the environmental regulations of the country of origin.

A catalogue record for this book is available from the British Library.

A catalog record for this book is available from the Library of Congress.

This book is dedicated to Vanessa Oakes.

Contents

General Editors' Preface

This series sets out to explore key performance practices encountered in modern and contemporary theatre. Talking to students and scholars in seminar rooms and studios, and to practitioners in rehearsal, it became clear that there were widely used modes of practice that had received very little critical and analytical attention. In response, we offer these critical, research-based studies that draw on international fieldwork to produce fresh insight into a range of performance processes. Authors, who are specialists in their fields, have set each mode of practice in its social, political and aesthetic context. The series charts both a history of the development of modes of performance process and an assessment of their significance in contemporary culture.

Each volume is accessibly written and gives a clear and pithy analysis of the historical and cultural development of a mode of practice. As well as offering readers a sense of the breadth of the field, the authors have also given key examples and performance illustrations. In different ways each book in the series asks readers to look again at processes and practices of theatre-making that seem obvious and self-evident, and to examine why and how they have developed as they have, and what their ideological content is. Ultimately the series aims to ask questions about what are the choices and responsibilities facing performance-makers today?

Graham Ley and Jane Milling

Acknowledgements

Movement and theatre have been lifelong passions of mine, and the time I have been able to spend over the years with movement experts, teachers, directors and performers has provided me with endless provocation, stimulation and friendship. I am very grateful to all of these fellow movers for everything they have contributed to this book through their enthusiasm, passion, dedication, thoughtfulness and criticism. I hope that I have done their work justice.

I would like to thank all those who agreed to be interviewed for this book for allowing me permission to use their words: Peter Elliott, Scott Graham, Steven Hoggett, Kristine Landon-Smith, Struan Leslie and Gareth Taylor. Their passion for and knowledge of this field has been an inspiration. Thanks also to Katy Morrison and Laura Grimes for their assistance with the transcription of the interview material. Numerous colleagues and students have provided challenging conversations that have informed the development of this book – and I thank them for their imaginative and critical questioning. A short section in Chapter 5 is drawn directly from my article 'Playing with history: Personal accounts of the political and cultural self in actor training through movement', in the *Theatre, Dance and Performance Training* journal special issue on Training, Politics and Ideology (5: 2), published by Routledge in 2014 (www.tandfonline.com/doi/full/10.1080/19443927.2014.907823). I am grateful to Routledge for permission to use material from the journal in this book.

My particular thanks go to Jane Milling and Graham Ley, the series editors. Their patience and understanding over the writing of this book has been saintly. Their editorial comments have been invaluable, as has their enthusiastic support for the project. I would also like to thank the editorial staff at Red Globe Press (formerly Palgrave) who have been wonderfully helpful over the preparation of this book: Kate Wallis, Lucy Knight, Nicola Cattini, Clarissa Sutherland and, most recently, Sonya Barker.

Finally, I would like to thank my wife, Vanessa, for her patience, love and wisdom, and Belle and Rubis, who have lightened my days and distracted me when I needed it.

1 Introduction: The Body in Theatre Performance and Training

A central theoretical position that informs this book is that the actor/performer's body has a cultural history and significance, as do the skills and techniques it acquires and uses and the processes through which such skills are taught and learnt. More importantly, what is central to this book is the belief that the processes that are variously used to teach, direct, share and perform those skills, and the ways in which the teaching practices and performance processes are conceptualized, also have a history and a social and cultural purpose. This book therefore engages in the complex and challenging activity of talking about the body – how bodies are used in theatre and performance, how they are created through theatre and performance, and how they can become products of theatre and performance. This is a complex activity because on so many levels the body is always evading our ability to pin it down through words.

Talking about the body necessitates talking about ourselves as embodied subjects. In places in this book, this will mean that, contrary to academic convention, it will be necessary for me, the author, sometimes to write from a personal perspective. To write in this way recognizes that movement is not just something that 'someone' does, it is something that 'I' do, something that I experience, and in a more profound sense something that I am. It is to recognize that, at the same time that movement enables me to be conscious of my being in the world, it also enables me to reflect on, to resist and to challenge the ways in which power operates on my own body and on the bodies of others. Writing about how the body functions as a way of knowing the world, as a means of representation of the world, and as something creating meaning within the world, will therefore sometimes necessitate that I write about my own experiences or from my own perspective.

For the purposes of this book, movement is broadly defined both as physical activity that is personal, intentional and expressive, and also as a set of established professional practices within the entertainment industry. One hundred years ago, forms of theatre movement practice and of movement training for acting and performance were quite clearly prescribed and largely traditional in nature. Performers would learn acrobatics, fencing, social dance, good posture, and perhaps even *pantomime blanche* (or silent mime), skills necessary for the stage but not directly related to the psychophysical techniques of acting as we might now understand them. These older physical skills would normally have been self-taught or acquired through instruction by older company members. Movement as a field of practice in its own right, until the early decades of the twentieth century, existed only as a marginal, low status and possibly eccentric set of practices.[1] Over the last century, the body and its capacity for expression through movement have been increasingly recognized as a central concern for the aspiring performer. The recognition of and interest in movement within performance during the twentieth century marks a significant change in the extent to which the body is acknowledged as an important component of subject identity representation and construction. There has also been a corresponding development in our understanding of how the body works in movement, its relationship to the making of meaning and its possibilities for communication.

The journey towards the recognition of a separate discipline of movement practice began with the development of a more scientific understanding of the emerging subject field in the late nineteenth and early twentieth centuries. This development was built upon the work of early European pioneers in the analysis of human movement such as François Delsarte (1811–1871), Émile Jaques-Dalcroze (1865–1950), Étienne-Jules Marey (1830–1904), Eadweard Muybridge (1830–1904) and Rudolf Laban (1879–1958).[2] Conceiving that there might be common principles that underpinned movement allowed practitioners to analyse movement in its own right and to construct regimes for training which enabled the student to make expressive use of such analysis. Such a development increasingly allowed movement practitioners to make a case for movement as a central skill necessary for the modern actor, and as central to the making and performing of good theatre.

Jacques Copeau (1879–1949) was one of the first theatre practitioners to recognize this development. Having witnessed Dalcroze's work on eurhythmics in the summer of 1916, he brought in a former student of Dalcroze, Jessmin Howarth, to teach movement to his actors. Later his preference changed to the natural gymnastics of Georges Hébert, but, in both cases, he saw the movement work as more than just a discrete set of skills; instead they offered the actor a way of understanding and expressing the dynamics of the drama they were presenting (Evans, 2018: 17–18, 26–27). By the mid-twentieth century, the work of Rudolf Laban and his followers was impacting on the training regimes of Michel Saint-Denis (1897–1971) at the Old Vic School[3] and the work of Joan Littlewood (1914–2002)[4] at Theatre Workshop, Stratford East (Littlewood employed Jean Newlove (1923–2017), a student of Laban, as movement teacher and director for her company). Laban's ability to link an analysis of the dynamics of movement (space, time, weight and flow) with the psychology of character made his ideas and practice particularly appealing for actor trainers and those interested in physically expressive theatre performance (see Mirodan, 2015). The growth of interest in somatic practices during the twentieth century, particularly after the Second World War, represents a recognition of movement, the body and its cultural significances, as far more central to our sense of self than had previously been the case. In 1956 Jacques Lecoq[5] (1921–1999) opened his international theatre school in Paris, which brought together the abstraction of movement developed by Marey and a recognition of the role of movement in our understanding of the world, as developed in the anthropological ideas of Marcel Jousse and the phenomenology of Maurice Merleau-Ponty (Sachs in Evans & Kemp, 2016: 51–58; Sherman in Evans & Kemp, 2016: 59–66). The school's internationalism, its focus on movement as a universal language, and its emphasis on collaborative creation link strongly to the themes of post-World War II humanism and spoke to a generation increasingly interested in the body's potential for theatrical and cultural expression. Other forms of movement and dance practice, such as contact improvisation and *parkour*, have opened up new ways to understand the body in movement. Such forms have further enriched movement practice and performance, also marking the shift of movement out of institutions and onto the streets and other sites and venues and challenging conventional notions of space, weight and touch.

Movement and Culture

We are seldom made aware of the ways in which the exercises we use to train ourselves, or the practices we undertake in order to perform, go to work not just on our bodies, but also on our professional selves (as performers and/ or teachers) and on our ability to negotiate meanings through movement and gesture in the wider world. Nor are we always aware of the history of such exercises and practices. This book does not deal with the provenance of these exercises, which has been examined elsewhere (Callery, 2001; Evans, 2009), but instead it sets out to examine how, within the field of theatrical movement, practice reveals theory and theory informs practice; looking in particular at where current theoretical and practical developments might be taking the training of actors' and performers' bodies and their engagement in performance.

We will look in general terms at the ways in which, and the contexts within which, the actor's body creates meaning and connects experiences: such as within the context of their training and education, and within text-based performance, devised physical performance (including circus and physical theatre), and mediated performance (for example motion capture within the context of film, television, theatre and online gaming). In doing so we will also examine how movement practice can be located within the various professional contexts for the actor/performer. Just as there is no such thing as 'the actor's body' (rather there are multiple bodies), so there is (despite what some practitioners might claim) no one definitive form of practice or mode of training. This book argues that in this sense the actor has to locate their practice both on a micro level (what works for them in terms of their sense of the personal integrity and authenticity of their movement work) and on a macro level (how others read what the actor intends, what the social and aesthetic significances are of their actions, gestures and performances). The inter-relationship between the micro and the macro is of course fluid and dynamic, and at the heart of the performer's work.

Each person has their own cultural history of embodiment, developed through the physical and social education of their bodies. In many instances, our bodies acquire ways of being that are shaped through habitual behaviours, social conventions, injuries, misuse or environmental influences, without our conscious awareness. My own experience of movement has involved varying degrees of training and performance in contemporary dance, biomechanics, circus skills, acrobatics, Feldenkrais Method and Alexander Technique, folk dance, military drill, tai chi, various sports, mime, mask work, clowning, Japanese movement rituals and African dance. In almost all of these activities I was setting out consciously to acquire skills that I believed to be of value to me in the context of my life and my performance practice at that time. I was sometimes self-taught, but often acquired these skills through instruction and repetitive practice.

The Cultural Context of Movement

When I trained in movement practice, what I did not always appreciate while I was studying was the cultural context of the training I was undertaking and the cultural significance of the processes I was allowing to work upon my body. This lack of contextualization is changing, but a historically and culturally aware process is still not the norm within most practical movement workshops and classes. Understanding how we perform surely should also relate to understanding how we were trained to perform, where we were trained to perform, and by whom. Training the body for performance creates effects that become visible and/or evident in performance; effects that are not simply evidence of skill and technique, but that also signify cultural heritage or levels of professionalism, for instance.

Within different cultural and industrial performance contexts, the features of training identified above may manifest in slightly different ways: movement direction within mainstream commercial or subsidized theatre may be delivered by an expert professional movement director, but that is not guaranteed and it may also be delivered by an experienced company member. A future study might valuably examine the extent to which other differences permeate mainstream and contemporary devised physical theatre practices. Are there differences, for example, between the ways in which movement correction is given (verbally or physically, by a movement director or a fellow performer)? How prominent is movement work within the warm-up, rehearsal and performance practices? Where does authority reside within the rehearsal studio; to what extent do economic power and industry hierarchy come in to play? How important is continuous professional development in movement skills? Movement participates in wider assumptions and practices within the world of theatre and performance; such assumptions and practices must surely reflect the socio-economic forces at play within the theatre industry. The examples examined in the chapters that follow attempt specifically to explore how these different contexts are reflected in the nature of the different forms of theatre and performance work.

Theatre training is essentially a twentieth-century phenomenon. Up until the late nineteenth and early twentieth centuries the vast majority of theatre performers learnt 'on the job' and through apprenticeship. The modernist project created a momentum that drove theatre practice towards method, form, style and experiment, and in doing so created a need and a desire for a modern approach to training and to professionalization. In response to the massive social shifts that took place across the industrialized nations during the early part of the twentieth century, the acting profession sought to acquire higher social status and align itself as an art form, not just a craft. In order to achieve this, it was necessary to take a more scientific approach towards preparation for a career on the stage. Training needed to be codified, categorized, systematized and, most notably, it began to take place outside of the theatre companies themselves – not just in conservatoire schools, as it had done in some instances already, but also in laboratories, retreats, studios and ateliers. The professionalization of the actor's body was paradoxically achieved in part through its removal from the theatrical context of the theatre company, in which the age-old model of the apprenticeship had thrived for so long. The other pressure came from changes in the nature of the theatre being performed. New plays in new styles demanded actors with new skills and new abilities. Several of the major innovators in actor training at this time (for example Konstantin Stanislavsky[6] (1863–1938), Edward Gordon Craig (1872–1966) and Copeau) were prompted to set up their own training establishments because they could see that actors already trained in the old ways simply would not be able to adapt to the challenges of the new drama that was emerging at this time.

Embodied Stories and Physical Performance Practice

This book attempts to bring together some of the dominant influences, issues and challenges relating to the actor's body, in training and performance. In order to do so, it will draw on a number of points of reference. Firstly, it will draw on books and articles both on and about movement practice and movement training. Secondly, it will examine examples of contemporary practice, through observation, interviews and case studies. In summary, it will look at the stories that are told about the trained and performing body, and at what stories are written onto/into those bodies, by whom and to what effect. An overarching conceptual framework for this approach comes from Arthur Frank's book *The Wounded Storyteller* (1995). Frank discusses how stories told of and through the body renegotiate our understanding of the ill body. I will aim to use a similar framework in order to consider how the stories we tell about and through the performing body connect our experience of movement, its training, its purposes, its cultural history and values, and its affects, as well as our experience of physically expressive performance. The book will examine the idea that in some important senses the stories that we tell about movement, performance, training and our bodies locate those concepts in our bodies in very important and meaningful ways, emotionally/intellectually, physically/somatically and culturally/conceptually. It will examine the suggestion that individual somatic experiences, however intense, should not be seen as 'deep' experiences except in so far as they become part of stories about and from the body, revealing our bodies to us in all their complexity. That is to say that the effect is not only somatic, but is also written on the moving subject's conception of selfhood. It is the participation of such physical experiences in the stories we tell of our embodiment that connects that experience socially, culturally, politically, such that the experiences 'make sense' of/with/within the student's or performer's body and the wider notions of the body within our culture(s). The journey from experience to consciousness to narrative construction of identity is also at the heart of the performance process, however it is configured. In the words of the formative psychologist Stanley Keleman: 'The body organizes sensations that arise out of tissue metabolism, and this is what we call consciousness. This somatic process is the matrix for the stories and images of myth' (1999: 5).

Frank writes about how modern medicine reconstructs the patient's understanding of their body through the form and language it provides for the stories that patients tell about their illness. By 'story' he means the narratives that patients construct in order to make sense of their experiences. From a reading of Frank, we can consider whether it might also be true to say that movement practice and movement training rewrite the student/ performer's understanding of their self (in much the same way as it rewrites their bodies and their voices) as a form of story and not simply as a set of experiences, tools or techniques. Creating the stories of the training in/of our bodies, for instance, could then be understood as a process of reflective transformation at the end of which the student should be recognizably an actor/performer. One of the students that I interviewed told me how his parents declared when he returned home from his acting school, 'Oh my God, you're standing like an actor' (Evans, 2009: 120). Not only are they recognizing something that has been written on his body, but they are also completing and confirming the story that he has been telling (for/to/about) himself.

Creating the stories of how we perform with our bodies often retells the formative events for our bodies, justifying our bodies' professionalization. As part of the training or performance process, students/actors tell themselves stories about what is happening to them, to their voices and to their bodies. The student actors' bodies and the bodies of trained performers, similar to the bodies of the patients that Frank writes about, are not just the subject matter of their stories, they are the very material on which they are written and also the medium of the writing. Roanna Mitchell (2014) reminds us of the ways in which powerful and dominant stories about our bodies, stories that configure the 'body as servant' (2014: 64), for instance, can as often as they are constructive and supportive be damaging and dangerous – in part because of this interweaving of writer and written upon.

The stories told by actors, performers and students are both personal and social, both physical and cultural: 'It is [the students'] past that now separate them, and they therefore seek to validate the new experiences which bind them together as a group' (Evans 2009: 122). The embodied stories of the student/actor's past become a 'problem' that they are required to identify, confront and rewrite. In UK conservatoires and actor training courses, neutral body work and somatic practices such as the Alexander Technique and the Feldenkrais Method are the processes at the heart of this relearning/rewriting (see, for example, the work of Vanessa Ewan at Royal Central School of Speech and Drama and Niamh Dowling at Rose Bruford College). Since the mid-twentieth century, the approaches of Jacques Lecoq, Rudolf Laban and F. M. Alexander have all been integrated into well-established regimes of movement training for the actor, and the success of these approaches is largely due to the ways in which they enable and support the student/actor[7] in relearning/rewriting their body's expressive potential. Other approaches, such as ballet and contemporary dance, have generally been sidelined as leaving too strong an imprint on the student/actor's body, movement and physicality. The flexibility intended by the neutral body approach which is at the heart of most conservatoire actor training writes a particular form of professional malleability onto the actor's body; efficient, pliant and responsive, the actor's body is prepared for the demands of the modern theatre industry. This flexibility represents an industry need for control of the actor as creative individual and for the actor's submission to efficient practice – both of which clearly reflect the demands of global capitalism within the international entertainment industry.

As the student/actor's body responds to the training, she tells stories about it in order to understand and assimilate the change, to make her transformed body once more familiar to her. This process becomes an important part of the acting process as the students/actors learn to create 'scores' of physical actions, which function to connect: their bodies; the social and cultural contexts within which their bodies are experienced; their inner experiences and how they feel about their bodies; the theatrical style within which they are working; and the fictive world of the characters they are playing. Telling embodied stories is the activity that makes sense of all of this information and of their role in performing it.

We cannot tell the story of the changes to our bodies, or of our transformation into other bodies, without the body as an active referent. The stories told about movement training and performance are also a necessary condition for the actor's body – it cannot be known as an actor's body outside of the stories that construct it as such. Listen to how one acting student at a conservatoire explains the way in which a movement sequence writes onto her body, hinting at the professional importance of this process: 'equally important is the repetitiveness of constantly doing the arm lift and the accuracy of it, just lifting your arm up, so when you do it on stage it's like blinking, it just comes' (Evans, 2009: 136). In my 2007 article on reflective writing, I suggest that creative writing and reflective narrative can transform our understanding of the ways that we write our bodies:

> [Creative] [r]eflective writing is [...] realigned with the body and not simply understood as a mental activity. The students' knowledge and beliefs are revealed and made present, but they are revealed in/through action and not alone through cognitive meta-reflection; they become present in action and practice; they are in this sense revealed as embodied and directly related to the students' creative expression. (Evans, 2007: 73)

The other side of the 'body-as-story' is thus a reconfiguration of how we might write about our bodies, our physical training, and our performance work. The challenge is to look at how students and performers can be enabled to write and read their own stories about their bodies, their embodiment and their use of and engagement with movement practice and the multiple stories around it and which constitute it.

Modernist approaches to acting have emphasized technique and a scientific analysis of the process of acting, an abstraction of the actor's process that provides a metanarrative of acting. This has happened alongside both the emergence of metaphoric clusters–ways in which movement in theatrical performance is conceived and constructed – and the association of forms of practice with specific names and with 'master' practitioners. Modernism and modern technologies of documentation and dissemination have enabled techniques to exist outside of bodies and to be shared without recourse to direct person-to-person transmission. These approaches represent a movement towards abstraction that strives to enable technique to be universal and to enable acting to be taught and acting problems to be diagnosed on an institutionalized basis. In this manner creativity is brought within the forms of production and of social control. The metanarratives at play in this context give authority and provenance to the teacher and to the conceptual understanding of the acting processes to which they adhere. Certainly, in Europe and America, this has meant that actor training has historically delegated responsibility for the development of the actor away from the actor herself and towards the teacher within the drama school or conservatoire. Modernism has led to the metanarrative of professionalism – which requires, embodies and reinforces abstract notions of artistry.

Professionalism has become influential as a concept in the higher education landscape and is not contested and interrogated enough within the academy. It exerts a formidable influence over how we view ourselves and how we view our training and performance work. It implies a particular understanding of depth and rigour with regard to acting skills and techniques, in which they are configured as tools and not as potentially critical approaches to (embodied) knowledge. Physical skill can thus easily become the outcome itself and no longer the process towards something else. Demand for actor training remains very strong. Despite recent evidence that the opportunities for actors are very sparse indeed and the financial rewards often pitiful for many (Merrifield, 2014), the applications for both university theatre courses and conservatoire actor training courses remain healthy. As training opportunities have become diversified and more fragmented (through workshops, collective groups, online communities, and private or alternative schools), what is of interest is the extent to which these alternatives offer opportunities for students/actors to hold on to, or to create, their own embodied stories in ways that might challenge the processes and the dominant narratives present in the traditional training and performance institutions. Can these alternative training and performance contexts help students/actors to find stories in which they are either no longer subject to forces which construct their bodies negatively (as too black, too thin, too fat, too old, too disabled, for instance), or in which their bodies can become expressive in ways that don't fit with the conventional professional narrative (for example physical theatre, *parkour*, immersive theatre, intercultural theatre)? As a student at the Lecoq School in the mid-1980s, I remember how the standard narratives of psychological acting were repeatedly denied to us by the teachers, how the *auto-cours*[8] required us to construct our own stories, how Lecoq used the story of his own sports experience to create the 'twenty movements' exercise, which in turn required us to create our own form of narrative on our own bodies. I valued this difference. But I was aware upon returning to the UK that these 'stories', these practices, had little or no traction in the mainstream theatre context at that time.

The challenge post-Stanislavsky, and even post-Lecoq, is to find a form of training in which the cultural history of these practitioners' work, what I elsewhere call their 'foundational practices' (Evans, 2014: 149–151), is revealed, critiqued and re-constructed by the student. In the context of Lecoq's pedagogy one might variously ask: 'Why twenty movements? Why sports movements? What would the twenty movements for the global twenty-first century acting student be? What might my own twenty movements look like?'

In order to open up critical dialogue around the dominant narratives of movement practice for actors, we need to find ways in which students/actors can identify: how the stories underpinning their acting came to be; what practices they are built on; and what bodies wrote them. Also, we will need to welcome the multiplicity and diversity of student/actor stories, however conflicting, as this diversity will better capture the totality of all the practices and concepts of acting and performance. We should not be afraid of encouraging students and actors to create their own stories around their practice and their embodied experiences. We should acknowledge that while stories will overlap, there is no metanarrative that should go uninvestigated, unresisted and unchallenged. As important as the embodied writing of stories is the act of reading them on the bodies of others and through a wide range of media. What should we look for when we engage with the work of others, and what exactly can and should that act of looking teach us? The skill of the actor can be understood not just as an ability to write stories through and of the body, but also as an alertness to the stories (personal, social and cultural) that other bodies hold. How, for instance, can we find better ways of exploring the intersection between forms of difference (for example age, gender, culture, ethnicity) where, at least initially, the embodied story and the manner in which it is written may feel strange?

Our bodies rewrite the stories of our training through their differences, through their occasional and perhaps inevitable unruliness, through our embodied reactions to the effects of that training and our acceptance of its wider narratives. Similarly, the use of stories within training and performance is not an option but rather an inevitability – if we do not recognize and make use of this as part of our practice, our bodies will still make up their own stories. Abstract concepts such as energy, skill and creativity arise from and encapsulate stories we use to try and explain how certain collections of physical activities and experiences work on/within us. Even intuition might be understood as a place where the story is hidden but still present and where narratives of tacit knowledge can circulate. It has become increasingly necessary for students and performers to understand how various stories reinforce or challenge abstract concepts of movement and the power mechanisms embedded within them. Making such stories our own is the challenge that we face as performers, as students and as teachers; and making those stories of our bodies our own, owning them in the fullest sense, is our moral responsibility. Ownership of our stories offers us a point of resistance, a place from which to attempt to rewrite – or unwrite – what has been written upon our bodies. In this context, processes in training such as the neutral mask can be understood as potentially enabling such 'unwriting'. The neutral body then aligns itself with William Haver's analysis of Deborah Britzman's 'queer pedagogy' as: 'a technique [...] which does not make the world familiar or comfortable [...] but which defamiliarizes, or makes strange, queer or even cruel what we had thought to be a world' (Haver, 1997: 291).

We might profitably look to digital media, not simply as a place where training and performance might, in the not-too-distant future, take place, but as a place where the embodied and written stories of actor training can circulate widely and be critiqued and challenged in a wide range of ways. This would not be to deny the ways in which digital media are themselves compromised by their own histories and constructions of reality and engagement; but nonetheless, digital media still provide interesting potential both to empower the student/performer and to resist a colonialization of the acting process.

The Plan of the Book

The structure and trajectory of this book works outwards from an initial examination of the dominant cultural models for the teaching and practice of movement skills, which are probably broadly familiar to most drama students and professional actors, towards those models that suggest different configurations of the relationship between the actor, the audience and the performance 'text' or event. The student/actor typically experiences movement and movement training in a range of contexts: text-based theatre; improvisation, dance and physical theatre; intercultural theatre practice; and in relation to digital performance within films, television and video games. In all these contexts, a number of themes come into play – issues of cultural difference such as gender, ethnicity and (dis)ability; issues around the relationship between mind and body, social perceptions of the body, and embodiment; issues around physical training/performance and its political implications; and issues around the effects of, and implications for, new digital media. Consideration of these areas of difference will be woven into the chapters of the book, and forefronted where appropriate. Whereas movement and the body has often been a central concern within contemporary experimental performance, this book sets out to consider practices as yet not extensively theorized. Focusing on theatre and performance practice that is well-known and established enables us to look in more detail at how performance and training replicates or resists social norms, and encourages us to question our assumptions about the radical potential of such work.

After the introduction, the second chapter therefore looks at how various movement practices have evolved in relation to the need for the actor to have a systematized approach to embodying both text and fictive character(s) generated through work on text. This is an area of work that was at one stage in the last century the dominant paradigm for actor training. As such it still represents a cultural position for movement and the body in relation to text, voice and the word that is worthy of careful examination. The chapter will critique the ways in which the standard practices normalize the body of the actor or enable difference to thrive and survive. The case studies within the chapter examine practice within the major subsidized theatres, the commercial sector and the leading conservatoires.

The next four chapters consider how movement work has been part of a transition from the dominance of text towards theatre practice that is more richly connected to movement as the source of the actor's expressivity and creativity. The body is also examined as an area of resistance, transgression, transformation and change. These chapters will look at the impact of improvisation, contemporary dance, circus and physical theatre on perceptions of the role and function of movement training for the actor. Whereas the second chapter considers the notion of movement as work (productive, purposeful, structured and 'owned'), these chapters will focus on movement as playful (disruptive, imaginative, carnivalesque), as transitional (involving crossover between influences and practices, such as the impact of dance on circus practices), as inter- and transcultural (offering a site for the exploration of difference and (ex)change), and as mediatized (presented on screen and/or mediated through digital technology). These chapters will include case studies of movement training practices that have been developed by a range of theatre practitioners. Finally, the conclusion reflects on the key concepts developed in the book and the implications for students and practitioners in terms of their own practice.

Notes

1. For example, the Street Acrobats and Risley Dancers mentioned by Henry Mayhew in his 1861 survey of London workers (1968 [1861]: 90–98).
2. See Evans (2009: 18–23, 27–29) and Brennan in Evans and Kemp (2016: 67–78) for more information on Delsarte, Dalcroze, Marey and Muybridge. See Bradley (2009) for more information on Laban.
3. Litz Pisk, movement tutor at the Old Vic School, was an important link between Laban and the Copeau tradition of acting training. For more information on Pisk, see Ayse Tashkiran's introduction to the latest edition of Pisk's book *The Actor and His Body* (2017).
4. See Holdsworth (2006) for more information on Joan Littlewood.
5. For detail on Lecoq, see Murray (2003 and 2010) and Evans and Kemp (2016).
6. This spelling is used throughout this book, in line with contemporary scholarly practice, except where the former spelling, Stanislavski, is used in book titles or quotations.
7. This hybrid term is used, when the context is appropriate, to represent both the trainee actor and the actor who has been trained as part of a continuum of movement development and expression.
8. Lecoq set weekly tasks for student groups to create their own responses to set themes. These would then be shared with fellow students and staff for critique.

2 Moving into the Mainstream

Mainstream Theatre and Movement – An Overview

In considering the role of movement performance and movement training within mainstream theatre, it is first necessary to establish what is meant by the term 'mainstream'. This is complicated by the fact that the mainstream is both culturally invisible (in the sense that it is the assumed norm) and constantly adapting and changing. As John Bull suggests, 'It is as if its constitution, its shape and its location were so obvious as to need no placement' (2004: 326). For many people in Western industrialized societies, the mainstream theatres (for example London's West End, New York's Broadway, the major state subsidized theatres of Europe) can be among the first places in which they experience live professional theatre, and are consequently the archetype for theatre practice. Mainstream theatre, if understood as both 'serious' subsidized theatre and large-scale commercial theatre, still accounts for the vast majority of theatre attendance in the UK. For actors, success in the subsidized theatre sector is still seen by many as an indication of achievement and status – an attitude reinforced by their training experience, their social networks, familial expectations and society at large. Although theatre produced within this definition of the mainstream may sometimes offer alternative social visions and may critique societal norms, it still does so within a generally conventional approach to the practice and production of theatre. Mainstream theatre is normally made in particular ways, within particular buildings and particular hierarchical structures of employment relationships. Within mainstream theatre, acting is predominantly seen as work – serious, purposeful, structured and 'owned'.

Bull sees mainstream theatre as partly defined by location and partly by text/performance/reception (2004: 328). This chapter will seek to explore how the tension implicit in this relationship between the spaces that mainstream theatre is made in and the processes used to produce it, as well as the experiences and attitudes of those involved in directing movement within mainstream theatre, play out within the field of movement and the actor's body. In so far as mainstream theatre is a powerful force in respect of popular taste it also acts as a significant influence on the curriculum of conservatoire actor training and to a lesser extent on that of schools and universities. As such, mainstream practice does much to determine dominant trends in both movement practice and movement training, and to sustain and defend those practices that, in the view of the mainstream theatre industry, best suit its needs at any moment in time.

Mainstream theatre practice generally draws extensively on the approaches developed by a limited number of twentieth-century practitioners. The dominant figure in this landscape is Konstantin Stanislavsky, and, to a lesser extent, others who have interpreted his work within their own national, social and cultural contexts (see Pitches and Aquilina (2017) for detail on the global dissemination of his practices). The Stanislavskian approach that the mainstream theatre industry and the conservatoires tend to utilize means that most movement work is already ideologically orientated towards naturalism and realism. Within this context, the movement practices employed generally stem from a small number of practitioners whose work can be easily assimilated into these dominant approaches to acting. Stanislavsky's System, and its later developments the Method of Physical Action and Affective Analysis (see Benedetti, 1982; Carnicke, 1998; Merlin, 2003), do not propose particular approaches to movement beyond the need for a certain level of facility. They require a body that is prepared, alert, aware, fit, flexible and responsive (Stanislavski, 2008: 355–380). His later focus on physical actions – 'small, achievable tasks of an outer nature' (Merlin, 2001: 17) – meant that intention, emotion and physical movement could all be integrated within the actor's work in the creation of a 'score' of physical actions, linking the physical life of the character with the text. His approach to movement and embodiment, as he describes it in *An Actor's Work* (2008), combines a psychophysical approach with more conventional training in dance, Swedish gymnastics, fencing and acrobatics (2008: 351). His ideal of the body that is 'compact, strong, developed, well-proportioned, well-built' (2008: 357) indicates the importance to him of a body that is recessive and efficient, movement that has 'definition and finish' (2008: 359), a body that draws attention to the actor's will and not to their physicality or physical difference. The movement practices adopted by conservatoires to achieve this facility include those developed by Rudolf Laban, Jacques Lecoq, F. M. Alexander and, to a lesser extent, Moshe Feldenkrais. Interestingly, these practitioners developed their ideas as a reaction against the mainstream of their times, as an attempt to challenge and reinvigorate practices that had become moribund and disconnected from the experience of contemporary life. The transformation of these processes of care and experimentation for the embodied self into training commodities and professional toolkits for the actor is a process that has over the years somewhat eroded their perceived radicalism. The relationship between the centre and the margins of movement practice is thus revealed as historically complex, fluid, politicized and generative.

The emphasis within large-scale subsidized and commercial theatre on text-based naturalistic performance means that the actor feels obliged to adopt an approach to movement that is systematic, consistent and reliable, as change and variation is not generally desirable within this industrialized performance context. Working from text to create a convincing, 'truthful' and endlessly repeatable portrayal of character has, for the last hundred years at least, been the dominant skill that actor training has sought to develop. If film and cinema eventually functioned to remove the need for such consistent repetition of a quality performance, it arguably did so only in a manner that reinforced the general value of such consistency.

Locating Mainstream Movement Practices

My intention in this chapter is to look at key locations in which movement training and practice is explicitly engaged within mainstream theatre in the UK. The chapter will therefore include a case study of movement practice over a specific period of time at a major international theatre company, the Royal Shakespeare Company (RSC), a case study of the work of a successful mainstream movement director (Steven Hoggett), and a brief review of conservatoire movement training. The breadth, profile and variety of the RSC's work, as well as its international status, its production standards and its relationship to both the subsidized and the commercial theatre world, make it an ideal example of mainstream practice. Steven Hoggett's career in movement direction is a useful example of the ways in which the mainstream sector has come to recognize the market value of the exciting and distinctive movement work developed by small- and medium-scale companies.[1]

The increasingly visible role of movement within the RSC and the commercial mainstream speaks to a wider cultural change that now places greater value on the physical. Movement offers ways of revealing and constructing meanings that are non-verbal and more directly related to our contemporary experiences of embodiment – using the expressive power of touching, carrying, holding, evading or letting go, for instance. The mainstream theatre, through its social, cultural and economic power, tends to normalize the relationships it portrays and the manner in which those relationships are portrayed. Within most naturalistic theatre over the last century this has meant that principal characters, declaiming from centre stage, have functioned to normalize relationships built around such social situations and to normalize the body and its movement as a less significant mode of communication than the voice. Laurence Olivier was, for example, renowned for the physical approach he brought to his roles – however, when John Gielgud and Olivier alternated Romeo and Mercutio in Gielgud's 1935 production of *Romeo and Juliet*, Alec Guinness remarked, 'We all admired John greatly, but we were not so keen on Larry. He seemed a bit cheap and vulgar, striving after effects and making nonsense of the verse' (Beckett, 2005: 39–40). Such attitudes have changed substantially in the new millennium, and the success of a production such as *War Horse* (National Theatre, 2007), which would have been unstageable without the use of movement and puppetry, indicates how far tastes have altered.

However, we will start with a consideration of the role of movement within UK drama conservatoires. How an actor moves is indicative of their personal training history and of their socio-economic positioning as a professional within the industry. The drama conservatoire is one of the options facing the student wanting to study acting. It is the dominant professional model and provides an intensive and focused professional training, recognized by the industry and affirmed by many successful alumni. The other options include university degrees in acting,[2] theatre and/or performance (which may stress self-guided study over practical classes, and are not generally recognized by the industry) or a range of alternative models including workshops, short courses and retreats (which struggle to provide sustained and consistent skill development). Conservatoires have responded to these challenges by seeking degree validation for many of their vocational courses, and adapting their offer to include courses in applied theatre (Royal Central School of Speech and Drama), physical theatre (East 15), or contemporary devised performance (the Royal Academy of Dramatic Art (RADA) and Royal Central School of Speech and Drama).

Movement Training in the Conservatoires

In my book on movement training for the modern actor (Evans, 2009), I describe the history of movement training for acting within the context of the conservatoire training establishments. Historically, formal actor training has had strong links with mainstream theatre in pretty much all of its forms. Early drama conservatoires were often connected to existing theatre companies; RADA[3] was founded by Herbert Beerbohm Tree in 1904 and was initially based at His Majesty's Theatre on Haymarket in the city of Westminster, with the primary aim of training actors for Tree's own productions.

Formal modern actor training, from its origins in the nineteenth century, inevitably focused on the bodies and the movements that were prioritized within the drama of the day. The range permitted was of course fairly broad – plays might include a wide range of characters – but it was nonetheless prescribed and policed.[4] The fact that the training establishments focused largely on preparing actors for a theatre dominated by conservative middle-class attitudes of course meant that the bodies developed and the movement skills learnt were primarily those which would be appropriate to middle-class theatrical tastes. At least initially this meant that the movement skills taught in such schools were largely limited to deportment, social dancing, fencing and stage combat: 'Joan Littlewood famously opined that the theatre training schools, and RADA in particular, taught "poise, propriety and 'tricks of the trade'"' (Shepherd, 2009: 7), effectively turning 'class style into an aesthetic value' (ibid.).

Many schools recognized the need to train actors in voice and speech long before they recognized a need to train the actor's body and movement. Historically, the lower status of movement within the drama conservatoire curriculum in the first part of the last century reflects what might be considered a typically middle-class inhibition with regard to physical expression and a belief that the true and lasting meaning of the drama can only be expressed through voice, speech and text. The institutional status of movement has historically had gender implications as well, with the majority of movement teaching being undertaken by women. All of this, together with a comprehensive history of movement training in the UK, I discuss in my earlier book, *Movement Training for the Modern Actor* (Evans, 2009).

Theorization of mainstream movement practices has been slow to emerge and to become established. There has been a significant sense in which movement training and direction, for much of the twentieth century, was considered a field of work for women and gay men and was largely ignored academically. All of the texts on movement prior to the publication of my own book in 2009 were 'how to' books that outlined technique with little or no explanation of underlying theory or critical analysis of practice. The reasons for this lie in part in the nature of the subject – the accumulation and passing on of embodied knowledge has worked best historically on a model of apprenticeship and practical study. The gender bias of the UK education system has meant that the particular blend of knowledges required for teaching movement (such as dance, physiology, choreography, historical dance and mime) seem to have been knowledges that women were more likely to be encouraged to acquire than men. There is also a pragmatism within mainstream theatre that emphasizes what needs to be done, and how, over why. Much of the sharing and discussing within the field of practice took place informally, between established tutors and their deputies and apprentices, and was largely unrecorded (see Conway, 2008).

Many of the leading teachers at UK drama conservatoires, were, until fairly recently, women (Shona Morris, Vanessa Ewan, Wendy Allnutt, Jane Gibson, Trish Arnold, Jean Newlove, Litz Pisk, Niamh Dowling, Jackie Snow, Lorna Marshall). Gaining a post was, until the last decade, a matter of working one's way in through part-time teaching and forms of informal apprenticeship. The recent rise in formal training for movement teaching (masters-level courses now exist at Central School of Speech and Drama and at Guildhall School of Music and Drama) has created a more professionalized route into teaching and increased the value of theoretical discussion and academic debate within the field. Interestingly there has also been a rise in the number of men now in movement posts within conservatoires, a change driven, no doubt, by shifts in the perception of the cultural status of movement. Most teachers juggle their teaching with periods of professional practice as movement directors in order to maintain their credibility as teachers and to explore their own creativity. It is important to recognize the substantial and important achievement of these women tutors, all of whom have contributed significantly to movement practice within their institutions and in the wider theatre industry.

The majority of student actors studying at UK conservatoires receive a movement training that focuses on the teachings of a small number of male practitioners. They may also experience some movement work based on the teachings of Jerzy Grotowski, Włodzimierz Staniewski, Tadashi Suzuki, Mary Overlie/Anne Bogart (Viewpoints), Eugenio Barba, Gabrielle Roth and others, particularly if an individual or guest movement tutor has a specific interest in one or more from this list. Movement training in the conservatoire classroom almost always has the overall aim of preparing the actor for the challenges of the mainstream rehearsal process; the difference is thus marked out between movement training for actors and movement as a performance approach for other (devised and/or physical) forms of theatre.

In the West, theatre movement training often has at its core what might be described as 'pure movement' work which focuses on the development of the student's understanding of the expressive dynamics of movement as movement. The movement principles of Rudolf Laban, for example, emphasize the development of the student actor's appreciation of space, time, weight, direction and flow. Lecoq's pedagogy focuses on the dynamics of push and pull, and the student's ability to identify with the world around them through movement. Lecoq uses sports movements to help the student build up an understanding of movement analysis and the ways in which movements can be transposed and transformed. In Russia and some parts of Eastern Europe there is a distinctive emphasis on sports training and physical fitness, stamina and flexibility. The work of Russian movement tutor Andrei Droznin, for instance, although based on the psychophysical principles of Stanislavsky, also draws on acrobatics, athletics, yoga, stage combat, calisthenics and coordination exercises (Allain, 2011). Droznin's work is typically physically rigorous and demanding. In Poland, the work of Grotowski is continued at the Grotowski Institute in Wroclaw and through the work of other companies such as Gardzienice and Teatr Pieśń Kozła (Song of the Goat). This work is less 'playful' than the practices of Laban and Lecoq; it is designed to remove the obstacles to the actor's physical expression of their inner impulses through exhaustive fine-tuning of their physical capabilities. In Finland, the Helsinki Theatre Academy includes the development of robust physical fitness through regular exercise and the use of the Cooper test[5] (Kumpulainen, 2012: 229–241).

What the UK conservatoires aim to do is to avoid the restrictive focus of the Eastern European approach to movement training, and, by providing the student with a range of experiences and a physical understanding of the underlying principles of several practitioners, to encourage them to make sense of this diverse range of techniques and methods for themselves. This is achieved partly through a process whereby the student is taught to acknowledge and understand their own physical heritage, and partly through the teacher's efforts to identify ways in which different techniques can be used to achieve the desired learning experience for the student.

The body and his [sic] imagination are [the student actor's] instruments. In his work, he is expected to become many bodies, each behaving differently from his own. He has to construct, inhabit and offer each character's body, with its multiplicity of known and unknown physical expression. (Ewan & Green, 2014: 3)

Alongside general movement practice, the acting student at a conservatoire institution can also expect to learn the marketable skills of social dance, stage dance, period dance, stage combat, and perhaps a limited amount of acrobatics, mask work, clowning and contemporary dance. Skills such as social dance and stage combat are enhanced by a core movement understanding but not reliant upon them. The value of such skills is related to the ability to fulfil certain actions (dancing and fighting) effectively, safely and appropriately for the demands of the play or production, not to their contribution to the students' overall ability to transform themselves into a believable character.

The close relationship between drama conservatoires and the traditional mainstream theatre industry is part of the attraction of conservatoire training for the aspiring actor. Roanna Mitchell has researched the extent to which student actors feel under pressure in such circumstances to achieve a particular body type, which they perceive as having strong market value in the theatre economy.

> Typecasting, beauty ideals, fashions of the body, and the perception of what kind of body is appropriate to perform a specific role – all of these contribute to the importance of the actor's appearance in gaining work, particularly in the commercial performance industry. Here a physical capital marketplace has developed, in which the dynamics of supply and demand are shaped by the number of actors with a certain physicality seeking work at one time, and by assumptions of what type of body is deemed appropriate to perform a certain role or character. (Mitchell, 2014: 61)

Mitchell argues convincingly that, within a variety of contexts within mainstream theatre, actors are encouraged to conceive of their bodies as marketable commodities and as instruments rather than as part of a body-mind that connects themselves as actor-artists to their roles within a larger industry. Within the theatre wardrobe department, for example, their bodies are measured and examined; film and television work may demand partial or full nudity, and sometimes physical intimacy or sex scenes.[6] Professional requirements for the actor's body to be 'on display' in such ways emphasize the need for a particular kind of physical fitness and body shape. It is important, therefore, to remind students that dieting, plastic surgery and working out are not the same thing as acting. Mitchell points out that the use of typecasting within mainstream theatre practice diminishes the importance of the transformational skills of the actor in favour of the actor's ability to match a particular type. In general terms, this kind of attitude portrays the body not as the starting point but as the end point of the student's journey. They strive towards a certain kind of body, rather than developing the expressive potential of the body that they have; all this, despite the very real care and attention that movement tutors give to supporting student actors' personal development. All movement training grapples with this tension between the demands of a voracious industry, the need to equip the student as a freelance professional, and a desire to empower the student on a personal level through enriching their understanding of their personal physicality and its multiple potentialities.

At the same time that actors' bodies are affected by the disciplining power of the training that they undergo, they are also affected by the performance spaces within which they undertake their work, the costumes they are required to wear, and their relationship to other bodies, all of which can also combine to commodify the body and fetishize its attractiveness if the training is not handled with care. The training practices for mainstream theatre outlined above provide an interesting perspective for the examination of two case studies of movement and mainstream theatre. These case studies will illustrate how traditional and non-traditional movement skills and practices are integrated into movement work within the contexts of a large-scale company and of freelance movement direction. They will also help reveal how the tensions between the industry's needs and the student's or actor's personal development can play out within this context.

Locating Movement within a Company Ethos

The Royal Shakespeare Company (RSC) received its royal charter in 1961. The company's origins can be traced back to the opening of the Shakespeare Memorial Theatre in 1875, since when the town had been home to an annual festival of Shakespeare plays. In 1958, Peter Hall became director of the Memorial Theatre Festival and led the movement towards its reorganization into the internationally important ensemble company that the RSC is today. Movement has a special status at the RSC. The company has a long history of employing many of the best and most experienced choreographers and movement directors, as well as offering opportunities for new movement directors to test their skills. For a spell from 2008 to 2013, the RSC was the only major theatre company in the UK with a dedicated movement department and a head of movement. Although its support for movement has subsequently evolved and has been reconfigured around integrated support for voice and movement, the company's long-term commitment to the artistic development of its company members and this particular example of its commitment to movement as an important part of its artistic practice is significant and worthy of examination.

Currently there are very few critical academic texts on the practice, history or genealogy of movement direction at the RSC, or in British mainstream theatre.[7] Struan Leslie (Movement Director for several RSC productions and Head of Movement at the RSC from 2008 to 2013) has written on choral movement in the context of his own work (Leslie in Macintosh, 2012), and Diane Alison-Mitchell has written about her experiences directing movement for the 2012 RSC production of *Julius Caesar* (Alison-Mitchell, 2017). Alison-Mitchell describes the job of the movement director[8] at a company such as the RSC as potentially including:

> dance and choreography; staging; building the ensemble; development of a particular dynamic such as space, rhythm, breath or touch; creation of a movement language; facilitating something that is from the actor's own body knowledge and extending their movement expertise; and looking after the general care of the actor's body and ensuring its preparedness for the physical work ahead. (2017: 147)

Ayse Tashkiran has written a chapter on Lecoq's influence on UK theatre movement direction (Evans & Kemp, 2016: 227–235) and an introduction to the latest edition of Litz Pisk's seminal book, *The Actor and His Body* (2017), that contains interesting details relevant to movement direction in UK theatre. In the meantime, reference to movement work in existing texts about the RSC is very limited or anecdotal, coming largely from autobiographical writings and the reflections of individual actors on their work on specific parts or during specific seasons. RSC directors and actors who have written about the staging of Shakespeare's plays make only passing comment on the role and value of movement; nonetheless, in the past, landmark RSC productions have required skills in Commedia dell'Arte (*Comedy of Errors*, 1963, directed by Clifford Williams) and circus skills (*A Midsummer Night's Dream*, 1970, directed by Peter Brook), as well as involving workshops with major practitioners such as Jerzy Grotowski (*US*, 1966, directed by Peter Brook). More recently productions have made integral use of a variety of movement skills in both the performance and rehearsal process, such as: Michael Boyd's complete cycle of the history plays (2007–2008), *The Song of Songs* (2012), *The Heart of Robin Hood* (2011–2012), *The Orphan of Zhao* (2012–2013) and *Julius Caesar* (2012–2013).[9]

Struan Leslie came to movement direction in the theatre through dance and choreography. He trained at the London Contemporary Dance School in the 1980s, where he was taught by first-generation Graham dancers.[10] He recalls that his dance training also included creative movement classes and animal study. Early on in his dance career he went to America to study with Nancy Stark-Smith and Steve Paxton, with Meredith Monk and with Trisha Brown, leaders in the new wave of postmodern dance practices emerging at that time in the USA. His education with Jane Dudley at London Contemporary was also clearly very influential:

> Jane Dudley used to teach a movement class, so on top of getting Graham technique, once or maybe twice a week we would do movement with Jane. She would get us to do creative movement, be washing machines, I remember, animal studies but from a Dance perspective. It's actually only really recently that I've learnt that Jane Dudley was involved in the Group Theatre[11] in New York in the 1930s, as what we would now call the Movement Director. (Leslie, 2012)

His sense of a developing practice that linked dance with theatre was stimulated by his choreographic experiences and led eventually to an opportunity to work with the theatre director Katie Mitchell.[12] He went on to make over 30 pieces of work with and for Mitchell: new plays, classic plays, operas, but interestingly no Shakespeare. Not coming from a background where he had experienced restrictive boundaries between movement and text, the traditional separations never seemed to have imposed themselves within his work and this provided an interesting starting point for his own practice and for his practice within the RSC.

The momentum behind a movement department at the RSC came from Michael Boyd (RSC Artistic Director, 2003–2013), who was clear that one of the things he wanted to do in his time at the RSC was to elevate movement to the same status as voice. The effect of movement becoming a permanent and visible feature of work at the RSC, as opposed to something that various individuals brought in on a short-term basis, was that practice could become consolidated and networked – both for actors and for movement practitioners. As Struan Leslie states: 'The thing that has changed [...] was that there is an opportunity to consolidate twenty-five years of practice' (Leslie, 2012). Being a part of a large organization, rather than just a freelance visitor, meant longer spells working with the actors and directors in the company, with the education department and with the broader ensemble. At the time, the RSC was also in the process of commissioning a rebuild of the main theatre space. The company made a decision that the rebuilt main theatre space, the Royal Shakespeare Theatre, would be constructed as a thrust theatre space, a horse-shoe auditorium capable of seating around one thousand people on three different levels, with the furthest seat from the stage no more than 15 metres from the centre stage spot. This is not typical for a mainstream theatre, although it is consistent with recent efforts to re-engage audiences more directly with the theatrical experience (for example, the success of theatre spaces such as Shakespeare's Globe, the Young Vic, and the RSC's Swan Theatre space in Stratford-upon-Avon). This significant architectural decision provided an excellent opportunity to consider how the new space made different requirements of the actors' bodies as well as their voices. It enabled both the company and the movement practitioners within it to build a much clearer picture of what each could offer and require of the other. While still in post, Leslie described how:

> As a freelance movement director coming into the company you would just work with that team of actors and maybe do a workshop for the education department. But now, for me, the work divides up into about four or five bits. There's work with the acting company and there's work with the broader company. With the acting company, there is training to work in our spaces with the Shakespeare text, then there is also working with contemporary text, exploring other forms, so that's some of the training work. Then there's being part of a creative team [...] and then support work for movement directors that come in to work in the company. With the larger ensemble, there's everything from setting up weekly core classes, devising workshops around health and safety, lifting at work, to working with the education department, doing workshops for the development department for fundraisers, for benefactors, works with events and exhibitions, work with marketing, so you are doing that all the time. I also sit on the artistic planning group which is just essential even if I am just listening; so, I'm involved in that. Then there's extra curriculum work, so there's the Birthplace Trust wants workshops, drama schools around the country who I believe I should be really seeing on a three-year cycle. I should be in every drama school [...] Then, as and when there is someone else in the department, there's their training and development. (Leslie, 2012)

Of course, the creation of the post and the department, despite their limited duration, was an important statement by the RSC that marked a much broader and wider recognition of the value of movement practice within society and culture. Nonetheless, the job clearly involved a level of advocacy both within and outside the company, just as much as it enabled the RSC to hold discussions with the external industry community that focused specifically on movement practice. Although this specific post and department no longer exists, the company still maintains a commitment to artist development, and to maintaining its connections with the professional development of the movement and physicality of the actors with whom it works. Strong links still exist with the conservatoires – Tashkiran combines movement direction work at the RSC with her role as a senior lecturer in movement and co-course leader of the MA/MFA in Movement: Direction and Teaching at Royal Central School of Speech and Drama, indeed several students from the MA programme have gone on to work with the RSC. Other movement tutors elsewhere in the conservatoire sector have similar links to theatre companies and other areas of professional practice (for example, movement direction for film and television, choreography, motion capture direction).

The challenge in providing such a consolidation and continuity of artist development is that of providing a core of fundamental practice which can underpin the actors' general development while at the same time not working against the practices that any freelance movement director brought in for a particular show might want to use.

> It's about establishing some fundamentals; so, the actors come in and we do an initial period [...] where we will spend six hours with the company, spread over a period of workshops, including a visit to the spaces in Stratford, whereby we will explore some of those fundamentals. The basis of the fundamentals is the '360° body', the idea of that total, holistic bodily connection. So, I guess it goes, 'My body, my body in the space, my body in relation to your body, and our bodies in the space, my body in connection with an ensemble and that ensemble's connection with the space'. (Leslie, 2012)

This is a problem that speaks directly to the way that power operates on the formation of the actor's body. The actor's body is individualized as a tool to be used by the director in the service of the production – mainstream actor training accepts general standards of technical competence, but achieves these through a multitude of means. In the context of commercial theatre production, this doesn't matter – the actor is left to deal with their own movement problems and otherwise does what the choreographer tells them – but in the context of sustained ensemble work, based within a specific set of spaces, this becomes more complicated. Some ways in which a coherent and consistent approach to movement can be maintained then becomes very desirable.

Fundamental movement work within a company such as the RSC, while not seeking to reconstruct the actor's physical self in the same way as a training regime, unsurprisingly seeks to build on the actor's existing ability and previous experience through work that will be familiar and will take them back to a useful and productive level of 'neutral' physical awareness, fitness, strength and flexibility. For Leslie, this meant adopting a pluralistic approach:

> I talk about Laban, I do Pilates-derived work that works on that, I do anatomical work, Somatics; I don't call them any of those things because I will work with them as they arise out of the need of a situation. [...] there is an absolute connection between the body, the breath and the space and those things form the fundamentals. (Leslie, 2012)

One of the other key issues within the company has been the integration of movement and voice. An abiding influence in this area has been the work of Cicely Berry (1926–2018), Voice Director at the RSC from 1969 to 2014. For Struan Leslie, her work 'has been absolutely fundamental in changing the way that people in British Theatre speak and therefore move, because speaking is as she says, words in action' (Leslie, 2012). Berry's work on the rhythm of words and text and on the physical dynamics of antithesis are areas that resonate for movement practitioners such as Leslie: 'the text is a provocation to movement in some way; because of its rhythmic structure, because of its melodic structure; and in this case that repeated vowel structure or the assonance' (Leslie, 2012). The continuing (even if now marginal) influence of Cicely Berry, and the manner in which experience is shared and built upon throughout the company's work and its history, means that the RSC has a privileged place in the mainstream theatre. It is still able to support the sustained exploration and development of practice around movement, breath, voice and text. Leslie speaks of a real sense in which this creates a shared ensemble knowledge, only really possible and available in a company that can stay together and that can foster a continual process of questioning and experimenting. Historically, one of the key problems with movement in mainstream theatre could be summed up as what Leslie describes as 'parking and barking', where movement was simply about getting into position to deliver the text. Such practice was and still is exacerbated by the size and scale of many mainstream theatres – the old Royal Shakespeare Theatre, before the rebuild, was somewhat challenging for actors in terms of the distance from centre stage to the upper circle; the technique and concentration required to communicate across that space didn't leave much energy for movement and physical expression. What the ensemble nature of the RSC enables is the time, space and resource to reach beyond this.

When it was founded in 1961 the RSC had a triumvirate: Peter Hall (1930–2017), Peter Brook (1925–) and Michel Saint-Denis (1897–1971). Saint-Denis, a nephew of the innovative French theatre director and pedagogue Jacques Copeau, had experience of setting up several highly influential training schools (for example, The London Theatre Studio (1935–1939) and the Old Vic Theatre School[13] (1945–1951)): 'As the left-leaning journal *New Theatre* saw it in its survey of London institutions in the mid-1940s, only one school trained actors for the future – namely Saint-Denis's Old Vic Theatre School; the rest merely trained for "today"' (Shepherd, 2009: 7). He was specifically brought in by Hall to develop a studio within the RSC that would develop new skills and new ways of working. In this sense, from its earliest days the RSC was attempting to draw on and integrate new practices. What Saint-Denis also brought to the company (at least for the few years he was able to do so while his health and the required funding lasted) was a commitment to preparing actors to be physically eloquent and expressive in ways that would be meaningful to the increasingly liberated audiences of the 1960s and 1970s. Saint-Denis' practice drew on the work he had done with his uncle at the Théâtre du Vieux-Colombier, with Les Copiaus (the group of young actors and students that Copeau took to Burgundy in 1924), and with La Compagnie des Quinze (the company Saint-Denis formed after the break-up of Les Copiaus in 1929).[14] He brought to his work a rigorous focus on the physicality of the actor, developed through silent improvisation, mask work, mime, chorus work and expressive movement.

Shakespeare and Movement

The performance of Shakespeare and other classic English drama has historically been dogged by associations with a particular kind of theatrical acting style. Perhaps classic renaissance drama does require, or at least invite, a particular kind of physical presence within the space, or offer an opportunity for certain patterns of movement and gesture. At its worst this might manifest itself in an attitude of swagger and bravado or of poetic lyricism. This kind of physical posturing might be encouraged by the flamboyance of the costumes, the excitement of the fight sequences, the grace of the courtly dances, and the speed of the rapid scene changes that pepper many of Shakespeare's plays. At its best, movement work within Shakespeare's plays integrates the kinds of alertness to space, proximity, rhythm and ensemble that such activities as court and popular dance and fencing must have (even implicitly) developed for the Elizabethan and Jacobean actor. One of the roles for the movement director, beyond that of simply choreographing dances and group scenes, might well be understood as that of identifying and addressing movement and gesture that is not inhabited by the actor/character. The movement director can assist the actor in working against their occasional need to 'show off' or ensuring that they do not fall back on bad habits. Actors playing minor roles in a large company such as the RSC may receive limited attention from the director, and clear instruction from a movement director can help them to avoid either insufficient attention to movement or clichéd gesture and action.

To some extent the changes to performance spaces at the RSC have not only reflected changes in movement practice and attitudes towards the body, but have also accelerated such changes. The original Other Place venue, when it opened in 1974, immediately demanded a very different physicality from the Main House. The actors' bodies were no longer distant from the audience, there was a more visceral and immediate quality to the performance event, and movement work could be subtler and more detailed. The Other Place was a natural consequence of the training and studio work that Saint-Denis had initiated in the 1960s. Leslie vividly recalls the differences he experienced as a visitor to both spaces in the early 1980s:

> I went to see Richard Pasco do Timon of Athens,[15] which was amazing and I think it still must have been the tin shed then. It was amazing, the images, I can still see it [...] The other thing was The Winter's Tale in the Main House, and [...] it made no connection with me at all [...] The Other Place of course is what I remember. (Leslie, 2012)

From Leslie's perspective, the RSC body is increasingly 'more aware. It's multi-sensory' (Leslie, 2012), and at least in part that must be the result of a more multi-directional relationship with the audience imposed by a thrust stage. Additionally, by 2012, the culture had changed such that, 'Now in actors' contracts it states that if you are called for a morning call or if there is a movement call and it's full company you have to attend' (Leslie, 2012). The contractual aspect is important – it makes concrete an institutional commitment. Michael Boyd, while he was director of the company, spoke of an industry scepticism around the notion of the theatre ensemble, a scepticism grown from:

> a theatre culture that is heavily influenced by the free market economy of the entertainment industry, where actors are encouraged to move like a commodity on the stock market, where any restriction of that degree of nimble flexibility is seen as leaden, and stifling. (Boyd in Radosavljevic, 2013: 39)

His blend of movement words ('nimble' and 'flexibility') with the language of capitalism and the marketplace is particularly telling. In the same interview, he talks of the benefits for the company of sessions with Pascale Lecoq and Krikor Belekian from the Laboratoire d'Etude du Mouvement at the Lecoq School in Paris: 'Most of the company found it really, really useful. Some found it pretentious and nothing to do with "what I do"' (Boyd in Radosavljevic, 2013: 37). Institutional leadership is clearly enormously important in (re)defining, defending and maintaining the role of movement within a mainstream organization.

This level of institutional commitment helps to transform movement practice from a tool that can effectively be ignored by student actors after the end of their second year of training into a skill that needs to be maintained, refreshed and developed on a regular basis – both individually and within the context of a company as a whole. The demands of working in a mainstream company like the RSC can easily take its toll on an actor and result in tiredness and in falling back on bad habits. As Richard Cave suggests, 'Actors [need] frequently to learn ways of caring for their bodies in the face of such demands' (Cave, 2015: 176). Somatic practices, such as yoga and the Feldenkrais Method are generally non-threatening to the professional actor, and allow a degree of individual responsibility for physical care while still operating within the context of the ensemble as a whole.

The development of movement practice within a company of the size and status of the RSC will always rely not just on what it can offer internally (in terms of regular movement sessions, warm-ups and work on productions), but also on its ability to bring in and integrate new practices and processes. This might happen through the influence of a particular actor:

> Katherine Hunter[16] is a big yoga person and so she was asking if there was a possibility of us doing yoga. So, we did some yoga and then had conversations about it, about how it works, and the relevance of that. (Leslie, 2012)

Clearly, even for such a large organization as the RSC, specific movement requirements might sometimes be identified that can only be addressed by bringing new working practices in, even on a short-term basis. The RSC is big enough to have the resources to do this – smaller mainstream companies (regional repertory companies, major touring companies or some commercial companies) rely on employing company members or freelancers who already have the relevant skills, or on bidding for additional funds to buy in specific expertise. Furthermore, because the RSC has the resources to put in place an artist's development programme and to keep key actors within the ensemble for sustained periods of time, it is able to reap the benefits from actors developing a range of skills: 'I think actors leave the RSC with more skills after than before they arrive' (Leslie, 2012). Accessing new ideas and practices is therefore an important part of the role that an artist development programme can play. Bringing in new practices is part of the process by which conventional practices are refreshed, challenged, renewed and even replaced. But there is a particular dynamic at play here: the cultural hegemony of the dominant theatre forms and practices means that certain new practices will inevitably struggle to be seen as anything more than an esoteric one-off, as an optional alternative, or they will risk being quickly subsumed into more conventional practice to the point where they lose their distinctiveness. In this way, the radical impact of new practices introduced into the mainstream can be diluted and the social, political and cultural challenges that they might embody become compromised. Practice that might emphasize collaboration, or cultural difference and diversity, might find that it is only taken up on a superficial or limited level and that the deeper changes to making and per-forming are not implemented. By the same token, not all new methods and practices may have lasting value – some (and mime, dance/theatre or *parkour* might be seen as historical and contemporary examples of this) may become fashionable because they are 'new', but have limited long-term benefits and may relatively quickly become unfashionable.[17] Without support and guid-ance, the actor may struggle to make sense of various different approaches and to find a way of usefully integrating them into their practice. In the same way, what may be useful at an individual level (yoga for relaxation and stretching) may not be useful in the context of ensemble work and the needs of a specific production or set of productions.

For a large national company like the RSC, there is also a sense of obli-gation towards the wider industry and its future development. The role of the movement director is often, but not always, a solo one. Working within the mainstream can be an extreme example of this – the movement director is still often called in only to solve specific 'problems': a dance here, a rou-tine there. But the mainstream, by its very size and scale, can also in some instances provide opportunities for movement directors to work more closely with company ensembles, directors, designers and individual actors. In some instances, movement directors may actually, or in effect, be key members of the company's artistic team (for instance, Cheek by Jowl and Jane Gibson; Frantic Assembly and Scott Graham).

What has been lacking, certainly within the UK, is a place where movement directors can come together and engage in conversation and the sharing and exchange of practice. In some respects, the development of the MA/MFA Movement: Directing and Teaching at Royal Central School of Speech and Drama, together with the International Community for Movement curated by Ayse Tashkiran, have helped start to create such spaces. More recently, in 2018, a couple of young movement directors have started a self-help network, MoveSpace (http://movespace.org.uk) to enable discussion and sharing. However, more still needs to be done to establish effective links between training, professional practice and research. In September 2010, the RSC, in collaboration with the University of Kent, offered an example of what might be possible with its 'In the Body' event, which brought together UK movement practitioners, some movement and actor training academics, and a number of students of movement practice, for an event that enabled UK practice to be shared and discussed, and that also provided an opportunity to experience and discuss the working methods of the Russian movement teacher Andrei Droznin[18] and some of his colleagues. Institutions such as the RSC and the National Theatre[19] have a key role to play in supporting such opportunities.

The mainstream theatre industry is a field in which practices and ideas are often heavily exploited for profit; even in the subsidized sector the generation of profit/surplus has become more or less essential for longer-term survival. The financial value of shows such as *Les Misérables* and *Matilda* for the RSC and *War Horse* and *One Man, Two Guvnors* for the National Theatre is significant. This means that individual movement directors and practitioners can experience substantial economic pressure to become protective of their work and their processes, making collaborative dialogues and exchanges more difficult to establish and maintain. The differences, often evident through and created by each individual's history of training (Laban, Lecoq, Alexander, contemporary dance, etc.), also participate in this economy of movement practice. Collaboration and the exploration of commonality are not necessarily as easy as one might think, and lack perceived value within the mainstream theatre industry.

It goes back to my dance school days, people who were at Laban didn't talk to people who were at The Place. In the same way as people who went to Lecoq are people who went to Lecoq, everybody's 'other' instead of identifying commonality. (Leslie, 2012)

Work environments that enable these sorts of exchanges would surely be beneficial to all. Large-scale companies such as the RSC and some of the larger repertory and production companies might find that enhancing the offer to actors and to movement practitioners (through collaborative workshop opportunities, for instance) would help to attract interesting people into their work processes to mutual benefit, as well as benefiting their actors and directors through skill and knowledge development.

The changing economic pressures on the theatre industry from online gaming, 3D cinema and HD digital television mean that audiences are also expecting something extra: 'more precision and more eloquent physical expressions and more multi-dimensional physicality' (Leslie, 2012). On the one hand these kinds of expectation can be seen to work against experimentation within the industry, but on the other it is clear that at least one way of realizing such expectations is by engaging in experimentation – the cost of development time and experiment can be recouped several times over if this process works. Audiences are increasingly excited by the imaginative physical solutions that movement can offer to complex staging problems.

Audiences also have cultural expectations of organizations such as the RSC. Changing audience demographics over the lifespan of such companies means that audiences now are more willing to accept different kinds of production and different kinds of actors. Over time, and thanks to the funding of training for students from disadvantaged backgrounds and to arts policies that support changes in casting practices, the cultural background of the actors (and the movement directors who work with them) has also changed. Audiences for many mainstream shows can expect to see more ethnic and gender diversity in the casting of productions, even if areas of difference still remain under-represented (Kean & Larsen, 2016). The economics of the acting profession unfortunately mean that it is still hard for someone from a disadvantaged background to consider such a career. An actor will typically need to consider the costs of attending a drama conservatoire, as well as being able to survive long periods of unemployment or under-employment (short periods of employment on relatively low wages). A movement director will typically have had to study dance, acting or movement to degree level (or equivalent), perhaps have undertaken some level of postgraduate training and education, and possibly also have had a period of apprenticeship and/or professional experience. In addition, they will have to cope with a peripatetic lifestyle and short-term contracts. These conditions certainly make it harder for people whose families are not able to support them, and who do not have alternative or independent sources of income or support. Many movement directors find it necessary to teach movement (at least on a part-time or occasional basis) and develop other forms of income-generating activity. The relative financial security of close association with a large company can clearly help to address this.

The consequence of the absence of people from disadvantaged backgrounds from various parts of the theatre-making process is that it is then more likely that the movements, gestures and physical cultures of these social groupings will either not be represented or may be misrepresented. Furthermore, if they do make it through to a successful career, such practitioners may find that they do so only by distancing themselves from their own culture's movement heritage and becoming absorbed into a predominantly white European middle-class heritage. Fortunately, many such cultural limitations are less restricting than they were 50 years ago, but it is worth noting that 50 years ago working-class student actors were at least able to apply for full student grants to support their studies.

Major companies have tried to address the challenges posed by an increasingly culturally diverse society. The RSC, for instance, has worked over the last decade to develop a colour-blind casting system (a complex and contestable process as will be explored in Chapter 5) as well as a nursery for company members with child-care responsibilities. Movement directors are now sensitive and alert to the many kinds of cultural difference and the relationship of such difference to effective movement work. This might involve considering the vocabulary and reference points they use in talking about and instructing movement work, as well as an openness to different forms of physical expression:

> The thing that I'm being clearer about is that the movement work aims to make a connectedness within your body, to your body, with the space, with the text, with the ideas, with the Director, with your colleagues. That idea of connectedness within your own body is only possible with your body. So, my body is different from your body; and this is quite a fresh way of talking about it. Instead of talking about neutral, as in postural neutrality, actually I just want postural connectedness – I don't want it, I seek for people to arrive at that, so that there's a connectedness. If that's connected then we have a connection between the body and the breath. So, the thing that I am making more and more clear to people is that I am not here to change you, what I am here to do is to make your body more connected and therefore more efficient and more flexible and more responsive to what's going on in the room. (Leslie, 2012)

Within the mainstream theatre industry, movement work will often involve more than just working on the general movement facility of the actors – it may include choreography, stage combat, flying and aerial work, perhaps even acrobatics. Not all of these would conventionally come within the remit of the movement director, and in some areas the demarcation of roles is very clear and even contractual – the movement director and the fight director might meet and talk, but one would not usually encroach on the professional work of the other. Equally the same person may simply not be equipped to fulfil so many roles to the level required: 'not all choreographers are movement directors and not all movement directors are choreographers' (Leslie, 2012). Inevitably this means that the possibilities for crossover and collaboration can vary markedly within the mainstream, and where it does occur it is likely to be limited by contractual issues, union concerns, health and safety issues and associated demarcations of responsibility.

Integrating Contemporary Collaborative Movement Practice

Struan Leslie's career trajectory speaks of the ways in which various techniques, which might not normally be associated with the mainstream, are drawn in from the margins to create an approach that can sit comfortably and meaningfully within the mainstream. A more recent example of this process is also evident in the experiences of Steven Hoggett. Hoggett began his career in theatre as one of the founding directors of Frantic Assembly.[20] After nearly two decades with Frantic, Hoggett took the decision to leave the company to pursue work as a freelance movement director in the UK and the USA. He has been movement director for a number of highly successful productions, including: *Black Watch* (2006, National Theatre of Scotland, subsequent revival and international tour), *Once* (2011, West End and Broadway), *American Idiot* (2010, West End and Broadway), *Rocky the Musical* (2014, Broadway), *Let the Right One In* (2013, West End), *Harry Potter and the Cursed Child* (2016, West End and Broadway), has been nominated for several prestigious awards, and won an Olivier award for his choreography for *Black Watch*.

Hoggett's experience speaks very much of the ways in which new approaches to movement and choreography find their way into mainstream practice. He recognizes that, despite quite significant cultural changes over the last 30 or so years, movement and physicality that is outside the existing conventions of musical theatre and standard acting practice is still not accepted as part of the vocabulary of mainstream theatre. He refers to the need to:

> sneak the information in, in a way that feels very generous and very steady, and quite simplistic [...] making sure you don't stride out too much. And that, if you are doing something beyond naturalism, that you are educating an audience in that first twenty minutes. (Hoggett, 2014)

Within the mainstream theatre world, audiences don't primarily go to see shows because of the choreography or movement work and are unlikely to know who the movement director is before the show, despite the fact that the movement may well be one of the elements that, after the performance, they recognize as integral to its success. Contemporary mainstream theatre producers and directors are increasingly enthusiastic about tapping into innovative practices. Some, such as John Tiffany,[21] with whom Hoggett now frequently collaborates, have actively sought out new practices and have recognized how movement work can help solve difficult staging problems. However, this kind of relationship is by no means always the case for movement directors, and without a clear understanding between all involved tensions can arise between traditional practices and new ways of working. If casting agencies and directors don't understand the processes involved in making innovative movement performance work, for instance, then actors may be contracted who will struggle to engage with the process. Additionally, producers may have to acknowledge the need to set aside time for new skills, processes and practices to be explored and developed, or for movement directors to audition the actors to ensure that they can adapt to a particular way of working and that they have an adequate level of physical ability.

Actors working within the mainstream may, in many cases, not have been required to work in new and different ways for a long time. In the commercial sector, there may be a strong company ethos within a production team, but that does not necessarily extend into ensemble ways of creating, rehearsing and making work, something some actors may never have been asked to do in the past. Patterns of working in commercial and mainstream shows may mean that actors are only required on stage for 15 minutes and spend the rest of the time in their dressing rooms; it is easy for that to be reflected in attitudes to rehearsal and in actors' approaches to movement work – what Hoggett describes at its worst as, 'they turn up, they do their turn, they don't move much [...] then they go sit downstairs, or sit down in the rehearsal room' (2014). Creating a physical language with a group of performers can become a complex and difficult part of putting on a show when the casting process takes only experience into account and not adaptability and creativity.

Hoggett is positive about the changes in attitude and physical ability that he sees within the industry:

> I think that performers are getting smarter to what the challenges of a modern theatre ecology are [...] it is about that training that you have at drama school, that physicality. And no matter how rich or spare it was, there are a lot of people asking that of [them] now, more than there ever were before. (Hoggett, 2014)

This undoubtedly reflects the fact that more movement work has been integrated into mainstream theatre practice over the last decade. Hoggett has, for instance, worked with directors such as Marianne Elliot (*The Curious Incident of the Dog in the Night-time*, National Theatre, 2012) and Vicky Featherstone (Paines Plough, National Theatre of Scotland and Royal Court Theatre, London) who are confidently adopting a more physical and collaborative approach to their whole rehearsal process. Hoggett sees this as a clear cultural shift:

> I think it's in everybody's mind now; there is something about the way, as an artistic community, that even though people want choreographers and movement directors in the room, they are actually doing it themselves anyway. And Rufus [Norris][22] is the same, Michael Mayer[23] is the same. There are lots of directors that you are not teaching anything, you are actually just working alongside them. (Hoggett, 2014)

The National Theatre production of *War Horse* is widely recognized as a game-changer in this respect, but, as Hoggett points out, this is not simply because of the puppetry and movement work, but because of the realization of a whole process that had movement work embedded at the heart of it:

> I think what was great about *War Horse*, is that between Tom [Morris] and Marianne [Elliot], they genuinely created a brand-new type of process. And she [Marianne Elliot] saw that through on *Curious* [*The Curious Incident of the Dog in the Night-time*] as well, where you don't see the joins between the different creative teams. (Hoggett, 2014)

In this sense movement direction has increasing capital within the industry through its ability to enable the creators and producers of shows to access a broader and wider palette of dramatic and theatrical expression. Producers, as always, are thinking about successful shows; movement direction has encouraged producers and directors to think bigger and bolder in terms of what might be achievable and stageable.

While Broadway and London's West End have historically been the homes of theatrical choreography, movement directors such as Hoggett have offered something very different and something that is increasingly perceived as having value. For Hoggett, America

> was always ready to look for people that weren't the normal, archetypal choreographer, but sit within that realm and have that title next to their name. America is greedy, and it's also intuitive, it's promiscuous, and all those things, so if you rock up and you aren't quite doing what the big names are doing, then they want to know who you are and what you are about. (Hoggett, 2014)

The mainstream is driven financially by the need for reliable and repeatable success. This drive, of course, generates very real tensions between recognition of the value of innovation and the need for a reliable and proven formula or process. Opportunities for movement direction can come about, therefore, either because the choreographer is perceived as being new and innovative (risky but high impact) or because they are considered to be able to do one thing well (specialist and predictable but reliable). Movement directors in mainstream commercial theatre are, as already noted, most often employed to work on specific projects; they seldom have a substantial degree of control over what they will do next. Furthermore, the desire for a familiar product can effectively mean that once well established, 'you end up doing the same piece over and over again with varying directors' (Hoggett, 2014). Any move towards valuing process rather than result within the mainstream is important in this context, as it mitigates against the formulaic and encourages a greater promiscuity of ideas and practices.

Hoggett describes how he feels comfortable with the opportunities that this cultural change has given him, and that he has noticed the change in attitude most particularly in the USA:

> America, well specifically Broadway, has felt more – not accepting, that's not the word – but certainly more open to work of the kind I've been doing. Now I don't know how far that tracks back, but I've been approached by producers in America quicker than I've been approached by producers here [in the UK]. And I don't quite know what the truth of that is really…But I have felt very relaxed there, and able to make bold choices on shows, where if I thought about the money involved in it, I might worry a bit. But I've never had to think like that. (Hoggett, 2014)

Certainly, the impact of globally successful shows that include a strong emphasis on innovative collaborative movement practice – such as *War Horse* and *Black Watch* – reflects an increased public awareness of, and interest in, theatre performance that uses innovative staging techniques to fully engage the physicality of the actor. As bodies within Western society have been allowed to become more openly expressive, and are less restricted by the clothes people wear and the social situations that they find themselves in, so audiences have been willing to accept performances within which the body and its movement is a central part of the theatrical event, its construction and its modes of meaning creation. The use of movement to create innovative new theatre productions reflects a growing industry realization that contemporary movement practice has cultural and economic value. Whereas the old models of movement direction and choreography relied upon performers being trained to be able quickly to pick up new sets of steps and movements, or upon movement 'numbers' being created to feature briefly at an appropriate point in the storyline, what these new productions demand and are built upon is a more collaborative and organic process, less easy to replicate on an industrial scale but giving a value to the individual performer's movement creativity that had not been acknowledged before. Hoggett believes that this is what contributed to producers just not seeing this new kind of approach coming:

> *Black Watch* is the watershed, really. That was the Americans looking at a show like that, playing across America three times, and them not knowing how that came about. [...] And that really was when the American producers started to wonder, 'What was that?', 'How are they doing that?', 'Who are those people?' (Hoggett, 2014)

Once the value of innovative and collaborative approaches that might solve complex staging problems has been realized, commercial and mainstream producers are willing to invest into what can sometimes be a lengthy development process. Disney, famously, for instance, were prepared to fund an extensive period of development for Julie Taymor to work on *The Lion King* (1997). Hoggett recalls a long trajectory on the American production of *American Idiot* (2009), 'where I did a year and a half of workshops, two years nearly, before we did our first version. And then it was another nine months before it was on Broadway' (Hoggett, 2014). Of course, the producers' investment is not simply altruistic, 'because ultimately, you need to get it absolutely right' (Hoggett, 2014).

As a result of these changes it is possible to see the community of movement directors and choreographers changing in some interesting ways. Where once this community would have been dominated by people with a strong dance background, there is a growing sense that that is widening out and that people are coming in to the community with a different or wider skill set. Points of contact still tend to be limited and fixed, and networks determined by who you work with and where. Work that takes place outside the pressure of the mainstream increasingly encourages collaborative approaches to theatre making and enables theatre artists and makers to be quite protective of this quality of their work. For Hoggett, his partnership in Frantic Assembly had meant that he and co-founder Scott Graham were able both to envision the kind of collaborative creative environment that they wanted, and to achieve it. Working now in the USA, he no longer has the responsibility of initiating and taking overall responsibility for projects – a big part of what was involved in running a company like Frantic Assembly. On one level this is restricting, but on another level he is able to focus on simply taking advantage of the resources made available for the work that he has to do: 'I don't have that level of responsibility in America, so I ask more of the immediate world around me' (Hoggett, 2014).

The commercial dynamics of the mainstream and the importance and significance of it for the career profiles of those drawn into these sectors mean that there are specific and particular forces that work on the bodies of those involved. The body has to be ready to work, responsive and adaptable, as might be expected; there are perhaps also conflicting imperatives both to stand out from the crowd and to blend seamlessly into the production aesthetic. Presence is required, demanded even, but not to the detriment of the overall effect. One balance point in this dynamic is around 'risk': 'Risk is just not something you have to ask someone to take in America, in a rehearsal room, certainly not in a development period or a workshop' (Hoggett, 2014). Hoggett understands this as culturally specific, identifying a greater willingness from American performers to push the boundaries:

I was definitely the product of my own misgivings, my own limits of what you'd ask for in the rehearsal room. And you could say that's about being loud, and uninhibited, and not necessarily being smart about what the movement director wants. On the other hand, it could be about saying 'if this space is safe like you say it is, then I'll try things that aren't safe'. We say that all the time. You know, normally, we don't have to deal with things that don't feel safe, don't feel palatable. (Hoggett, 2014)

But movement work, it seems, must always fluctuate between that which is controlled, understandable and willed, and that which is disruptive, unplanned, abject and unruly if it is to retain the authentic qualities that connect it with our lived and current experiences of our bodies. Hoggett's reflections reveal this tension and place it within the complex context of the mainstream actor's body. This relates very directly with public and professional conceptions of what being a 'proper' actor means. Within the mainstream there can often be quite firm and sometimes fixed and refined notions of 'the actor' – perhaps most restrictively so in the UK, which has a long history of what is, somewhat uncritically, referred to as 'great acting'. The actor's body becomes fixed within this kind of professional and cultural ecology, losing its adaptability and its potential to move between and across forms. Risk in the rehearsal room is one thing, risk within the realm of a professional career is something that seems to be perceived as much more dangerous.

> I know exactly what I am going to go see if I am going to see a Helen Mirren performance, and she will always deliver. But, she is never going to be in *Chicago* – well maybe she will be! But that's the kind of thing where wouldn't it be interesting if some of our lot were asked to do those kinds of roles. I was thinking the other day about a dance piece I really want to make – a pure dance piece – and one of the characters, the perfect piece of casting, is Ian McKellen. And I was thinking, maybe I should ask Ian McKellen, in my 'un-brit' way, because he would be extraordinary in it. (Hoggett, 2014)

The body of the mainstream actor can become limited by too closely defined notions of craft, by what can become (particularly in some cultures and some industry contexts) very fixed notions of what it means to be an actor. Movement directors within mainstream theatre cannot change this directly, but only impact upon these forces through making opportunities for change available as and when they arise. This need not directly subvert the actor's core processes – they may still see themselves as essentially following a Stanislavskian approach to developing a 'through-line' for their character – but it does require the actor to be less rigid or dogmatic in the ways that they find physical expression for their choices, and more interestingly in the ways they understand movement as a dynamic and generative element in that process.

Ayse Tashkiran, in her writings on movement direction (2016 and 2017), identifies the role that some other important movement directors have played in changing what is possible within mainstream theatre practice. Claude Chagrin, for instance, who trained with Jacques Lecoq from 1959 to 1962, provided the movement direction for the seminal National Theatre productions of Peter Shaffer's plays *The Royal Hunt of the Sun* (1964) and *Equus* (1973), two productions that made vivid use of the actors' physical skills. For *The Royal Hunt of the Sun*, Chagrin found a way of turning Shaffer's enigmatic stage direction – 'They cross the Andes' – into a piece of grand and impressive theatrical performance; for *Equus*, she brought to theatrical life the six horses at the heart of the story, with actors in wire horse masks conveying their looming presence through movement and posture. Movement direction, particularly within the context of the work of major mainstream companies, has thus historically reflected a growing trend to integrate voice and movement within a broader, more physically engaged and engaging vision of the play in performance. The process has taken time, but has reflected the influence of key movement practitioners and the gradual changes in theatrical taste.

Movement directors have, particularly in these instances, been genuine pathfinders over the last half century. They have enabled and supported mainstream theatre to enrich its modes of expression and production; they have brought influential changes to the processes of preparation and rehearsal; and they have encouraged actors to bring the increasingly rich range of skills that they develop through their training on to the stage and in to the service of the play. Just as much as in any other field of theatre practice, they have drawn together the rich history of movement, responded to the complex changes of cultural taste, and sought new ways to unlock the expressive potential of the actor.

Conclusion: Chapter 2

As John Bull states, '[mainstream theatre] is continually altering its shape by assimilating elements originally conceived as alien, or even in opposition, to it' (Bull, 2004: 327). Movement and physical performance practice is increasingly seen as adding value to mainstream theatre production, as the experiences of Leslie and Hoggett attest. Innovation through movement has its own cultural capital, constructed in relation to changes in aesthetic taste that reflect deeper changes in social attitudes to the body and to what we do with our bodies. However, the innovative and often collaborative practices that are brought in to the mainstream from small-scale theatre practice also have an effect that might be described as viral (in the sense that the 'host' is changed in subtle but significant ways through the process of 'infection').

If Hoggett is able to open up spaces within commercial theatre development and rehearsal processes that enable collaborative practices to be employed in genuine and productive ways, then it would be encouraging to think that that same set of practices might resurface later on and that others might feel more confident in developing similar approaches within their own work methods and production contexts.

The historical separation of movement from acting, directing and voice over the last one hundred years or so is changing. Movement is, as we have seen, increasingly perceived as integral to productions and to the achievement of the overall vision for the play. The MA Movement course at Central School of Speech and Drama now includes opportunities for movement directors and trainee directors to have periods of exploration and discovery together that are important steps in establishing the vital role that movement can play in modern theatre practice. Perhaps we might be seeing conventional power dynamics shifting at least a little and the movement text, physical ensemble and dynamic physicality of a production becoming at least as important as the written text and design.

The demands that the mainstream theatre industry makes on actors' bodies can easily be construed as the embodied effects of capitalist economics – the need to be fit, trim, athletic, attractive, voluptuous and so on, or the need to respond quickly and professionally with a recognized level of skill. Although drama conservatoire students probably feel the operation of these forces on their bodies more and more acutely as they approach graduation, their training also attempts to provide them with the means to address the negative effects of such pressures. Vanessa Ewan and Debbie Green's recent book on movement (Ewan & Green, 2014), as well as the work of practitioners/researchers such as Roanna Mitchell, offer support and advice for student actors as to how they might deal with these pressures. Indeed, it may be that, at the time of writing, non-conservatoire routes into the acting profession are less alert to these pressures than the conservatoires themselves. Although the rise of performance studies has seen a growing awareness of the body as a means of meaning-making, as the source for performance creativity, and as a site for cultural resistance, this has not necessarily gone hand in hand with an awareness of the pressures within the industry. The increased emphasis on employment and employability across the higher education sector could also be fuelling an environment in which critical interrogation of the nature and politics of the theatre workplace is less likely to happen. A more critical approach to the operation of employment and employability on the student/actor's body and to attitudes towards movement training would now seem to be timely.

Notes

1. The National Theatre produced Complicité's *Street of Crocodiles* (1992, and West End transfer). Frantic Assembly contributed movement direction to *The Curious Incident of the Dog in the Night-time* (National Theatre, 2012, followed by West End transfer and national/international tour). It is arguable that these texts would not even have been considered stageable without the contribution of practitioners whose expertise in movement came from their experiences developing their own movement practice outside of the mainstream.

2. As of April 2018, the UK UCAS (Universities and Colleges Admission Service) website listed 46 degree courses that included 'acting' within the title, of which only seven were at conservatoire institutions.

3. It was initially known as the Academy of Dramatic Art; the Royal Charter was not granted until 1920.

4. Outside of licensed dramatic performance, the policing of what was acceptable was still rigorous. For instance, the naked bodies on display in the nude *tableaux vivants* at the Windmill Theatre, London from 1932 had to remain motionless in order to remain within the law – a clear association in law of movement with lewdness and abjection.

5. The Cooper test is a test of physical fitness, designed in 1968 by Kenneth Cooper. The test typically involves assessing how far the participant can run in a set period of time.

6. Vanessa Ewan and Debbie Green include a section in their book on actor movement (2014) that explicitly deals with nudity and sex scenes in relation to movement and safe practices. There are also movement directors who specialize in the direction of 'intimate' scenes on stage and screen (see, for example, Intimacy Directors International: www.IntimacyDirectorsInternational.com and Theatrical Intimacy: www.theatricalintimacy.com).

7. Alan Brissenden's 1981 book, *Shakespeare and the Dance*, is still the only significant academic publication to analyse dance and dancing within Shakespeare's texts.

8. For a general outline and discussion of the role of the contemporary movement director in UK theatre, see the video 'What is a Movement Director?' (National Theatre, 2014).

9. There has been little or no critical investigation of the significance of this movement work and these developments to the RSC's movement practice in general. The CAPITAL Project (Warwick University/RSC, 2005–2010), for instance, involved some exploration of the ways in which objects (such as prompt books) might contain valuable traces of performance practice, and also included Lucy Cullingford's work on 'Interrogating the Renaissance through Dance'; however, the project resulted in no published material on movement practice, and focused on historical practice over contemporary performance. *The Song of Songs* was a movement-based theatrical adaptation of the eponymous text from the Bible,

directed by Struan Leslie. *The Heart of Robin Hood*, written by David Farr, was an exuberantly physical family production, directed by Gisli Örn Gardarsson from the Icelandic company Vesturport. Movement and the body in relation to the RSC's 2012 productions of *The Orphan of Zhao* and *Julius Caesar* are dealt with in detail in Chapter 5.

10. Dancers who trained with the highly influential American dancer and choreographer Martha Graham (1894–1991)

11. The Group Theatre was a New York theatre collective, formed in 1931 by Harold Clurman, Cheryl Crawford and Lee Strasberg. The group pioneered an approach to naturalistic acting, based on the work of Stanislavsky. The Group Theatre had ended by 1941.

12. Katie Mitchell OBE (1964–) is a British theatre director renowned for both the detail of her work and her innovative and ground-breaking approach to performance making.

13. There is hardly a drama conservatoire or professional actor training course in the UK that has not been influenced by Saint-Denis' work to some extent. His influence on actor training in France, Canada and the USA has also been profound and lasting.

14. For more detail on the work of Jacques Copeau, see Evans (2018).

15. Richard Pascoe played Timon in the RSC production of *Timon of Athens*, directed by Ron Daniels, in 1981.

16. Katherine Hunter was an associate artist of the RSC from 2008 to 2011. She performed in a number of RSC productions, including as Cleopatra in *Anthony and Cleopatra*, and as the Fool in *King Lear*.

17. Mime is a fascinating example of this. For a period in the late 1970s and the 1980s, mime was very much in ascendancy. By the late 1980s and the early 1990s there were a substantial number of UK mime and physical theatre companies, supported by an umbrella organization Total Theatre (formerly Mime Action Group), and mime was recognized by the Arts Council as a discrete field with its own funding stream. By the late 2000s and the early 2010s mime had virtually disappeared as an art form, with only a small number of artists still referring to themselves as mimes.

18. Droznin is a leading Russian movement teacher. His work draws on Stanislavsky's theories, and makes use of sequences of challenging and difficult physical exercises. Details of his work can be found in Allain (2011).

19. The National Theatre has recently produced a set of videos describing the work of the movement director and the role of movement within its productions. You can search these at: www.youtube.com/user/ntdiscovertheatre.

20. Hoggett co-founded Frantic Assembly in 1994 along with Scott Graham and Vicki Coles (now Middleton). Hoggett and Middleton have now left the company; Scott Graham is the current artistic director.

21. John Tiffany (OBE) began his career in theatre as literary director at the Traverse Theatre, Edinburgh. He went on to work with Paines Plough and the National Theatre of Scotland. His major productions as director include: *Black Watch, The Bacchae, Let the Right One In* (all for National Theatre of Scotland), *Once* (Broadway and West End), *The Twits* (Royal Court) and *Harry Potter and the Cursed Child* (West End).

22. Rufus Norris was an associate director at the National Theatre from 2011 to 2015, since when he has taken over as the artistic director.

23. Michael Mayer directed the Broadway production of *American Idiot* (2010) for which Hoggett provided movement direction.

3 Movement, Play and Performance

This book is proposing 'play' as a type of activity that is deeply rooted in performance, and closely linked to movement and the body. It is understood as a form of human behaviour whose rational justification is not necessarily required; in which the pleasure, unpredictability and excitement of physical engagement is at least as important as any outcomes; in which physical imagination is at least as important as rational intention; and in which meaning is present but always fluid and embodied. It is in this sense not only an activity but also an attitude towards activity. I intend in this chapter to look at the ways in which the concept of 'play' might challenge conventional rational paradigms for the processes of physical performance.

The term 'play', as used in this chapter, is not intended to refer to the theatre games of Clive Barker (1977), Chris Johnston (2006) or Keith Johnstone (1979), nor to the general games theories of Roger Caillois (2001) and Johan Huizinga (1980), though there are clearly some associations with these reference points, as theatre games and games in general share important features with the notion of play proposed here. Play as discussed in this chapter is more in tune with the play that John Wright discusses in his book, *Why Is That So Funny* (2006: 27–47), something 'absorbing, beautiful and pleasurable to watch' (2006: 27): it is about experiencing the world through the body, with a sense of openness, imagination, flexibility and availability. Play is not about pre-supposing structures or meanings for action and gesture, but about allowing the imagination and the body to work together to explore how and in what ways structure and meaning might emerge. This kind of play, as we will see, allows performers to transfer creatively between the internal and the external dimension, between different kinds of action and gesture, between different imaginative worlds. As Wright puts it, 'Play occupies a liminal world between the actual and the imaginary where anything can become something else and metaphors breed like rabbits' (2006: 30). In this sense, it is one very important model for the relationship between the body and performance, and a model that also opens up all sorts of possibilities for diversity and inclusion. Play can, in addition, be disruptive, particularly in relation to discursive constructions. It at once acknowledges the power of discourses and the power structures that work to shape our activities, while at the same time suggesting – even requiring – a sense in which there is much that discourse cannot capture or pin down and that therefore remains 'in play'. It is as easy to define 'play' as it is to describe how to ride a bicycle. For some useful discussion on the subject, I refer the reader to Wright (2006), Lecoq (2000), Coletto and Buckley (in Evans & Kemp, 2016: 112–118), Gaulier (2006) and Murray (2010: 215–236).

A playful and disruptive approach might, at first glance, be seen as antithetical to the systems and methods of Konstantin Stanislavsky, approaches that have become the dominant model for actor training and performance practice. However, a close reading of the development of Stanislavsky's training methods from the start of the twentieth century into the 1930s reveals a transformation from an approach which placed rational analysis of the logical through-line of the character's objectives at the heart of the actor's process towards a new position, where the actor engages first and foremost with the character's physical action; the character's emotions would then emerge from this action. Although Stanislavsky never abandoned the importance of the through-line of the character's objective, his changing emphasis from the System to the Method of Physical Action, and later to Affective Analysis, does point towards the realization of a different kind of coherence: one based on the body, its actions and its psychophysical logic. As Bella Merlin states: 'Stanislavsky found that the actual living bodies and imaginations of his actors themselves could unlock the intricacies of a text quickly and inventively' (Merlin, 2003: 160). Stanislavsky's eventual recognition of the importance of the body's place in the development of theatrical performance was, unfortunately, overshadowed by the importance given to emotion memory in the development of the Method by Lee Strasberg. The emphasis placed on the body and on physical action by Stanislavsky's Russian disciples, such as Vsevolod Meyerhold and Maria Knebel, was not acknowledged in the West until much later in the century, by which time the Method had become well established, in America in particular. Several authors have written in depth about Stanislavsky's later emphasis on action – for example, Benedetti (1982), Carnicke (1998) and

Merlin (2003) – but his work is still more strongly associated with the performance of text, the training of the mainstream actor, and the body as an instrument. In such a scheme, the world is understood by the thinking subject who then expresses their reaction to the world through their actions, gestures and words. In his later years, however, Stanislavsky's ideas were closer to those of William James and the behaviourists (see Whyman, 2008: 59–60), and he appeared to be more comfortable with the idea that physical action and engagement of the body would precede emotion and intellectual response.

This chapter seeks to examine the implications of acknowledging the body not as an instrument but as the primary way in which we know the world and as central to the processes through which we express that knowledge. For these reasons, this chapter focuses on the work of one particular group of practitioners who represent a 'playful' strand of theatre practice that stands in partial alignment with and partial contrast to psychological realism. This strand runs from the early twentieth-century French theatre director and pedagogue Jacques Copeau, to the more recent work of the French theatre teachers Jacques Lecoq, Philippe Gaulier[1] and Monika Pagneux.[2] This approach to play and to performance is distinctive in that it has consistently followed a very clear and carefully set out pedagogy, with a strong sense of an educational journey, all designed with 'play' as a driving principle.

Although Lecoq has had a significant influence on the development of professional actor training for the mainstream theatre, both he and his former students[3] also emphasize the importance of playfulness and its role within the actor's creative use of the body. This section will first look at the general notion of physical play and its particular development through Lecoq's pedagogy. It will then examine one area of actor training in which Lecoq's principles of observation, mimicry and transformation are extensively used by mainstream theatre training – animal study. Animal study has for several decades been a core part of traditional actor training courses, although rarely critiqued and never subjected to detailed analysis. This is in part because it can easily be perceived as trivial, anti-intellectual, irrelevant to text work and as placing too much emphasis on the non-human. This section will examine whether and in what ways animal study brings to the surface significant issues around performance, movement and the body that have greater importance than has previously been acknowledged. This will lead to discussions of ways in which animal study enables concepts of what it means to be embodied and human to be opened up and interrogated in new ways.

Jacques Lecoq, Philippe Gaulier and 'Le Jeu'

For Lecoq and Gaulier, the body both offers and responds to a different kind of logic and sense-making than the psychological realism commonly associated with Stanislavsky. In their teaching, the student connects their actions and gestures through a set of guiding principles that are driven by the physical associations between various kinds of gestures and movements and their dynamic qualities. Such a playful and disruptive logic has its roots in the work of Jacques Copeau, in the French surrealist movement of the early twentieth century (in particular the work of Antonin Artaud), and in Lecoq's background in physical education and sports therapy. For Lecoq and for Gaulier, the playful body represents a form of poetic engagement with the world and with the nature of theatre performance. From a starting point based on play as a form of engagement with the world, their teaching extends, through a range of basic training exercises, into dramatic territories such as clowning, Commedia dell'Arte, and bouffon, where improvisation, imagination and irreverence are central, both historically and in terms of how these territories relate to contemporary theatre and culture. For the Lecoq School, this means that frequent opportunities for students to create their own theatrical vision is critical. Jos Houben believes that 'what distinguishes the Lecoq training from any other theatrical training as I know it is that it is a school for creators' (Houben in Barker, 2012). Since the 1960s there has been a rapid expansion in the development of improvisation as a form in its own right and within physical theatre practice in particular (see Frost & Yarrow, 2015). Similarly, the contemporaneous rise in the popularity of somatic practices, contemporary dance and contact improvisation represents another strand of the development of the playful body in performance and in training over this same period. The work of Johnstone, Barker and others emphasizes the notion that performance cannot be solely textual and rational but must also be physical, intuitive, instinctive, spontaneous and playful if it is to liberate the performer's creativity and engage all of their expressive resources.

For Lecoq, play is a theme drawn from his experiences in sport as a young man (Evans 2012b: 165–170), enriched by his sojourn in Italy between 1948 and 1956, during which time he studied and taught Commedia dell'Arte and worked with Dario Fo (1926–2016) on satirical theatrical sketches. It is a theme that speaks to his inclinations and interests as a teacher and director. Physical imitation and transformation provide the central process for Lecoq in the actor's training/education and the performer's practice. For Lecoq, the starting point lies in a process of opening up the body to physical expression generated in reaction to the world around us – he refers to this as 'mimodynamics' (see Lecoq, 2000: 46–52). It is through allowing the impressions made in this way to play upon our bodies that change is created and transformation achieved.

> It's about searching deep down and finding the deposit that is the result of things that we have observed (impression). For example, let's take our impression of a tree. In bypassing the concepts and personal responses that we have to a tree, we can find a physical sensation that allows us to experience the dynamic life of a tree. It is this sensation that should act as a reference point in making the tree come alive. It is as though one side of our skin is used to connect with the exterior world and the other side to connect with our interior world. (Lecoq, 2006: 112)

This approach is not a complete rejection of psychology so much as a proposal that embodied engagement with the physical environment comes at an earlier stage than the performer's psychological engagement. However, if his pedagogy is similar to Stanislavsky's Method of Physical Action in this respect, it should not be assumed that Lecoq's teaching is simply a variation on Stanislavsky's. Although the training at Lecoq's School in Paris begins with what he calls 'psychological *replay*' (2000: 29), from this starting point the students then move on to explore what Lecoq calls '*le jeu*': 'the point when, aware of the theatrical dimension, the actor can shape an improvisation for spectators, using rhythm, tempo, space and form' (2000: 29). For Lecoq, although play may sometimes come very close to 'replay', ultimately it allows the actor to transform or extend reality, though always rooted in the performer's embodied understanding of the world. One early exercise at the school is an improvisation entitled 'The Childhood Bedroom' (Lecoq, 2000: 30–31). In this exercise, the student enters a childhood bedroom which they 'rediscover'. They find a toy with which they spend time playing before they come back into the present moment and leave the room. Although the exercise might be considered to have individual psychological resonances for the student, it is the dynamics of memory and remembering, of the imagined space, and of childhood play that are the focus of the exercise – what happens to our bodies and our movement at the moment that the memory engulfs us and takes us back to our own childhood, and how that transposition is effectively created and communicated in performance. As a student at the school in the early 1980s, my own recollection is that this exercise helps the student to recognize how memory, childhood and play have their particular dramatic rhythms that can communicate powerfully through the body. Emotion is of course present in the exercise, but the emotion is not dominant or controlling;

rather it is played (imagined, imitated, transferred and transposed) through the student's movement. In this sense, play does not diminish the emotion or trivialize it – as might be implied by a conventional understanding of the word 'play' – rather it deepens the dramatic potential of the emotion and enables it to be used creatively. 'The contents of a memory are secondary in [Lecoq's] view of the creative impulse. What is more important is how the energies implicit in the memory are manifest in the body' (Lutterbie, 2011: 58).

Play in the sense described above also enables structure to be developed, explored and transformed. This can start through pushing the situations, characters and interactions to the limits of their rhythmic, dynamic and spatial possibilities and interactions. At this point the student can move beyond psychological realism and start to make connections based on other elements of dramatic form and structure. The hungry man can start to eat himself, the lover can fly across the room, many can express the feelings of the one. Before moving on to dramatic forms, however, the student undertakes more detailed explorations of play through the use of the neutral mask and identification with the world around them (elements, materials, animals). The neutral mask helps the student to identify and remove everyday tensions and movement habits from the body. This in turn enables the student to become more aware of the interplay of movement dynamics in the world around them and of their responses to that world, including identification with it. This kind of identification takes place through the mimodynamics that Lecoq has introduced from the start of the course and that permeates all the teaching. It is this profound yet playful approach that enables the student to move with ease from embodying an element to human characterization and to explore the theatrical potential of such a transition. The neutral mask also encourages a state of discovery, openness, and what Lecoq referred to as *disponibilité*, a state of balance, equilibrium and readiness from which all movement begins. It is thus clear that for Lecoq not all knowledge is rational, intellectual and logical – 'the body knows things about which the mind is ignorant' (Lecoq, 2000: 9). The connecting principle behind Lecoq's teaching is movement/stillness – everything can be understood and transformed through this principle. In the words of Lecoq's lecture/demonstration, '*Tout bouge*' ('everything moves').

Play is central to Lecoq's work with the neutral mask. The mask places the student at a fulcrum point from which movement begins. Richard Hayes-Marshall, a former student and teacher at the Lecoq School, refers to neutrality as 'a condition such that, if the actor finds himself [*sic*] there, he doesn't know what he will do next' (Eldredge and Huston in Zarrilli, 1995: 122–123). It is this moment of uncertainty and possibility, where balance is about to turn into imbalance, that marks the point where the neutral mask and play overlap and intersect. The student discovers the rules of play at the point at which they have to come into action in order to respond to the world they are engaging with. When Lecoq challenges the student in the neutral mask to respond to the exercise of looking out at the sea, the student reaches into their embodied knowledge of the world in order to find the response that is needed. In the absence of the actual sea they use their physical skill and their embodied knowledge to recreate the rhythms of the sea in movement. In doing so, in the sea's absence they begin the process of understanding how physical play functions, how mimodynamics enables identification, transposition and transformation.

Lecoq's mimodynamics owes much to the work of the French anthropologist Marcel Jousse (1886–1961). Jousse proposed that the act of physical mimicry is the primary language of humankind, and is central to the way that the environment works upon the human subject and the manner in which the human subject responds. Edgard Sienaert argues convincingly that, for Jousse, play is central. It is worth quoting Sienaert at length, as what he says about Jousse has direct relevance to any understanding of Lecoq's notion of play.

> Play, then, is the osmosis of man [sic] and the reality that imposes itself upon him, it is the way by which reality is progressively instilled into him from childhood. It is this act of playing out, this play, that is at the origin of all art, for man needs to reproduce what he sees. He cannot but play out, he cannot do without art. Unlike the anthropoid, however, the anthropos can, through his bodily gestures, in an orderly fashion and in order to master them, consciously replay a perceived and intussuscepted gesture. This capability to re-play a once perceived reality in its absence, to re-present something past, is unique to man and it is memory that allows him to do so and thus makes him unique: through memory he replays experienced reality stored in him, through memory he conserves and transmits consciously his past actions and reactions and so is enabled to shape his future according to the experiences of the past. Memory is the reactivation of gestures previously internalized, shaped, played in us with the cooperation of our body. (Sienaert, 1990: 95)

In this sense, Lecoq's work with the neutral mask is not simply a process that enables the student to engage imaginatively with their environment, but it is also a process that enhances the student's physical memory and their ability to (re)play their environment in the future. As Jousse himself puts it:

> A genuine anthropological need, resulting from the law of Mimism, impels [the anthropos] to become, somehow, all things, even as they are being spontaneously imbricated and interacted.

He [sic] does not become, as is the case with independent 'plastic poses', a series of living but immobile statues, without any link between them. No, there is no 'cutting up'. Instead, by virtue of a dynamic and muscular flow, the successive interactions of the universe are incarnated within him without any break in continuity.

One could say that he never finishes replaying what has as a matter of course been played within him in a finite way. His ability to 'compose', to 'de-compose', to 're-compose' gestual interactions is infinite. Quite unlike that of the anthropoid, his curiosity is universal and mechanistic, in the sense that he is impelled, in spite of himself, to realize *how* everything plays before him so as to ensure that everything can be exactly re-played in him. (2000: 82)

Lecoq's training, in this sense, is a training for life as much as for theatre. What Lecoq adds to Jousse's concept of gesture is the possibility of transformation – the idea that through our bodies we can not only know the world and remember it, but also transform and change it. If this is so, then the more profound the challenge in terms of physical transformation, the more profound will be the potential change to how we understand, configure and interact with the world we live in.

This kind of playfulness has its own logic – for Lecoq, play is made possible through the student's grasp of the principles of rhythm, tempo, space and form. As with most forms of play, rules and parameters either emerge or are already present. However, while much has been made of the rules that make play possible, less attention is paid to the ability of playful activity to subvert rules and to resist the ways in which power can operate within and through game structures. This will be explored in more detail in the section on animal study later in this chapter and in the section on disability in Chapter 5. However fixed or flexible the rules of play are, they not only create the parameters in which play takes place but they allow for a degree of understanding between players and between players and spectators – an awareness of the type of game that is being proposed and enacted. For Lecoq, Gaulier and Pagneux, play also creates and sustains what Lecoq calls *complicité* – a relationship that is best described as a mutual enthusiasm for the transformative, disruptive and creative potential of play between actor and actor, and between actor and audience. *Complicité* is not just an acknowledgement of the fact that a game is underway, but also a willingness to allow the game to change, develop and disrupt what is happening. Connections, sense and meaning are made through playful connections that break across rational and conventional sequencing and association. Movement can lead to movement, through connections that are to do with the body's anatomy or the rhythm and dynamics of an action. The imagination can be led by the body. Meaning becomes more fluid and less fixed. Absence or minimal use of language enables and facilitates this semiological fluidity. Meaning is still present, but less restricted and more contingent. Lecoq is sometimes described as a mime teacher, but mime is a distraction in relation to this aspect of his work. Traditional notions of mime conceive of a form that strives for the linguistic capability of sign language, where images and ideas are clearly signalled and understood. Lecoq's sense of mime is more profound than this. Although he taught what he called *pantomime blanche*[4] as one element of the dramatic territories explored in the second year at the school, we have already seen that his practice is actually based on a more profound notion of movement, encapsulated in the mimodynamic process. This embodied approach to developing a form of physical imagination reflects a changing attitude to the actor's work on text. As Callery points out, the scripted text is no longer the fixed element in the theatrical idiom in this context (2001: 8). Although the Lecoq training includes addressing various dramatic texts as well as writing for the theatre, his approach aligns best to texts that are flexible enough to allow for the body to play with the meanings that the text seeks to bring to life.

Gaulier and Pagneux, although both distinguished and influential teachers in their own right, can also be seen as working within the broad framework of Lecoq's concept of play. The connection that they share through Lecoq means that despite their differences, all three have a common sense of the importance and value of play and make use of it in their teaching. As Murray points out, for Lecoq play is the driver for creativity; actors able to play, who understand how to play, bring a 'spirit of invention, generosity and openness' (Murray, 2010: 223) that is deeply rooted in the body. Play is closely linked to 'physical dynamics, rhythm and the laws of motion' (2010: 223). Whereas this set of principles is embedded across Lecoq's training, Gaulier has decided to teach play (or *le jeu*) as a separate and distinct part of his training, a course that students can take on a stand-alone basis. For Gaulier, play has a deeper, more profound and poetic importance – it is 'the source of everything: of the pleasure and desire to be an actor' (Gaulier in Murray, 2010: 224). The link with pleasure is important for Gaulier; it also refers to the need to avoid excessive tension and effort, and straining after the right action. Pleasure for Gaulier is closely linked to pretending, to imagination and to provocation and teasing – all of which play an important part in his style of teaching. Pagneux's work echoes this, but her particular emphasis is on what Murray refers to as 'a quality of attention' to movement and on the playful relationships within the body itself as much as between bodies (Murray, 2010: 226). A telling example of Pagneux's approach might be the description Murray quotes from Annabel Arden of how Pagneux taught acrobatics at the Lecoq School. She would match students of different abilities together and ask the more talented acrobat to mimic their partner:

> first, the poor student would improve, second the gifted acrobat would find a new expressivity and humanity in the movement, third a possible improvisatory dialogue and relationship would emerge so that a scene could be played between the two, using the dynamic of their difference. It was all play – that was the secret. (Arden in Murray, 2010)

Across their several approaches to play, Lecoq, Gaulier and Pagneux explore towards a common purpose – placing play as an attitude to the body, to the activity of performing, to the environment and space within which one acts, to one's fellow performers, and to the processes of creating, that is quintessential to the nature of theatre.

Although Lecoq and Gaulier are strongly associated with this particular notion of play and their work has done much to define and promote it for the contemporary student and performer, it would be quite wrong to imagine that the concept of play does not also have a wider history in relation to the actor's physicality and that 'play' is not evident in other theatre cultures and in other countries. Meyerhold, for instance, asserts that: 'An actor can improvise only when he [*sic*] feels internal joy. Without an atmosphere of creative joy, of artistic *élan*, an actor never completely opens up' (Meyerhold in Callery, 2001: 71). Benedetti notes that for Stanislavsky, 'Tempo is not speed and rant but an ability "to juggle easily with even the strongest of emotions"' (Benedetti, 1988: 144) – implying the importance of a light and flexible approach. Indeed, for a number of key practitioners, the notions of joy, play and *élan* describe both an important impetus into movement and a certain attitude towards that impetus. Where Meyerhold talks of joy, Brecht in his writings refers to *spass*, which can be broadly translated as 'fun'. For Brecht, *spass* was important as an attitude towards performance (Brecht, 2015: 25–31). This attitude helped create the sense of distance from events and characters that he valued. He also understood that playfulness breaks the control of psychology and allows new meanings to become evident, perhaps meanings that might otherwise be suppressed or disapproved of. Play has a long history of offering a space to be subversive and resistant to dominant ideologies.

The next sections will explore an area of movement work where the performer or student can be confronted with a significant challenge in relation to the ideas examined above: animal study. Movement work on animal study is based on the actor exploring a process of physical transformation into an animal. The actor is challenged to enter into a deep and profoundly physical imaginative play with their body and its rhythms and dynamics, with how it occupies and inhabits space and with how it interacts with other bodies. Animal study is thus a particularly eloquent example of the relationship between play, transformation, embodiment and movement.

Animal Study, Movement and Play

Almost all actor training programmes in the UK, and indeed many such programmes around the world, include animal study as a part of their curriculum. It is interesting to consider where this element of training comes from and what it has offered the trainee actor over the years. There is of course a long history of the actor's embodiment of animal characteristics in performance. The earliest human performances may well have been shamanistic re-enactments of animal behaviour as part of an attempt to understand and represent the natural world around them. It is certainly possible that animal impersonation was part of the 'tricks of the trade' of popular performers across the ages, including the actors of the Italian Commedia dell'Arte. Modern Commedia teachers and practitioners have pointed out the way that different Commedia characters seem to make use of animal movements – the chicken, the monkey, the bear, etc. (Rudlin, 1994: 37–39). However, there is little evidence of animal study as part of any formal scheme of actor training until the early twentieth century. It took until the beginning of modern systematized actor training for these skills to be separately identified and recorded. There is very little mention of animal study within early actor training texts, although Jean Benedetti mentions in his biography of Stanislavsky that he had used animal improvisations as part of his work on Maeterlinck's *The Blue Bird*, in August 1907. Benedetti notes how, 'On August 21 Nemirovich had written to his wife with cynical amusement that [the actors] were all imitating dogs, cats and cockerels and were mewing, barking and crowing all around a delighted Stanislavski [*sic*]' (1988: 169).

Despite Stanislavsky's experiment, one of the first examples of animal study becoming a formal and established part of professional actor training is Jacques Copeau and Suzanne Bing's early work at the École du Vieux-Colombier, the school attached to his Théâtre du Vieux-Colombier in Paris. This work most probably began during the school's 'exile' in America for the Vieux-Colombier Theatre's 1917–1919 tour. Copeau recorded various exercises in his note-books, and the entry for 16 June 1918 reads: 'Observation of animals', and later 'Study of La Fountaine's Fables' (Copeau, 1990: 34–35) – many of La Fountaine's fables centre on stories of animals. This short reference almost cer-tainly refers to some exercises in animal mimicry and improvisation. Copeau and Bing (his assistant who initiated and developed many of the pedagogical innovations) shared a fascination with children's play, which would also have drawn them towards this kind of imaginative exploration. Bing took respon-sibility for classes on improvisation and mime within the school, especially in its later stages when the work focused on teaching relatively young stu-dents (including Copeau's own daughter Marie-Hélène). In the context of this younger and smaller group, it is highly likely that playful exercises such as the imitation of different animals might have been further developed and refined.

Just prior to Copeau and Bing's work in the Vieux-Colombier school, early advances in photography had meant that the study of animal movement was becoming more and more sophisticated. Étienne-Jules Marey (1830–1904) was a leading French figure in the use of early photographic techniques to cap-ture the movement of animals, as outlined in his influential books *Le Vol des Oiseaux* (1890) (*The Flight of Birds*) and *La Machine Animale* (1873) (*Animal Mechanism*). The work of Marey and of the English photographer Eadweard James Muybridge stimulated new interest in the ways that humans and animals moved and enabled more detailed analysis of the dynamics of movement. In so far as their work attempted to capture movement it not only participated in the development of cinematic photography, it also emphasized the rhythmic dynamics of movement rather than its sculptural qualities. In this sense, the emphasis started to turn from how bodies looked towards what bodies do.

Copeau and Bing may well have been aware of Marey's work, and conse-quently alert to the sense in which representation of the world need not be through a closely observed and positivist reconstruction, such as is the case in naturalism, but through a form of representation enabled by dynamics, rhythm and movement. Bing's work was also inspired by the educational experiments of Margaret Naumburg, a progressive American educationalist whose work explored the value of play in children's imaginative development. The work of Copeau and Bing's young students eventually flowered into the-atrical creation in 1924, when Copeau took the decision to leave Paris and the Vieux-Colombier and retreat to Burgundy with a troupe of young actors and students. Copeau's nephew, Michel Saint-Denis, became a key member of this new company, often taking charge while Copeau himself was away trying to raise funds. The group, known by the local people as Les Copiaus, continued with many of the exercises that they had developed in Paris and on tour in America, including the animal exercises. They developed what we would now understand as devised theatre, combining mime, song and movement to create performances that celebrated life in the rural communities in which they were based. When the company was disbanded by Copeau in 1929, the core of Les Copiaus stayed together under the direction of Saint-Denis, eventually forming as the Compagnie des Quinze in 1931. The new company toured internationally, including a successful run in London where they performed André Obey's play *Noé* (Noah), which included animal work. The success of this tour led to Saint-Denis' decision to relocate to London, where there was enough interest and support for his work to enable him to set up a school, the London Theatre Studio, where he could continue to train actors according to the pedagogy that had been developed by Copeau and Bing. Despite the interruption of the work of this studio by the onset of the Second World War, its impact was significant enough for Saint-Denis to be invited to join in the creation of the Old Vic Centre in 1945 which was to include the Old Vic School.[5] The curriculum at these schools included traditional elements such as voice, text work, rehearsal process and stage combat, but it also drew on Saint-Denis' early experiences and included mask work, mime, improvisation and animal study. In the UK, within a few decades, these curriculum changes had become widespread and animal study was established practice within actor training. By the 1960s, for many theatre trainers, the actor's transformative potential was no longer simply constructed from voice, posture, costume and make-up, but from the actor's whole physical potential, limited only by their imagination.

The rise of mime as a theatre form in its own right after the Second World War also maps this cultural change. By the late 1970s mime had emerged from its roots in Paris as an offshoot of Copeau's work; nurtured by Étienne Decroux, his former pupil, and Jacques Lecoq, who had worked with his son-in-law Jean Dasté, mime was now a successful art form in its own right. Pupils from the Paris schools run by Decroux, Marcel Marceau[6] and Lecoq returned to their home countries and proceeded to embed this work into their own performances, into work that they were asked to direct or choreograph, and into their teaching both within and outwith the existing training provision for actors. While mime as a form of theatre had declined to near obscurity by the end of the 1990s, the emphasis on the transformative potential of the body remained, and has become a central tenet of actor training in the late twentieth and early twenty-first century. The influence of Copeau, Bing, Saint-Denis and the French mime teachers on the development and dissemination of animal study has been a crucial, significant and important element of the general transition towards a more movement-centred approach to training of the actor. The reason why animal study have become so central relates to the ways in which such movement exercises refocus the nature of theatre transformation away from psychology and towards a sense that this is what bodies do. The next section examines this premise and the extent to which contemporary theory enables us to better consider how this playful process might be understood.

What Bodies Do – Animal as a Way of Doing

Movement training and movement performance emphasize what bodies do. They place the focus firmly on the activities of the body – its dynamics, rhythms, use of space and weight: they are located in the physical world and although movement can be abstracted into its elements (as for example in Laban's efforts), it can never be wholly abstracted, and always draws us back again to our lived physical experience: 'We know nothing about a body until we know what it can do' (Deleuze & Guattari, 1988: 257). At the same time, movement allows, as Deleuze and Guattari argue, for a process of transformation and a fluidity between 'bodies'. In animal study, notions of character are almost entirely physicalized and embodied; the actor (re)composes their bodily rhythms and dynamics, what Deleuze and Guattari describe as the 'affects' of their body, in order to take on the movement dynamics of the animal. In so doing, they enter into new knowledge about their own body and about bodies in general. The actor redefines their body as 'animal' through a technique based on the manipulation of its 'affects'.

Deleuze and Guattari directly relate the notion of 'affects' to the process of acting when they refer to the work of the actor Robert De Niro in a film sequence in which he walks like a crab;[7] what they argue is that 'it is not a question of his imitating a crab; it is a question of making something that has to do with the crab enter into composition with the image, with the speed of the image' (Deleuze & Guattari, 1988: 274). This statement resonates with Rudolf Laban's reference to 'the image of a beehive as a source for a city street scene', in which he describes how '[a] group of performers could begin by improvising movement as it might occur on a busy street, keeping the image of a beehive in mind' (Bradley, 2009: 32). What underpins both these forms of rhythmic and dynamic transformation is the ability of humans to adapt and change their 'affects' or efforts. As Laban puts it, 'the effort characteristics of men [*sic*] are much more varied and variable than those of animals' (1980: 10). For Laban, this means that humankind 'is able to command a far wider range of effort possibilities than any animal possesses' (Laban, 1980: 13). It is this quality, therefore, that enables a process of consciously applied transformative play to take place.

This transformative ability brings into play an acting process that emphasizes the image, the bodily composition and the physical dynamics over psychological identification. Such a process, at least in part, challenges the conventional dominance of character-based psychology in acting; the student/ actor is able to inhabit a different world of representation in which character objective becomes less important than speed, rhythm, space, weight and flow. At this point the theatrical possibilities for the actor expand rapidly.

Despite the deconstruction of the human/animal distinction proposed by Deleuze and Guattari, there is a strong sense in which animal study maintains the primacy of the human gaze, thus creating what Merleau-Ponty refers to as 'a world in which every object displays the human face it acquires in a human gaze' (2008: 54). There is evidence of this form of anthropocentrism in Laban's statement, quoted above, about effort possibilities. For Merleau-Ponty, the difference between animals and humans is one of 'coherence'. For animals, 'the world which they occupy – insofar as we can reconstruct it from the way they behave – is certainly not a coherent system. By contrast, that of the healthy, civilized, adult human being strives for such coherence' (Merleau-Ponty, 2008: 56). This coherence, for Merleau-Ponty, is a function of human consciousness and reason. Laban seems to propose a position similar to Merleau-Ponty's when he suggests that '[a]nimals are perfect in the efficient use of the restricted effort habits they possess' (Laban, 1980: 10). He asserts: 'No one has ever seen a cat strut with a horse-like gait' (Laban, 1980: 11), confirming his belief that 'each animal genus is restricted to a relatively small range of typical qualities' (Laban, 1980: 10). For Laban, humans are able to demonstrate a higher level of compositional sophistication: 'Man's body-mind produces many kinds of qualities. He can jump like a deer, and, if he wishes, like a cat' (Laban, 1980: 11). This mimetic skill is something he suggests only humans are capable of using consciously and creatively, a position that broadly echoes the views of Jousse described earlier in this chapter. Laban's beliefs are representative of the principles underlying most European and American forms of animal study for actors.

Although it draws on this consciously applied mimetic ability, animal study offers the student/actor a distinctive coherence of its own, based on a logic of the dynamics of the body. This physical coherence, as previously argued, is a challenge to the dominance of rational logic and realist psychology that runs through most post-Stanislavsky forms of actor training. The practices of Laban and Lecoq have been used to provide movement training within Stanislavsky-based approaches to acting; however, animal study is one area in which their practices take a significantly different direction to naturalistic acting pedagogy. Lecoq's teaching replaces the logic of psychological causality with the logic of *le jeu* or 'play', in which connections are made through the physical imagination. Laban also sees enormous value in play, as a 'great aid to growing effort capacity and effort organisation' (Laban, 1980: 14). Both Lecoq and Laban position play, and a child-like capacity for physical engagement in play, as central to their visions of movement. McCaw argues that for Laban, 'the child is the human in its purest state, a state similar to "the noble savage" who has not been polluted by Western society and its life-denying values and practices' (2011: 75). This set of tropes, discussed in more detail by Evans (2009), clearly locates animal study alongside practices that reject urbanization and Western rationalism, at the same time that they are underpinned by forms of colonialism and humanism. The animal body can, as a result of these tropes, commonly be perceived as unthinking, 'savage', child-like – its 'otherness' a potential challenge to human predominance and to the supremacy of the rational mind. Such a set of assumptions raises complex issues around primitivism and potential racism that need to be resisted, rejected and critiqued.

Another issue to consider with animal study is the extent to which a focus on domesticated and caged animals can lead to student work that becomes too safe and 'tame'. For Laban, domestication is a process that enables the analysis of movement: 'In domesticating animals, man [*sic*] has learned how to deal with efforts, and how to change the basic effort-habits of living beings' (Laban in McCaw, 2011: 275); however, this same domestication can also lead to performed animal behaviour that becomes too quickly and uncritically humanized. The humanization of the animal is in tension with a desire within theatre and performance practice over the last century to rediscover the visceral physicality of animal movement, a search that has been driven by a rejection of the intellectual in relation to the body, and that can be seen in the work of Artaud, Grotowski, La Fura dels Baus and De La Guarda. 'Animal' is, within such contexts, conceived of as a mode of being in which the impulse is uninhibited and unsullied by civilization: 'In character work, you focus on intention, going for something and wanting something. That's what animals have; they just are what they are going for. When you watch an exciting actor, they are animalistic' (female actor, cited in McEvenue, 2001: 125).

Understanding animal movement was part of an early twentieth-century scientific and technological revolution; it is, through Marey, Georges Demeny (1850–1917) and Muybridge, closely related to the early development of photography. Capturing the essential elements of animal movement became a process of understanding not the 'spirit' of the animal but its physiological composition (rhythm, dynamics, coordination). The ability to observe animals in this way, to view them as no longer a part of everyday life but as a subject for scrutiny, is part of a wider change whereby '[a]s cities grew and societies became increasingly mechanized, animals were displaced by machines and relegated to spaces where, as rarities, humans could look at them' (Orozco, 2013: 18). Removed from the sphere of human life, animals were the quintessential objects of scrutiny for movement, as their lack of speech signalled (to the modern sensibility) an inability to reason, and emphasized the extent to which they were subject to their embodiment. When people play animals (in the classroom or on stage), they construct the body as caught in a dialogue between the-body-as-representational and the-body-as-a-mode-of-being, each of course continuously redefining each other (Orozco, 2013: 26). The hybrid human/animal of the animal study becomes 'a way of understanding the human and the animal' within a continuum of being (Orozco, 2013: 29). In the animal study, the student/actor can enact becoming/being animal in a manner that asserts human animality in ways that language (with its inherently human complexities) cannot.

The process of becoming/being animal within the animal study is, of course, inherently theatrical. It is a process of transformation that is visibly performative. The relationship between animals and human is revealed through this transformation and thus also revealed as not fixed or essentialized, but understood as performative and fluid. At the same time, the becoming-into-animal also performs the student/actor as, like a domesticated or caged animal, a potentially subjugated other, trained to perform for our pleasure. Animal study, while traditionally useful for the student actor, thus raises many questions. Does animal study increase ethical and environmental awareness, or does it only develop the personal somatic awareness of the student? Is it just instrumental, or does it create a more profound learning experience? Do students learn something subtly exploitative and exploiting as they replicate the image of an animal ultimately controlled and dominated by humans?

Animal study seldom fully encompasses notions of danger, risk and violence; aspects inherent in the life of most animals. The work tends to be, perhaps for understandable reasons, contained and controlled in ways that mean the focus is on technique and somatic experience, not ultimately on the natural life experience of the animal. Animal study in this sense represents an aesthetic and cultural challenge to the student/actor, in so far as they may struggle to really respond to the process if their sense of what is believably animal and aesthetically pleasing is too fixed and conventional. As Lee Strasberg states,

> for people who have very strong physical conditioning in ballet and in dance, we find that at a certain point the breakthrough comes with the animal exercise. It has a strange effect on many people who have a very strong physical routine. It goes counter to their sense of beauty. (in Cohen, 2010: 35)

Through animal study, the animal becomes readable in a world where it does not belong (Orozco, 2013: 72); but, ethically, it should do so in a way that also enables it to write its own way of being. Playing an animal reproduces the way that performance works and makes meaning – the 'real' animal is not present, but indicated, signified and kinaesthetically initiated into the space. The challenge for the actor is to allow themselves to come as close as possible to the 'real' animal that is not present, and to leave their human selves as far behind as possible. In this manner, they may be able to experience a world of behaviour that is deeply physically 'playful' and that through its very nature continually challenges actor training concepts and practices that are built only on an instrumentalist understanding of the body and its potential.

Animal Study in Practice: Writings on Animal Study and Training

We can see how the overarching conceptual frameworks outlined above operate in practice when we examine the writings of various tutors and practitioners on the processes they use for the delivery of animal study. For most movement trainers, the starting place for animal study is in the structure and movement of the body. The student/actor starts by getting a sense of the animal's 'weight, size, proportions, breath, rhythm and the primary control of the animal' (McEvenue, 2001: 122), they explore the 'rhythms and centers of the body associated with another creature' (Krasner, 2012: 49); thus, they understand the points of difference, the otherness of the animal and the challenges to their own habitual movement patterns. But this investigation of the animal's physiology is only the starting point – Lee Strasberg, for instance, exhorts the student/actor to 'try to feel what the tiger feels. See the bars of your cage. Feel the unrest' (Strasberg, 1987: 74). Thus, through a form of physical empathy, the student/actor is encouraged 'to break down physical inhibitions, develop body awareness, and assume shapes not included in socially accustomed behaviour' (Krasner, 2012: 48). Animal work, in this way, 'helps the actors to use their bodies and avoid over-intellectualizing' (Krasner, 2012: 48), dropping inhibitions and stepping aside from the relative complexities of words and language. Again, we can see how the body takes precedence over the mind, the impulse for movement drops from the head to the spine and the pelvis (Darley, 2009: 66). Lecoq recognizes the challenge of getting students to completely engage with this process, pushing them past the physical inhibitions that function to maintain the humanity of their movement:

> At the start of this work, some students reject contact with the ground; they avoid supporting the whole weight of the body on their arms, they try to use just their fingertips. In doing so, they are trying to maintain balance on their legs, only pretending to walk on all fours. Not until they meet the ground on its own terms, and make full contact with it, can they progress. (Lecoq, 2000: 89)

While the process of animal study and the deep reconnection with the body it enables can be a liberating physical experience for many actors, allowing them to step aside from socially constructed modes of behaviour relating to class and gender, the effects of such liberation can only be sustained if the student/actor can establish an embodied critical awareness that can realize the significance of such a change. Observing how gender functions for animals, for example, needs to be carefully handled so as not to reinforce repressive human gender stereotypes or to make hasty assumptions about gendered behaviour among animals. We need to remember that our notions of 'nature' and 'natural' are as socially constructed as our notions of gender and race. To re-coin a phrase that Laban uses, this implies a particularly sensitive and integrated form of ethical 'movement-thinking' (1980: 15).

For most movement-based trainers, trips to the nearest zoo to observe animals 'in the flesh' are either compulsory or very strongly encouraged. Part of the value of this work lies precisely in the way that it develops creative links between close observation and imaginative embodiment, between the student/actor's outside world and their inside world. Darley describes how, within animal work, the body and limbs of the student/actor seem to become like antennae (2009: 66–68), hinting at the extent to which animal study sensitizes the body and brings the nervous system somehow closer to the surface, bypassing the tendency to rationalize and self-criticize. She describes how '[t]here is no pressure to be the animal, but gradually the internal image expands in the actor's human body, inhabits it, fills it' (Darley, 2009: 70). Connecting the internal and the external in this way is part of what makes the student/actor's experience of animal study a form of journey into 'strangeness' (2009: 74). Darley describes this as a similar process to being in a mask or to the kind of transformation that costume can bring: 'Transformation is the profession. The beauty of animal work is that it is the costuming of the very guts. Animal work as I have described it is about dressing up with extraordinary attention to detail from the inside out' (Darley, 2009: 78).

Unfortunately, few actors are required to achieve the same level of transformation and physical commitment again, after completing their animal study. As Clive Barker once lamented: 'I have sat in on an animal class in which there was fine, imaginative work performed using animals as a basis for extended characterization. I enjoyed the work – but when and where will I see it in a theatre[...]?' (Barker, 1995: 105). Only in the context of performance capture for films such as *War for the Planet of the Apes* (2017), or for productions such as *War Horse* (National Theatre, 2007), might such skills be directly required. Otherwise animal study, for most actors, simply becomes one option out of many for developing character in text-based plays. When Dymphna Callery writes: 'Playing around with the idea of characters as animals is highly productive' (2001: 212), my attention is drawn to the reference to 'playing around', words which might imply an assumption that this is an adjunct to the real business of acting.

In the light of concerns raised earlier about 'domestication', the reliance on the zoo as a site for animal study is surely also problematic. When Callery suggests that the students should first be allowed to 'explore the extreme limits of the physical characteristics of these animals, so the room resembles a zoo' (2001: 212), it is interesting that she identifies 'the extreme limits' of animal study with a zoo. Surely a zoo is a place where containment, control and human dominance are quite demonstrably preserved and made manifest in the way animals are forced to behave. While a zoo might help the student learn how to observe animals' physiology and movement dynamics, it also, at the same time, embeds a set of ideological assumptions into the act of looking. The issue of artificial containment within zoos is often overlooked, with only Snow recognizing that it is also important, given the difficulty of observing animals in the wild, 'to make sure that the students watch television, DVDs and other technologies, so they can see the animals in their natural environment, observing their intra- and inter-species relationships, catching their own prey and looking after their young' (Snow, 2012: 122). Such a reliance on media would, however, mean that once again the experience of the animals is only partial (no smell, for instance) and mediated, but it does open up a wider sense of the animals' movement and behaviour in a more natural environment. It is perhaps telling how little attention is often given to the environmental context in which animals are observed and then presented (the zoo, the classroom). These are spaces that carry significant symbolic meanings and where interactions are structured in particular ways. The implicit lesson for the student/actor is that context is not relevant to understanding movement, only the qualities of the movement itself.

For both Callery and Snow, animal study is not just about physical release, but is also about enabling the student/actor to develop an 'idea of the "otherness" of characters' (Callery, 2001: 212), and to '"become" an animal as a means to making a physical transformation into a character' (Snow, 2012: 122). As Lee Strasberg describes it: 'You must do things the human body isn't accustomed to' (Cohen, 2010: 34). This sense of 'otherness' is in part physical and in part socio-psychological: it speaks to 'the total lack of self-consciousness that animals have' (Snow, 2012: 122). Animals' lack of inhibition ('animals will do everything in public that we humans would do in private' (Snow, 2012: 123)), though not perhaps as simple a quality as might be commonly believed (notions of private and public are very human concepts), might be seen as a useful attribute for the student/actor, who must learn the professional skill of being uninhibited in performance. The animal study distils the process of acting to a pre-verbal act of uninhibited transformation into the other – connecting (again) with the play of the child and with some element of theatre's possibly shamanic origins. It contradicts and resists human withdrawal from the animal, standing against traditional Christian resistance to anthropomorphy. It is probably culturally more easily aligned with pantheism and the symbolism of Asian religions (Matthews, 2011: 75), all of which can be seen as philosophical and religious belief systems that reduce the psychic distance between human and animal.

The animal typically lacks the pretension of humanity; it does not conceive of itself as other than animal. Lee Strasberg recognizes this quality when he states that he sometimes uses an animal exercise because it 'helps the actor avoid emotion or self-consciousness in order to get a sense of himself [*sic*] without emotional or mental associations' (in Cohen, 2010: 34). There is a quality in the eyes of the animal that the student/actor can consequently find difficult to recreate; a quality that is conscious without the self-consciousness that one typically associates with humanity. In private conversation, the actor and teacher Jos Houben recalled Jacques Lecoq once stating: 'Laughter is falling; except when a horse falls'; a statement which while seemingly opaque actually captures quite well something of the way in which the animal *is* rather than *wants to be seen as*. The human that falls is often self-conscious (and funny because of that self-consciousness); the animal that falls is desperate, ill, dying or exhausted. This borderline of self-consciousness and performativity also marks the point at which animal study per se ceases to have value – the humanization of the animal is virtually inevitable in order for the performance to make sense in such a sense-making and self-conscious medium as live theatre.

Animal study reinforces the physicality of acting and reasserts a relationship with a fundamental sense of what it means to be and to become. For this reason, its place within the overall programme of actor training regimes is generally assured. It enables the student to attempt to experience play and transformation on a deep and profoundly embodied level. Its location within the scheme of training is usually carefully considered. In general, it comes within the first year of training, when the student/actor is still (re)forming their sense of self-as-performer, but not so early that the student has not started to loosen up that sense of self and explore its transformative potential. What I have sought to argue in this section is, however, the importance of a critical evaluation of the ideological assumptions embedded within the practice of humans becoming animal and the contexts within which they do so, in considering how we make best use of animal study and how it is taught. Animal study reveals to us some profound truths about our own embodiment, offering to reconnect us with aspects of our being-as-animal that society has often denied to us in the past. For these reasons, as will be argued throughout this book, we must now apply a clear critical perspective as to how such movement work is taught, where and with what level of critical awareness.

Conclusion: Chapter 3

Play enables the body to speak to us and through us. It is a form of activity that is also a way of being, an attitude to life and to performance; theorists such as Marcel Jousse (2008) and Johan Huizinga (1980) suggest that it is a very important and fundamental way of relating to our environment. More than other forms of and attitudes to physical activity, play brings more clearly into focus how we can use our movement and our bodies to understand and to transform our relationship to the world. Although play-logic is distinct from the conventional forms of rational logic, it is unwise to assume that play is anti-intellectual or that it is in some way unthinking. During play, the conscious mind may not be willing action or creating meaning in the way in which it might do in other circumstances, but the conscious mind can still be reflective during the act of play – noting and associating what is going on, marking meaning as it emerges: 'Presence [...] entails being at once active *and* receptive, spontaneous *and* disciplined, animal *and* human' (Magnat, 2016: 229).

Play is strongly associated with childhood and immaturity, largely because it rejects, subverts and ignores established rational knowledges of the body and it is consequently perceived as being unproductive. Indeed, the paradigm of the child is very much present within neutral mask work – a key element of the Lecoq-based approach to movement training for the actor (Evans, 2009: 90–92). The student and/or actor is not, however, literally returned to their childhood in such work; rather they are bringing in to action a particular attitude which they may not have employed since that time in their lives. Play is also associated with animals – 'Animals play just like men [*sic*]' (Huizinga, 1980: 1) – which might also explain a similar set of assumptions around the lack of meaning, productivity, value and significance in play. But when we examine what happens when actors attempt to play animals, we can see that this is also a space in which actors are able to come into a particularly fluid and liberating relationship with their body and their movement. In *Theater of the Oppressed* (1979: 130–131), Augusto Boal (1931–2009) describes his use of a game in which participants imitate animals, using only their bodies. For him the important thing about the exercise is the full engagement of the body – something that he suggests post-industrial subjects are not used to experiencing. Frances Babbage relates this to Boal's discussion of 'muscular alienation', the ways in which forms of work activity in modern society construct the body as alienated from its full potential. In this context, the 'animal' game is part of a process that 'reveals familiar habitual patterns and encourages exploration of alternatives' (Babbage, 2010: 316).

If performance is at some level about an act of transfer – of taking experience from one realm into another – then we should take note of play as a space within which this act can take place and as an attitude to action which facilitates such practice. Play presents the actor with access to pleasure within their labour, challenging the assumption that performance must always be hard work: 'When I was a young actor [...] I used to bang my head against doors like a sledgehammer until they would open. Now, I just play. I look for the joyful thing' (Mark Rylance in Logan, 2010). Caillois defines play as free, separate, uncertain, governed by rules and make-believe (2001: 9–10); however, he also claims that play is unproductive – 'creating neither goods, nor wealth, nor new elements of any kind' (2001: 10). In the sense that play has been used in this chapter, it is certainly possible to see play as free, as circumscribed by time and space, as uncertain and imaginative despite the inevitable rules, but is it true to say that it is unproductive? Play can produce important effects for the performer and their understanding of how their body (or should it be bodies?) can be used. Play can create resistance to dominant knowledges and practices of the body, reframing the mind–body relationship as a body–mind relationship and enabling performers to measure their bodies and the expressive potential of their bodies against new sets of criteria. In this sense, play marks the fluidity in practice of the body as a concept.

Notes

1. Philippe Gaulier (1943–) studied for two years with Lecoq before becoming a member of the teaching staff. He also worked as a performer, writer and director, in particular with Pierre Byland in the 1970s. From 1980 to 1987 he ran a school with Monika Pagneux in Paris. He continued teaching at his own school from 1987 to 1991 (Paris), 1991 to 2002 (London), 2002 to the present (Paris suburbs), as well as running international workshops.
2. Monika Pagneux (1927–) was a member of Mary Wigman's dance company and worked with the Circus Knie before moving to Paris in the early 1950s. She began at the Lecoq School in 1963 and remained there as a teacher until 1979. She also worked with Peter Brook at his International Centre for Theatre Research and studied with Moshe Feldenkrais. After the shared school with Gaulier (see note 1), she has worked independently, offering workshops around the world.
3. As well as Gaulier and Pagneux, several other former students of Lecoq have set up their own successful schools: Thomas Prattki (LISPA, Berlin); Lassaad Saidi (École Lassaad – International School of Theatre, Brussels); Berty Tovías (Estudis Berty Tovías, Escuela Internacional de Teatro, Barcelona), Paola Coletto (The School for Theatre Creators, Padua, Italy), Dody DiSanto (The Center for Movement Theatre, Washington, DC), Pig Iron Theatre Company (Pig Iron School for Advanced Performance Training, Philadelphia, PA), Rodrigo Malbrán and Ellie Nixon (La Mancha International School of Image and Gesture, Chile), for example.
4. A historic form of mime in which gestures take the place of words in the telling of stories. For more detail, see Evans, 2015.
5. The impact of these two schools on drama conservatoire training in the UK was to be enormous and lasting. Former colleagues and students went on to become not only successful actors and directors, but also the directors of several existing and new drama schools (George Devine, John Blatchley, Norman Ayrton, George Hall, Duncan Ross). Saint-Denis was also later involved in the formation of the Juilliard Drama Division in New York, and L'École Supérieure d'Art Dramatique du Théâtre National in Strasbourg.
6. Marcel Marceau (born Marcel Mangel) (1923–2007) was arguably the most famous of the French mime artists. He studied with Étienne Decroux, and developed his own style of white-faced illusion mime with which he toured the world.
7. This refers to his role as Travis Bickle in the film *Taxi Driver* (1976).

4 Doing Movement Differently: Dance and Circus – Danger, Touch and Sweat

The previous chapters have examined some of the ways in which movement might offer insights into how the body 'performs' and how it participates in creative activity within conventional theatre practice. However, the body is, as I have argued already and elsewhere (Evans, 2009), also a site for and of resistance, transgression, transformation and change. It is an important location from which individuals and groups can assert their sense of difference and the significance(s) of using their bodies differently. This chapter will examine some movement practices that, while they are part of the wider theatre and entertainment ecology, also offer challenges to conventional theatrical notions of how the body communicates, signifies, and enacts its own presence.

Historically, approaches to movement training within the drama conservatoire system have focused on movement work that does not draw attention to itself in performance. This kind of movement work is framed within a naturalistic approach to acting, which tends to disguise or conceal the techniques it uses. As we have seen through previous chapters, this position has been subject to challenge over the last 50 years as attitudes to physical difference have altered, as interest in non-naturalistic approaches to movement have grown, as modes of theatrical production have changed, and since awareness has increased of the multiple ways in which bodies and movement are capable of signifying meaning beyond what can be communicated through words. New approaches to movement training and movement performance over this period have drawn on practices such as contemporary dance, New Circus, acrobatics, somatic practices, and a range of intensive physical training techniques. Most of these techniques and practices have remained outside 'mainstream' actor training and performance practice. This chapter will examine the impact of forms such as contemporary dance, New Circus, *parkour* and physical theatre on perceptions of the role and function of movement for the contemporary theatre performer.

The emphasis on the physical that these forms of performance offer sets up new paradigms for theatre performance that emphasize: the politics of the body; the increasing cultural emphasis given to physicality, physical danger and risk; heightened physical experience; different ways in which bodies can collaborate with each other; and new ways in which the body partakes in the making and breaking of meaning. This chapter will focus on examples that reveal how movement practices such as those listed above have migrated into theatre contexts and been used to explore, develop and express new understandings of how the body performs. The case studies will examine how such approaches to movement offer new and alternative paradigms for the body as a locus for performance and for professionalism.

The development of movement performance has included a long process of cross-fertilization between different areas of practice. It is the potential of movement-based work to offer a locus for cross-disciplinary migration that has made it an area that is important in challenging and revitalizing performance and training practice. Working across disciplines opens up questions around the cultural construction of the performer's body. The inclusion of physical practices from other fields can either work to reinforce dominant paradigms for the body (for example, where the ideologies embedded in social dances function to strengthen the hold of traditional conceptions of gender and class) or to undermine such paradigms (for example, where women fence and men dance expressively). For the performer/student, the opportunity to bring new practices into play on their body is often invigorating and creatively stimulating, and can work in tandem with a desire to find new connections between their experience of movement and the theatre context within which they work or seek to work.

This chapter will examine some of the physical performance practices that have emerged over the last 20 years as part of this landscape. One case study will look at the work of Frantic Assembly, a company which over the last two decades has integrated a variety of performances practices including: contemporary dance (contact improvisation), sport (boxing), physical theatre and *parkour*. The chapter will also look at the emergence and development of New Circus over the last few decades, and the ways in which other performance practices have integrated with circus skills and practices. The aim will be to explore the significance of the processes involved in transmitting such knowledge and performing and producing the work.

Different Disciplines

There are some important distinctions and definitions that need to be established in respect of some of the key terms used in this chapter. The word 'discipline' relates both to a field of practice or study and also to a notion of rigour, strictness and even regulation. The danger, of course, is that too much of the latter can too quickly and too easily become restricting and limiting; even so, without discipline, work can become vague, imprecise and confusing. Michel Foucault has alerted us to the ways in which disciplines of practice become restrictive and come to represent the exercise of power and knowledge in ways that control us and that reflect societal structures and power systems. If disciplines of movement practice represent paradigmatic concepts of the body in performance, then clearly there is value and importance in examining the spaces where new and/or unusual practices might challenge those paradigms. A number of terms have emerged to define the various relationships available between disciplines. The definitions proposed in relation to teaching and pedagogy by Carr et al. (2014: 6) are perhaps as useful as is necessary for this chapter. They suggest that: 'multi-disciplinary' refers to those from different disciplines engaging in a shared activity; 'cross-disciplinary' refers to ways in which one discipline can be described in terms of another; 'trans-disciplinary' refers to practice that blurs discipline boundaries; 'collaboration' refers to work in which participants work together but from within their own disciplines; 'integration' refers to practitioners sampling each other's practice; 'intra-disciplinary' refers to collaboration within a discipline; and 'inter-disciplinary' refers to situations in which participants across different disciplines work with each other and explore different practices through shared activity.

Thus, this chapter will, in these terms, be exploring how knowledge and understanding within one field can be applied to another field (cross-discipline), how traditional discipline boundaries might be blurred or ignored (trans-discipline) and how combining disciplines can result in new knowledge, understanding and practice (inter-discipline). Inter/cross/trans-disciplinary performance work should not be seen as simply placing a bit of dance/circus/*parkour* in the middle of a conventional piece of theatre; it is about how and to what purpose new or different practices can deeply inform the ways that movement is used within a specific performance. Poststructuralist, postmodern and feminist performance theory have questioned the ability of single discipline practices to address the complexity of contemporary society. Inter/cross/trans-disciplinary theatre performance practice is arguably better able to represent different perspectives (geographical, historical, racial, cultural, gendered) and indeed the very notion of difference. Tamasha Theatre's *The Arrival*, devised in 2013 for a UK tour, for instance, combined theatre, circus and music in order to find a theatrical language through which to discuss migration, difference and displacement. Steven Hoggett and Scott Graham of Frantic Assembly capture quite eloquently the ways in which companies setting out to work across disciplines and emerging from ad hoc training regimes both struggle with and benefit from the lack of clear structures within such a field:

> The early days had us looking for an artistic process, much defined by the demands of the people we worked with rather than by us. We were feeling our way but realised quickly that our lack of experience and theatre training was actually liberating. We knew nothing of the important practitioners, other than Volcano, DV8 and a few others. Knowing nothing of, for example, Artaud meant that we were not beholden to a set of values or a defined process. We were absolutely free to try things out without dismissing a previous manifesto. There were no arguments about the directions of the company because they veered away from a classical line or suddenly contradicted themselves. It was all steered by gut instinct. (Graham & Hoggett, 2012: 7)

Over the last 50 years, the increase in university theatre, drama and performance courses, together with the willingness of art schools to accommodate live art and performance as forms of arts practice, have variously supported the development of performance work that explores the liminal spaces between and on the edges of traditional discipline boundaries. In the UK, workshops and festivals such as the International Workshop Festival, London International Festival of Theatre and London International Mime Festival, as well as regional events and opportunities such as the National Student Drama Festival, have also helped to promote this area of work and to encourage the international exchange of practices, ideas and working methods. Because of the nature of these influences, training opportunities have tended to be relatively low intensity (projects or modules on university courses) or ad hoc (one-off workshop opportunities). For the companies interested in working in this way, this also means that new company members can be hard to find – conventional recruitment methods don't necessarily work for performers with an eclectic range of skills and possibly little or no formal training. The audition process will also be different – as Frantic Assembly suggest, you cannot just put people through the same old hoops; a more open and collaborative approach is needed (Graham & Hoggett, 2012: 5).

Frantic Assembly

Frantic Assembly is a physical theatre company formed in Swansea in 1994 by Scott Graham, Steven Hoggett and Vicki Coles (now Middleton). They met as students at Swansea University and, inspired by workshops with Volcano Theatre Company, they decided to launch their own troupe. Their work was not particularly Welsh or Celtic in any easily recognizable way, but it certainly drew strength and purpose in those early days from not being in London (they were forced to tour), and from a history of physical performance practice in South Wales (such as that of Cardiff Laboratory Theatre, Paupers Carnival, RAT Theatre, Brith Gof and Moving Being). Working at a distance from London, and even from the Welsh capital, Cardiff, enabled them to avoid and challenge the conventional critical and commercial markers of success. Graham relates how 'it felt anti-establishment in a kind of way [...] it wasn't about the canon, pulling a play off the shelf and doing that; it was about making work, being artists and feeling like you were a little bit more guerilla' (2015). Starting from such a place enabled them to maintain and profit from a marginal position, to nurture an idiosyncratic and distinctive theatre voice, and to avoid easy pigeon-holing for an important period of their early development.

Early shows, including a 'Generation X' trilogy (*Klub, Flesh* and *Zero*), were largely devised by the company in collaboration with a writer, Spencer Hazel. After 2000, the company began to work with a range of established writers and also with external directors/choreographers (for example Liam Steel, who directed *Hymns* in 1999, was at that time an associate director of DV8). The company's work is marked by a blend of dance, movement, gesture, text, music, video and design. Wanting to speak to the interests of their own generation, they actively sought to avoid what they saw as the performance clichés of conventional theatre and to make use of dramaturgical, structural and presentational devices drawn from the culture around them – music videos, clubbing, DJ sets, adverts and films. Frantic represent a popular alternative to the conventional use of movement in mainstream theatre and to the more extreme and provocative work of Volcano. Their work is accessible, and has a strong following among theatregoers of their own generation and younger. They were, from the start, drawn by the excitement and pleasure of using dance and movement within theatre:

> I think we probably started in a very naïve and exuberant fashion, movement was everything and we just wanted to throw movement at it. The more we looked at movement, it became a part of the potential to move that was exciting rather than the movement itself. (Graham, 2015)

This attitude meant that they were, from the start, confident in allowing the movement work to be at the forefront of their devising process and their performances.

Frantic have not been afraid to maintain their particular style of movement work as a distinctive and important feature of what they do and who they are. Far from becoming a barrier for them, this open and embedded use of very particular movement approaches appears to have been an important part of their appeal to their audiences. Whereas the semiotic codes of mime now seem a little too obvious for the early twenty-first century audience, the complex and multiple meanings and significances available to directors, performers and audiences within Frantic's style of work seem to have created and, so far, maintained an important and significant degree of social and cultural relevance. For Frantic, the use of dance and movement has enabled them to explore innovative ways of staging complex situations in visually engaging ways. In *The Believers* (2014–2015), the company deliberately set out to explore what happens when notions of memory and truth become unsettled. Through the rehearsal process, they explored flipping the whole space by 90 degrees at one of the points in the play when the emotional stakes reach a peak. As well as being a very visual and physical representation of a moment of dis/reorientation, it also affected the performers: 'Their bodies feel very different. They have to hold themselves differently [...] it helps them because the world is different, something has changed' (Graham, 2015). This same approach informed the company's involvement in the National Theatre production of *The Curious Incident of the Dog in the Night-time* (2012 and subsequent tours), where their movement work enabled the production to find ways of representing the life-world of an autistic teenage boy.

Frantic began work at a time when the formal training opportunities in the UK for those seeking to work in this particular form of dance/theatre were practically non-existent. They recognized that they needed to learn and acquire performance skills, techniques and compositional methods, but they had only a partial understanding in the early days as to what those components were.

We just wanted to devour the experience and we knew that working with dancers and choreographers would provide that. What we had to offer was enthusiasm, openness and bravery. I think if we were to recognize what the component parts were, that might have terrified us. That would have shown us what we were lacking. We would never use the word technique. We were quite afraid of the word technique. And that's not to say the work doesn't possess technique, I think you do have to understand the mechanics of balance and power, and all of those things, but I think we understood technique to mean a certain kind of house style [...] That's what we were scared of. And also, we were inspired by something that appeared to be much rawer, and we thought there was a value in that and we wanted to present something that was genuinely raw. (Graham, 2015)

The result for Frantic was a kind of 'DIY training', which they self-managed through the decisions they made about who they worked with and what they worked on. Though generally less concerned about theatre history and theory and more concerned about where this journey was taking them, they were not unaware of what was on offer elsewhere. What might superficially seem to be a naive approach to training was actually a smart way of maintaining the freedom to choose what they needed when they needed it. In fact, the 'need' was very real for them – the work they did had to connect for them and their audiences if they were to survive – and the concept of learning through making links connects very clearly with the way that they make work – building from clear tasks and simple instructions, learning through devising and rehearsing, touring and performance. Graham argues that, 'in any contact improvisation or any kind of duet say, there should be three people involved at least, one of whom is the audience' (2015); this suggests an approach that is always considering and acknowledging what the audience might be understanding or experiencing by the actions and movements that are being performed. All of these elements produce an approach that has clearly emerged directly from the experience of touring and performing to different audiences on a regular basis.

Although the initial impetus for Frantic Assembly came from their early experiences with Volcano Theatre, they were also interested in the ways that they could bring their personal fascination with film, music videos and contemporary dance music into the work and into their making and creating processes. Their approach to collaboration was that everyone involved, from whatever background, could and would engage across the range of disciplines and starting points within the rehearsal space: 'We want lighting designers to engage with the choreography, designers to engage with the music and all of this to happen as early as possible' (Graham & Hoggett, 2012: 8).

This kind of collaborative process, of course, takes longer – typically a Frantic show can take six weeks to rehearse instead of the usual four. Choreography of the movement sections inevitably involves more time, especially as the work is sometimes choreographed with performers who may have limited dance experience and the choreography may need to be integrated with text and other elements. In the early days, this approach helped establish a distinctiveness and freshness, and was particularly attractive to a young audience who were as unfazed as Frantic were about mixing up disciplines and blending in things from their own life experience. Frantic have written about how they realized 'that any skills we picked up could be exploited to help keep the company afloat' (Graham & Hoggett, 2012: 9). Sharing, collaborating and working across disciplines was both an entrepreneurial necessity and a way in which they could accelerate their own artistic development; it also created an ethos for the company, an ethos that connected with a wider mood and that has subsequently informed their long-running commitment to enabling and empowering others to get involved in making this kind of inter/cross/trans-disciplinary work: 'It is clear that the way we stumbled into theatre has influenced our desire to bring others into it' (Graham & Hoggett, 2012: 10).

In these respects, Frantic are similar to many of the physical theatre companies that emerged in the late 1980s and early 1990s. The development from mime and performance art in the 1970s to physical theatre in the 1980s was a movement away from a formal delineation of different performance modes and towards a more integrated approach that drew together dance, movement, mime, mask work, improvisation, text, martial arts and sport in formations that spoke to the needs and interests of the performers and audiences at that time. Frantic, perhaps a little bit 'tongue in cheek', have claimed: 'We are not even sure what the physical theatre genre is' (Graham & Hoggett, 2012: 15). The reality is that physical theatre can probably only be understood as a range of practices and processes; Murray and Keefe (2015) refer to physical theatres in the plural for precisely this reason. In stating that they draw their inspiration from the contemporary cultural practices around them, Frantic are not denying the importance of history and theory, but sidestepping their immediate effects. They prefer to engage with history and theory through the ways in which both are already integral to and integrated into 'everyday' life. This has kept their work highly accessible, but it has led to a perception in some quarters that it is not political and not ideologically or intellectually challenging. This perception will be examined in more detail below.

Constructing work from the building blocks of physical tasks, Frantic have developed a devising and rehearsal method that fits well with their approach to collaboration, and to inter/cross/trans-disciplinary working. Choreography/direction is not imposed, dancing in the conventional sense is not required, meaning-making is temporarily deferred within the initial phases of the process, but the performance material grows out of movement sequences developed, shaped and structured by and with the performers. It is worth quoting Graham and Hoggett's detailed description of this process:

> We initially create the kernel of the idea and test this to see if it is interesting enough to us and if 'it has got legs' – whether it will stand up to scrutiny and be interesting to anyone else. This 'testing' is pretty much talking about the idea, letting it sit for a while and then returning to it with a wiser head to see if it still excites us.

> Then we take it into development with as many of our collaborators as possible on board. Here we flesh it out and hopefully come out with a much bigger idea that would then go into the rehearsal stage where a full script would be presented. This might take a couple of years. It might not sound like devising to you but it is the way we work.

> All devising is broken down into tasks. These remain bite sized and self-contained. They never set out to encapsulate the whole production idea or solve the entire demands of the text. They are always as simple as we can make them. They are merely building blocks that are created to support more blocks.

> By setting tasks you allow your performers much more creative input into the devising process without burdening them with the responsibility of creating the whole thing. (Graham & Hoggett, 2012: 16)

This approach has in large part developed out of the company's exposure to the working methods of a few of the choreographers that they have collaborated with (for example Liam Steel and Juan Carruscoso):

> They recognised the need to simplify things for us, to see what we could do and then use this. We responded to their use of rules and parameters and have taken this process on as our own. [...] In rehearsals we never teach 'steps.' The moves come from what the performers find they are capable of through the specific tasks set. (Graham & Hoggett, 2012: 16)

The dance practices that have influenced Frantic the most are those associated with contact improvisation and the New Dance movements within Britain and America over the last two decades, as well as the dance/theatre work of the German choreographer Pina Bausch (1940–2009). Bausch's work has had a profound impact on dance/theatre in the UK. Her work focused on attempting to 'reinvest dance performance with the personal and political concerns of the individual performer' (Buckland, 1995: 371). In doing so, it encouraged companies such as DV8, Volcano and Frantic to draw on whatever was needed, 'in order to communicate their experiences and concerns, unconstrained by the conventional performance lexicons of either dance or theatre' (Buckland, 1995: 371). As Alex Sierz notes (2017), Frantic found that starting from where they were as young people in the 1990s, as well as locating themselves as performers within the styles and formats they chose to use, unleashed their own creativity and also engaged the Generation X[1] audience demographic that they wanted to appeal to: 'I think we were very much drawn to stories about us' (Graham, 2015). For Frantic, this meant ditching some of what they saw as the conventional approaches to theatre making. Using their own names for the characters they played on stage, for instance, created a sense of honesty, immediacy and emotional depth (Sierz, 2017: 4), while at the same time unsettling their audience's sense of where character ended and performer began; it was what was happening on stage that was important. The notion of character as disassociated from a simple fictional identity but nonetheless strongly associated with the presence of the performer's body on stage somehow spoke to a generation who instinctively felt that there was something wrong with what they were being told about their identity elsewhere in the cultural marketplace. As Buckland writes about DV8:

> There are no 'characters' in Dead Dreams [Dead Dreams of Monochrome Men by DV8, 1988]. The performers adopt no personas. They are defined on stage in terms of their actions: by what they do. This means that in terms of their subject matter and the physicality with which they have chosen to represent it, the body becomes both the mode and the subject of the performance. (Buckland, 1995: 375)

Sierz notes that Frantic worked hard in devising and rehearsals to avoid 'deviation into actorly speech' (Sierz, 2017: 4) – the same also applied to their movements. Although they drew on choreographic structuring devices, the movements themselves were almost entirely drawn from everyday, accidental, informal gestures and actions – brushing past someone, a touch, briefly holding hands, a hug.

In interview in 1999, Fern Smith stated how, for Volcano, formal dance technique seemed potentially to desensitize the body and introduce a narrative of technical accuracy that curtailed the potential for complexity, immediacy and diversity. She recalled how, when Nigel Charnock was directing

Volcano, 'he'd go away and then we'd be touring a show and he'd come back and he'd say, "No. The movement's getting too good ... it's getting too dance like"' (Smith in Evans, 1999: 140). There is a similar tension in Frantic's work – within a more recent show like *Things I Know To Be True*, which has toured extensively to established venues, there might be a sense in which the movement work has become too well performed. On the other hand, one of the things that made *Lovesong* seem such a strongly emotional show was that the audience were more aware of the effort (and, in some cases, the struggle) involved in the movement work for those actors playing the older couple (Sam Cox and Siân Phillips).

New Dance and contact improvisation offered physical theatre companies like Frantic Assembly a way to represent a contemporary understanding of individuality, togetherness and identity through movement vocabularies and compositional devices that were no longer shaped and controlled by culturally dominant forms of dance and theatre. Lloyd Newson of DV8 states very clearly how strongly the need to be able to represent difference and individuality was felt by those working in this field at this time:

> I am very frustrated by the lack of individuality and character that is being presented in dance. I am so bored with work where everybody has to be the same – like the same person, which is often the choreographer. I want to see individuality, I want to see characters on stage, I want to see people experience things. (Lloyd Newson in Meisner, 1992: 10)

This emphasis on some kind of authentic experience underpins not just the work of DV8, Volcano and Frantic, but can also be seen in the work of other theatre practitioners in the 1990s, such as performance company Forced Entertainment and writer Sarah Kane. Their activity marks changing attitudes towards physicality, embodiment, pain, pleasure and sexuality, and a desire to represent these qualities in ways that are more fluid, immediate, exciting and recognizable for their generation. Their work sits in contrast to the majority of commercial and subsidized mainstream theatre, within which the expression of the sexual, the intimate and the emotional has tended to be largely verbal and/or intellectual. Sexuality, if present at all in mainstream performance, is usually implicit, rarely openly celebrated and hardly ever allowed to be visibly 'other'. DV8, Volcano and Frantic have explored new ways of using movement that allow sexuality to be present, expressive and richly complex.

This is an important respect in which the physical theatre practice of Frantic (and Volcano and DV8) is different from the other dominant influences in

UK physical theatre during the second half of the twentieth century, such as the French mime tradition (Copeau, Bing, Decroux and Lecoq) and the Russian/Polish tradition (Meyerhold, Chekhov and Vahktangov/Grotowski, Barba and Staniewski). At the heart of the French tradition is the ability of the actor to transform through movement and, in the case of mime, to employ the semiotic significance of movement and gesture. At the heart of the Eastern European tradition is an intensely physical approach built on Stanislavsky's understanding of ways in which the actor identifies with the role, on the actor's integrity and sincerity, on a deep sense of authenticity, and on a desire to unearth an essentially human, pre-performance mode of behaviour and action. The traditions that have influenced Frantic are those that allow and encourage a particular focus on the relationships between people and on the ways in which people perform their identity. This strand differs from the French tradition's notion of ensemble and the Eastern European notion of authenticity – its (apparent) lack of history placing more emphasis on the 'nowness' of its movement practices and on the physical relationship between performers.

It is in relation to these differences that the work of DV8, Volcano and Frantic has been able to challenge and explore the relationship between movement, gesture and gender identity in ways that the other forms of physical theatre have tended to ignore or be less concerned with. Contemporary fluidity around gender identities is at odds with the fixed notions of gender identity implied by the neutral mask, for instance. In Lecoq's teaching neither the neutral mask work nor the clown overtly raises gender as an issue (even though gender is clearly present and available within the neutral mask work; the school uses both a 'male' and a 'female' neutral mask). Indeed, it might be argued that gender and sexuality for both Grotowski and Lecoq (re)present a set of problems or distractions, and are not generally recognized as opportunities for creative exploration and expression; this is something that will be discussed in more detail in Chapter 5.

By contrast, sexuality, physical intimacy and the pleasure of movement are often visible in and central to the work of Frantic. Frantic's style of movement is seen by some as imposing a particular style on their performances. In so far as this is true, such overt use of movement is an intentional but subtle act of subversion. Movement is performed so as to signal its own presence, and in addition to signal the presence of sexuality and physical intimacy. It 'announces' itself – but with a release of pleasure, with confidence and energy, and not with self-congratulation or pomposity. Movement in these contexts reveals hidden tensions, desires, regrets and associations. This confessional quality operates as a dramatic trope; the performance, the spoken text and the movement all revealing something that had otherwise remained hidden and that would require a form of courage, of tacit permission from the listener, to expose in the open. This trope tends to create a sense of intimacy with the audience; there is an element of personal risk and danger (physical and confessional), and a degree of mutual moral complicity (the testimony – verbal or physical – always operates to implicate the listener/observer).

Buckland invokes Foucault, to remind us how 'power flows through the channels formed by discourse to reach, penetrate, and control individuals right down to their most private pleasures, using the negative methods of refusal and prohibition, but also the positive ones of excitation and intensification' (1995: 377). The work of DV8, Volcano and Frantic enables movement and the body to be examined as locations and processes through which power can be revealed, examined and challenged on personal, political and social levels. Of course, each of these companies responds to these possibilities in different ways. Acknowledging and celebrating the physicality, the eroticism and the sexuality of movement; revealing how touch, contact and movement resonate with meaning and potential, particularly in relation to gender, this style of work is not only confessional in tone, it is also subversive of the power structures that place it within the confessional. It is so because it brings desire into play, and it opens up and reveals the effects of consumption and power on the body. It is not just sexual desire that is being referred to here, but desire as the sense of a fulfilment that is withheld, desire that measures that gap between how we want our bodies to be and how they are, between how close we want to be to other people and how close we actually are. In this respect, a big part of the meaning of the work of these companies is in *how* they perform as much as in *what* they perform, and in when movement doesn't happen as much as in when (and why) it does.

> I am more excited about that moment before [movement] happens when the audience are screaming for it to happen or the characters are screaming for it to happen, because I think that sometimes it is just as exciting to deny them that, than to give them that. (Graham, 2015)

For many critics and academics, this aspect of Frantic's work can be misconstrued as a lack of meaning – this kind of movement is seen as deferring meaning, it is movement that is the expression of physicality for its own sake. But Graham is suggesting that this style of movement is certainly not meaningless; it is movement *as* meaning, not movement *for* meaning. It is what he refers to as movement 'vibrating with meaning' (Graham, 2015). These reverberations and disruptions are perhaps more easily discernible within the work of DV8, but they are also present in the work of Frantic if less immediately visible and less overtly political in intent.

If movement is not grounded in some form of meaning, then the danger is that it will become commodified, viewed only as a product such that any subversive intent is not revealed. Buckland (1995: 377) points out that too much emphasis on the body can result in sexual desire and the possession of the object dominating the audience's reception of the performance event. To what extent could this criticism be levelled at the work of Frantic? Is the work too rich in desire, intimacy and physical excitement? It is the presence of tenderness and vulnerability within the work, the emphasis on the relationships between bodies, and the space that is made for these qualities that becomes important and necessary if we are to understand Frantic's work as more than commodification of the body – as these qualities allow desire the possibility of some form of fulfilment and move the audience/consumer beyond excitement and/or titillation and towards a richer understanding of the kinds of meanings that movement can evoke beyond the semiotic and beyond struggle. Once again, the attitude of the performer, the choreographer and/or the director towards the movement work is as important as the movement work itself. It is also essential to be clear about what modes of physicality are being challenged and how.

The forms of dance used by Frantic, Volcano and DV8 are drawing on a style of performance that is clearly influenced by Pina Bausch's work in its directness, its blending of the everyday and the abstract, and its strong sense of the personal. They are also influenced by some of the European dance choreographers who emerged in the 1980s such as Wim Vandekeybus and Anne Teresa De Keersmaeker, both of whose work emphasizes physical exhaustion, repetition and the blending of dance with everyday actions. Vandekeybus was closely associated with what became known as 'Eurocrash' – a form of dance which construes 'the body as an emotional battlefield, and performance as a kind of extreme sport' (Mackrell, 2007). There are clear resonances here with the performance ethos of DV8 and Volcano and with some of the early work of Frantic. Buckland draws our attention to the emotional risk to the individual in this kind of work (Buckland, 1995: 377); but that risk is counter-balanced by the physical and emotional intensity and authenticity that such work generates. Graham describes how Frantic felt inspired by Volcano's fearless approach to movement – 'all energy and honesty' (2015) – and by DV8's ability to create movement-based work that was 'funny, remarkable, stunning, exciting and very masculine of course' (2015). Graham identifies the importance of what Lloyd Newson articulates as a lack of 'waft', implying that what both he and Hoggett were attracted to was an approach to movement that was direct, purposeful, lacking in any artificiality, and grounded. There could of course be gendered connotations within an attitude to 'waft' and movement – some of which will be addressed in Chapter 5. This mix results in a situation within performance in which '[t]he body is engaged with as a site of risk, of danger, of pleasure and of uncertainty. The body holds and withholds, reveals and lies, protects and betrays. Authenticity and truth are at issue, but never decided' (Evans, 1999: 140). Improvisation is central to this kind of performance work. Using improvisation facilitates and encourages, sometimes even demands, rejection of that which is conventional and familiar.

Playfulness and pleasure operate within Frantic's work as a way to invert Volcano and DV8's strong commitment to performance 'authenticity'. Frantic's physicality challenges the performer in what seem initially to be similar ways to the work of DV8, and yet, through its playfulness and pleasurability, their work simultaneously lightens and qualifies the intensity that can infuse some of DV8's and Volcano's work. Volcano's early work emphasized what might be referred to as the 'angry grapple' (to borrow from Judith Mackrell (2007)), pursued with a relentlessness that is impressive and compelling but limited in its meaning. Ultimately, despite a physicality that might be misconstrued as simply signifying the sincerity of the body, Frantic's shows are often about the difficulty of getting to the core of one's experience of oneself or one's experience of other people. Buckland (1995: 378) cites Doris Humphreys and the arc of 'fall and recovery' – a longing for security and a desiring for risk. This dynamic, so powerfully expressed through movement, has spoken strongly to new sets of audiences for the work of Frantic Assembly. Movement in this context embodies a different form of desperation, one that can be quiet and tender as well as frenzied and impetuous; it achieves this by seeking to find an eloquent balance between danger and safety.

Frantic's work is not as overtly political as that of DV8 or Volcano. Both of these companies have used dance and movement in order to address very specific issues (for example societal homophobia in *Dead Dreams of Monochrome Men* (DV8, 1988) and Marxist politics in *Manifesto*[2] (Volcano, 1994)). In Frantic's work, the politics are enmeshed in the way that the work is created and performed rather than in the choice of content and narrative.

> We're not didactic and part of my process of making a show is about listening. Listening to actors, listening in the greatest sense, listening with my eyes, taking it in and trying to learn something. Going in with a didactic position, I am not particularly interested in that. I think it's a particular type of theatre that is done very well by some people, but I think my interest in the politics lies somewhere differ-

ent. Presenting Othello[3] in the way we did is, I think, political, because it shows that this work is for people like you, like this, and it can be performed by people like you and those people are strong, in terms of younger women for instance, and also that their fall is just as great as any general's fall. (Graham, 2015)

What Frantic share with companies like DV8 and choreographers like Pina Bausch is a politics of making. The creative process, while overseen and led by the artistic director(s), is deliberately collaborative. Task-based activities are used to generate significant quantities of material that can be selected and integrated. The material thus recognizes, draws on, and validates the life experience of the performers as well as that of the director(s) and writer. It also creates a shared sense of responsibility and deliberately removes the actor from an otherwise individualized approach to their role within the rehearsal room: 'By inviting people into the creative side, I think it actually liberates them' (Graham, 2015). In this way, these companies aim to embody their politics in the way that they work as much as explain it through the content of their work.

In addition, this style of performance making also emphasizes close physical contact, the importance of touch and the sharing of weight; it does so in part to challenge social mechanisms that seek to control how such interactions work and make meaning, and also to undermine simple distinctions between what male and female performers can or cannot do. In drawing on the techniques developed within and associated with contact improvisation, they are drawing on a dance form which, as Cynthia Novack noted, is inherently democratic and which provides a direct and practical critique of traditional dance aesthetics (see Novack, 1990). Contact improvisation assumes a performance ecology that offers and celebrates empowerment and integrity within physical relationships, that recognizes the physical as creative, and that opens up for inspection the ways in which movement is important in understanding who we are and how we interact with each other. For Graham, the important thing is that 'there is a process that is very much alive in the room, and it's not about just what you do on your own but it's about how you relate to other people' (2015).

The physicality of Frantic's work is not in opposition to politics or intellect. The club culture from which they drew some of their early inspiration was a social dance phenomenon that placed new value on 'endurance, participation and emotional engagement' (Evans, 1999: 139), but it was also important as a political statement about how, where and in what ways bodies could come together and dance. The particular physicality that Frantic employed meant that bodies were 'not experienced reflexively but as the site for conflicting investigations of the physical experience of life' (ibid.). All of which argues that while not overtly political, Frantic's work should nonetheless be seen as part of a wider cultural change that viewed the personal, the physical and even forms of movement as potentially politically charged.

Frantic Assembly, Movement and Text

What Frantic's work picks up on is a cultural shift that has realigned movement and the body in relation to speech and text. Mark Smith writes about how the 'trope of physicality overpowering the verbal' repeats itself through Frantic's work (Smith, 2013: 104), and about how the company explores the ways in which physicality both expresses and overcomes a sense of inarticulacy and the struggle of dealing with intimacy and vulnerability. Graham notes how even the early shows embodied politically orientated questions about why a generation of young people 'were happy to spend their time and energy and money on an experience that they weren't getting somewhere else' (2015). This was a generation who were 'happy to cut themselves free from reality [...] it was mostly fun, mostly kind of open and warm. It was certainly political because it became outlawed' (Graham, 2015). If there is a final sense in which Frantic's work might be considered political, it is perhaps in relation to the people they invite to come and see it and the people they seek out to work with. They audition through workshops rather than through conventional auditions. They have spoken to several generations of young audiences in a form that is accessible and exciting. Their 'Learn and Train' programme has encouraged many young people to believe that they can make theatre and that they are capable of performances that they would previously have thought beyond them. Frantic from the start embraced something of a 'punk' aesthetic – 'we have always said that you can do this [...] just throw yourself in and try' (Graham, 2015). Their first show, *Look Back In Anger* (1994–1995), was a deliberate attempt to invert the canon, in the same way that punk music had done about 15 years before. An additional 'punk' element is the extent to which the bodily and physical expression of the performer is not a finished and defined object, a product of expensive training and an expression of virtuosity and expertise. If there is still a roughness about the movement, something that marks it as separate and different from professional dance work, it is that quality which allows the performer to connect with the people/bodies observing and to do so in a particular way that subverts at least some of the cultural conventions around traditional dance or theatre performance: 'What is added is risk not technique, energy not grace, desire not fulfilment'

(Evans, 1999: 142). This ethos has stuck with them, and even now, when Scott Graham talks about trying to define the Frantic method, his words echo the spirit of self-efficacy that informed their early approach:

> I think it is about openness and a desire to always find the simplest and most successful way to start and to build on that in simple and accessible steps. And to always be listening and looking out for potential and inspiration. (Graham, 2015)

In order to make the kind of physical theatre of which they dreamed, Graham and Hoggett have had to develop a dramaturgy of movement that might also work alongside and align with a textual dramaturgy. They describe in their book how the movement vocabulary of their shows typically emerges from the collaborative generation of fragments of movement sequences as opposed to larger, more sustained sections. This is an approach that brings musical and choreographic structural devices in to play as well as more conventional devices that might align movements with text or with themes underpinning or contrasting with the text. Hoggett has stated how:

> We construct[ed] our [early] shows around the principles of a DJ set, taught to us [by Andy Cleeton] when we made *Klub*, where the idea is to manipulate the audience/crowd by guiding them through peaks which gently break down only to bring them up further and repeat to fade. We used this method not only in constructing the soundtracks but also in our arrangement of text and physical sequences as well as crafting openings and finales which are treated in isolation. (in Evans, 1999: 141)

The blending of everyday gestures and movements with actions and sequences that can be more abstract serves to undermine any sense of virtuosity for its own sake: 'There does not appear to be any attempt to be or become "expert" within the limitations of a conventional dance or theatre aesthetic; that is to say to be more graceful, more technically precise or more "careful"' (Evans, 1999: 137). The use of the everyday gesture within the building blocks for performance also illuminates the everyday, revealing its rhythmical qualities, highlighting its potential resonances and, through repetition, allowing the audience to dwell for a little longer on its significance. Repetition can of course signify anxiety, frustration, anger and ennui, but it can also create moods that are contemplative, intimate, tender, elegiac, erotic or mournful. Graham speaks about the richness that comes from not aiming for a particular meaning, but allowing what is created to reveal (often multiple) meanings, including those not originally intended.

I am just absolutely fascinated by how complex a single moment can be when you ask the observer what it is. [...] I love words, I adore the work of writers, but I am most interested in those moments where nothing happens but an audience gasps because they have brought something to it, and you have created that. [...] I think my approach in the rehearsal room is about recognizing that power and keeping those moments alive and not crushing it through words and certainly not crushing it through movement. (Graham, 2015)

Mark Smith also writes of the ways in which this kind of approach employs and generates a sense of 'group-mind' in which the performance company (and, one might add, the audience) become attuned to each other and to the work at hand. This is an approach, as Smith (2013: 200) points out, that is shared with a number of companies from this period, including Complicité and Forced Entertainment. The postmodern suspicion of metanarratives of meaning seems to have led to a determination instead to create stage images, sequences of performance material, that invite and allow multiple meanings and interpretations at multiple levels of emotional and intellectual complexity. One example Graham gives is from *Curious Incident* – despite the inclusion of some spectacular lifts and moments of flight, it is, for him, the complex and multiple meanings circulating around attempted moments of touch between father (Ed) and son (Christopher), moments where we see the father reach to make contact with his autistic son, only for the offered moment to be ignored. It is these embodied moments that resonate most deeply within the movement dramaturgy of the production – the movement work is precise, but the meanings are open and generative, with touch echoing throughout the production as a metaphor for communication or its absence.

Within Frantic's work, speech and text are sometimes tellingly located alongside sections of intense or focused physical activity. This creates a specific effect, whereby the performer's attitude to the text is changed. The concentration and/or energy required for the movement work both distracts them from becoming too 'actorly' in the delivery of the text and also grounds the delivery in a presence supported by the intensity of the physical work. Movement and speech become both immediate and performative; the sensation and the act of moving and speaking in this way become both complicit and significant in constructing the social and subversive power of this physical theatre work.

Enacting risk and danger clearly resonates within the work of companies such as DV8, Volcano and Frantic Assembly. It can be empowering for the individual in terms of the development of their physical confidence, but it can also, if not approached with care, inadequately acknowledge the personal and social politics of space and proximity, or of assertive physical action. Opening up spaces for participants to discuss and to interrogate their gendered and social experiences of this work is important. The work of Frantic, DV8 and Volcano at least brings movement into this socio-political arena – the work is challenging enough to develop physical confidence in the participants, and through that very challenge it provokes the participants to engage critically with the meaning and significance of that experience. This is one of the benefits of working across different forms of performance – the ground is immediately unsteady: 'Many dancers and actors are not interested in exploring new ground: they say, "Give me the steps" and "Where's the script?"' (Newson in Giannachi & Luckhurst, 1999: 110); cross-disciplinary work challenges more than just these art form expectations, it can also challenge the foundational experiences that participants of any background have of movement and physicality.

Contemporary Circus

If the body in performance is a site of/for desire, then circus, perhaps more so than dance and theatre, is a form that most eloquently captures and expresses the performing body as desiring and desired. Rather than using physicality to embody meaning, as in physical theatre, circus shifts the emphasis towards presenting the physicality of the performer as a form of end-in-itself – its muscularity, flexibility, strength and dexterity are the very heart of the circus event. New Circus has done much to reassert the circus performer as subject rather than object. Whereas the circus performer's body has historically been an object which has had various remarkable things done to it, over the last 40 years or so it has begun to challenge itself as to whether it can or should mean or say more than what it already is (Zaccarini, 2009a). The challenge for circus is meaning. What does it mean in and of itself? What might it mean within different/other contexts – in relation to live art, dance and theatre? How can it become more meaningful?

For some time, dance and physical theatre have borrowed and exchanged practices and processes, and for some time new and alternative circus work has found spaces for itself within mime and physical theatre festivals. The clown, the acrobat and the juggler have, during the last 100 years, provided various points of crossover with theatre performance. More recently the aerialist has become a point of contact with dance (for instance in the work of Motionhouse, who now refer to themselves as a Dance-Circus company). In so far as these boundaries have existed between forms, they have been in part created by the funding and organizational bodies who have struggled to determine where to put circus – either locating it as part of a portfolio of 'combined arts' or alongside a larger and more established art form such as theatre. As with mime, which was for many years treated in a similar way, this tended to hinder the overall development of the form in its early years of funding.

The last few decades have seen the successful growth of a number of formal UK training schools for circus arts – in the UK these include Fooltime, now Circomedia (Bristol), and Circus Space, now the National Centre for Circus Arts (London). The challenge for these institutions has been the tension between training students with the technical skill required by the industry and helping the student to develop their own creative voice and a sense of what they might be able to say through circus. Circus artist and scholar Paul Zaccarini points to the dominance of product over potential: 'They think they need to leave the school with the act that will make them [...] Process isn't taught. Just get to the trick' (Zaccarini in Ellingsworth, 2009). In a sense, circus is stuck where mime was in the early 1990s. Because it is more spectacular and the skill levels are more visual, more extreme and more dangerous, it continues to conquer its shortcomings. But those shortcomings are still present and if not addressed may eventually undermine any attempts by circus arts to be more than a sensational form of family entertainment.

The traditional training methods for circus skills objectify the circus performer – they become 'stuff to be moulded' (Zaccarini in Ellingsworth, 2009). This training approach, Zaccarini states, tends to make circus repetitive – emphasis on the skill distracts the student from any consideration of why they have chosen their specialism and what it might possibly have to say. Technical drilling in circus skills may not allow for creativity 'to be taught within the actual technique itself' (Zaccarini in Ellingsworth, 2009). Zaccarini approaches circus through psychoanalytic theory. He speculates that, in this sense, circus has ultimately to be about the performer's self as the creative subject. The circus act, in his view, is not an act of interpretation, as in dance or theatre; thus, the challenge for the circus artist is to know what it is that they are trying to say, and to grapple with why and how circus might be the best means to say it (Zaccarini, 2009a).

In so far as physical theatre contributes to circus training, it may be something that is used to frame the circus skills and the event of the students' performances, possibly contributing narrative content. It is, as has been mentioned already, the clowns, the tumblers and the acrobats who have made the migration away from the sawdust ring. If physical theatre training has appropriated the clown and the tumbler, it is most often because of their potential to encapsulate wider dramatic meanings and to develop valuable levels of awareness, nimbleness and dexterity. Historically, the connections between circus and physical theatre over the last century have been strong. Jacques Copeau, in setting up his School in Paris in the 1920s, recruited the Fratellini Brothers[4] to teach clowning and other circus techniques, as he recognized the value of their skills in timing and physical precision and admired their ability to construct comic routines. Jacques Lecoq, at his international school in Paris, included work on clowning and tumbling; like Copeau, he realized how important agility, awareness and complicity with the audience could be for the creation of contemporary physical theatre. Grotowski drew on tumbling and acrobatics within his physically rigorous training regimes. Meyerhold saw the circus as a model for the kind of acrobatic, athletic, open and popular theatre necessary for a new revolutionary society.

On one level the heroic and spectacular skills of the circus performer offer a powerful dramatic metaphor. The endless repetition of their act might be seen to confirm that, despite its virtuosity, it means nothing and goes nowhere; it performs a kind of Beckettian tragedy. In this sense, it is physical theatre *in extremis* – pushed to the point where it can only repeat its own beautiful, brave and spectacular physical presence. The successful act cannot end; it must repeat itself again and again. What gives it meaning is not its success, but the possibility of failure and injury or death – the audience gasp, not just at the successful trick but at the relief (or even disappointment) that failure has been obverted; 'the closer we get to failure the more applause we get' (Zaccarini, 2012). The poetic resonance of circus in part resides not just in the possibility of failure, but in the faultless repetition of its beautiful dance over the abyss, night after night. However, the bodies of circus performers, already developed to be strong, flexible, poised or agile beyond what society expects, extend the 'otherness' of the physical theatre performer's body (whether male/female, of whatever ethnicity or age) into a form of exoticism that circus finds hard to subvert or challenge while it remains focused only on skill.

Zaccarini proposes that the challenge for the artist is 'to maintain an authentic relationship to their craft' (Zaccarini, 2012). This is most directly pertinent to the circus artist, who is challenged by Zaccarini to explore what it is that draws them to their circus form and how that form offers them opportunities for making meaning from their performance. This resonates with the earlier Frantic case study, which also explored the need for the physical theatre performer to focus beyond the skills that they might acquire, and to interrogate what issues those skills open up and how they enable the performer to tap in to meanings intrinsic to the nature of the physical skills they are using. As in physical theatre, skill and virtuosity can only take the performer so far before they collapse in the face of inevitable failure (how good can you get before you must fail?). At some point, and perhaps especially within such physical work, it is the performer's very rawness, fragility, vulnerability and humanity that are most important and that must not be forgotten or repressed. Certainly, one might argue that this was a dead-end that illusory mime failed to avoid – at a certain point, the technical finesse of an artist such as Marcel Marceau becomes pointless. Jacques Lecoq recalled learning to walk on the spot as a mime technique and then presenting this skill to an elderly Italian actor, Agostino Cantorello, who announced: 'Che Bello! Che Bello! Ma dove va? (*It's good! It's good! But where are you going?*)' (Murray, 2003: 84). I can recall seeing Marceau perform in the early 1980s and being astonished by the precision of his technique and yet totally unmoved by his performance and confused as to what the greater significance of this presentation might be. It is of course acceptable and sometimes appropriate to master technique, but not within a context that then denies the possibility of giving the technique meaning, of allowing intellect and creativity a place.

Zaccarini suggests that circus isn't about being someone else, it's about doing your own act, telling a personal story. He focuses on the artist's relationship to themselves and to the ways in which they can free themselves from a repressive concept of circus in order to act as a creative subject doing something *with* circus. There is also a need to release the circus performer from the social and cultural constraints that confine what they can do and what kind of artist they can be. The construction of a new act, however liberating for the circus artist, however expressive of their own creative motivations, has to exist within a performing arts industry that still promotes and upholds certain assumptions and expectations with regard to the performing body. In order to realize its subversive potential, circus practitioners must consider the context within which work is created and presented, who is enabled to present what work, and for whom is that work made available. Circus can also operate to subvert the normal through its excess – the body is taken to its limits: of dexterity, agility, strength, flexibility, precision, endurance and elasticity; all seemingly regardless of age and gender. If the circus performer is, in Zaccarini's terms, identifying a particular skill or technique with which to then express their sense of being in the world, it is equally the case that we cannot ignore the choice of circus as a form. Its excessive successes and excessive failures, its existence on the borders of acceptability (travelling, transient, transformative), all place it where family entertainment meets the macabre, the bizarre, the surreal and the dangerous.

The growth in what might usefully be referred to as alternative circus over the last 50 years exists in an interesting relationship to the growth of physical theatre. As with some elements of physical theatre, some of the earliest clear examples of alternative circus work emerged in France and came to prominence in the 1960s and 1970s. Jérôme Savary (1942–2013) launched The Grand Magic Circus in Paris in the mid-1960s, a company that sought to mix theatre, circus and performance to create extravagant live performance events. The surreal, popular and extravagant nature of Savary's work deliberately undermined and subverted the jaded commercialism of the conventional circus of the time, but did so using circus's own techniques and structures. For a long time, circus history has been the context that has justified choices of act and the nature of circus presentation, and this has played to the maintenance of some surprisingly resilient traditions (the ringmaster, the clown acts, the trapeze artists, the tightrope walkers). However, more recently, new and alternative circus has encouraged and enabled circus performers to make performances in a wider range of contexts and for a wider range of purposes. Sometimes that has included open, public spaces – such as the performance events in the Millennium Dome/O2 Arena and the opening ceremonies for the Olympic and Paralympic Games in London in 2012. In other instances, it has taken place within more intimate and conventional venues, albeit spaces that might resemble the circus tent in terms of informality, transience or roughness. But in all these instances, contemporary circus has attempted to grapple more precisely, more directly and more physically than its traditional antecedents with its nature and with what it can 'say'.

Many of the alternative circus companies started in the 1980s, about the same time that physical theatre in the UK hit its stride and the alternative comedy scene started to take off. These companies saw circus as a way to challenge the restrictive and increasingly corporatized society around them. As with many of the physical theatre companies operating in the UK in the 1980s, they took some initial inspiration from the punk aesthetic – rough, irreverent, comic, tongue-in-cheek, deconstructing audience expectations and the traditions of the format. Sometimes (for example in the case of the French circus company Archaos (1986–1991) and Argentinian performance company De La Guarda (1993–present)) this would include using loud rock music, as well as content deliberately designed to shock the audience – for example nudity, simulated sex and violence, and extreme physicality. In other instances, it was about presenting an alternative kind of show that challenged the conventions of circus and of society – through performances and workshops that took circus into fringe theatre and community arts spaces. NoFit

State Circus (formed in 1986) describe, albeit in terms that echo some of the more romantic notions that circulate around circus performers, how, for them, 'The circus are the strangers who live amongst us – and if we run away to join them we are throwing off our inhibitions, our conventions, the rules of settled society' (NoFit State Circus, 2018).

Ra Ra Zoo (1984–1994) was a seminal example of an English alternative circus group that attempted to blow the cobwebs off from conventional acts and present work that spoke more directly to fringe theatre audiences – crossing the line into theatre, comedy and performance art. Tumblers and acrobats, such as the inspirational Johnny Hutch (1913–2006), brought their circus experience into the world of physical theatre during this formative period. Hutch, for instance, worked with physical dance/theatre troupe The Kosh, as well as with the RSC. More recently aerial work has become particularly popular. It was part of the work of the Argentine group De La Guarda that integrated aerial performance with a kind of immersive clubbing experience for the audience. It has been used by choreographer/director Mark Murphy (formerly of dance group V-TOL), as well as being the central feature of work by New Circus companies such as Ockham's Razor (formed in 2004, by graduates from Circomedia in Bristol). Flight seems to have become a particularly resonant metaphor for several practitioners over the last decade or so. Soaring and swooping through space, becoming weightless and ungrounded, the performer no longer simply displays strength and agility – they also become graceful, fluid, even ethereal. In so far as this may represent a cultural shift away from weight and groundedness, it also relates to the growing use of CGI and performance capture in films and online gaming and the 'superhuman' movement performances that these technologies enable.

Just as the work of Frantic and Complicité has entered mainstream theatre venues and practices, so circus practice has, over time, entered into the entertainment mainstream. Beyond obvious examples of this kind of impact, such as the musical *Barnum*, it is also worth noting the success of Cirque de Soleil, which, from its origins as a small alternative Canadian circus operation, is now a global franchise, thoroughly immersed in the economics of international touring and global casting. While narrative line does exist in Cirque de Soleil's work, it does so as a device for stringing together what are still largely conventional circus acts and its 'otherness' is no longer subversive or radical, but instead mildly exotic and comforting. In 1999, I was appointed as the external examiner for a Certificate of Higher Education in Circus Arts which was run by Circus Space (NCCA), validated by Central School of Speech and Drama, and designed as part of the training programme for the performers recruited to create the performance in what was then the Millennium Dome (now the O2 Arena). As well as developing traditional circus skills, this course also involved the students in the creation of devised performance pieces that drew on but were not simply structured around the student/participant's technique and circus capabilities. However, by the time the final show arrived, the political imperatives for a popular and largely populist show and the sheer scale of the venue demanded a show that was low on complex narrative and high on visual spectacle and impact. Interestingly, some of the core of the Millennium Dome company went on, in 2001, to form The Generating Company. This troupe did attempt to make more complex and challenging work. They are still operating, but now reside in France. Beyond large-scale spectacles and occasional experiments such as Tamasha's *The Arrival* and Bristol Old Vic's *A Monster Calls* (2018), there is still little evidence of successful integration between circus arts and mainstream theatre performance.

Other Circus Bodies

As with dance and physical theatre, the question also arises: what space is there within circus for bodies that do not fit the conventions for the physical/circus performer? How can non-conventional performance subjects use these forms to find what they need to say? The circus body and physical theatre bodies have participated in some respects in the creation of an idealized athletic/acrobatic performing body, a body that has shaped cultural expectations of the physically expressive body within performance – not unlike the ways that expectations of the social body have also been shaped by the influence of music videos, sports and even pornography. The development of New Circus from the 1970s onwards has helped to question the bodies that are enabled and permitted within this field. The introduction of new bodies went hand in hand with a willingness and desire to question what circus might be about. As Zaccarini recalls:

> With the advent of New Circus, we trace a clear distinction between a traditional circus that is for the most part purely formal and a new circus placing as much importance on the content as it does on the form. New Circus challenges the notion that circus is not about anything other than tricks. (2013: 20)

This has also extended into an interest in the potential of circus to integrate with other forms of performance (live art, physical theatre and even mainstream theatre). Former RSC Artistic Director Michael Boyd remarked a few years ago that he had 'bumped in to a real appetite for language and narrative at places like Circus Space in Hoxton, a desire to sustain an idea beyond the theatrical equivalent of a three-minute pop song' (Boyd in Radosavljevic, 2013: 37). Such a remark reflects the desire of circus performers to cross discipline boundaries. Zaccarini, however, is resistant to the integration of circus into a wider field of performance, and sees such a move as detrimental to circus finding its own voice:

> The circus subject has something to say for itself, it has an account to give, but it cannot do so on its own terms if it needs the validation of an Other. If it responds to the circus, looks back at it for validation in its execution of the prescribed aesthetic of the tricks of circus, if it responds to theatre, by using an imaginary character to justify its real action, if it is conditioned by the opera to be a symbol, or commissioned in the pop video to be an augmentation of the value of the product being sold, then the subject is effaced and the power of its relationality diminished: it becomes an object. (2013: 195)

His proposal for an approach to circus that emerges from a 'pure' application of circus skills in the determination of the performer's individual artistic voice arguably fails to recognize the complex web of performance histories and cultural reverberations around these skills and techniques. In seeking to isolate them ontologically, there is a danger that they lose the resonances that help to give the work richer meaning. Circus, after all, cannot escape its own sociocultural location. In whatever form it takes and however it is presented, it cannot lose the histories of its cultural significance and the role it plays within the wider social frame.

The Australian New Circus company, Circus Oz, founded in Melbourne in 1978, is an example of a troupe directly seeking to address and challenge the idea of circus as an apolitical form. They were one of the first New Circus companies, setting out from the start to bring an overtly political agenda to their shows and to establish a commitment to collective ownership. This political stance extended beyond content to the inclusion of non-traditional circus bodies: 'The company rejected the balletic idea of a perfect, ideal body, embracing instead a philosophy of difference and actively incorporating a wide range of diverse body types among their performers' (Lavers & Burtt, 2017: 308). Lavers and Burtt suggest that: 'Circus has a long history of positioning itself on the margins of society' (Lavers & Burtt, 2017: 313); and they identify that, in Australia, this marginality had the power to evoke a sense of freedom that spoke powerfully to a colony rejecting the old world. The arrival of this kind of circus practice in the UK heralded opportunities for circus bodies on the (social, cultural and, in colonial terms, geographical) margins to bring their own messages of resistance to play on what was a largely European tradition. This diverse and inclusive new vision was perhaps most noticeably and publicly realized in the Paralympics Opening Ceremony in London in 2012. The development of community circus in the UK over the last two decades has increased opportunities for a wider range of people to explore the possibilities for self-expression through circus and has encouraged the development of new forms of apparatus to facilitate such work.

Conclusion: Chapter 4

The global success of Cirque de Soleil demonstrates the ways in which the performance industry can assimilate new practices in order to generate profit. The negative side of this rapid expansion of circus practices has been that it has become more institutionalized (schools, bureaucracy, company structures, funding, etc.) and has lost some of its former freedoms and possibilities. The more the status and profile of circus rises, the more it needs to be alert to the socio-cultural trends that will seek to construct it as increasingly white, middle class and exclusive. Circus can resist this gentrification in many ways. It is by its nature constantly dealing with, challenging, and disrupting two key constraints – cultural norms (what it is appropriate for men and women to do) and socio-biological norms (what it is possible for men and women to do). The danger of circus, the permanent 'potential risk of a tragic outcome' (Bouissac, 2012: 31), although controlled and staged, sets it aside from the relative stability of mainstream theatre. Circus acts as a game in which the outcome is predictable but never certain and the stakes are high. The cultural narrative is of the human ability to confront the impossible – a series of risks and dangerous challenges which they overcome.

The lifeblood of the circus is the audience's vicarious investment in the risk and danger of the circus acts. The flipside of the glory of flight – as the trapeze artist lets go in order to be caught again, or as the *corde lisse*[5] artist tumbles down the rope towards the floor – is the moment of the fall. The act of the fall generates intense attention through the raised level of risk and the anticipation of injury or death. This intensity inducts the audience into an experience of empathy with the performer and functions to draw the audience into the performer's psychophysical experiences and enhance the kinetic empathy between performer(s) and audience. Bouissac (2012: 96) identifies stability as central to notions of safety. Challenging stability generates anxiety and uncertainty.

Frantic, in the same spirit, use an exercise that they refer to as 'I'm Falling' – in which each participant is free at any time to shout out their intention to fall to the ground, requiring the rest of the group to catch them before impact. Falling acts as one of circus and physical theatre's key metaphors and poetic images – weightlessness, movement, danger, trusting/releasing/no longer being in control, group responsibility, *jouissance* are all brought in to play, giving body to the excitement, poetry and transformative power of movement through its inherent proximity to danger, injury and even death.

Central to the work examined in this chapter has been an examination of the cultural and theatrical significance of danger and truth. Both circus and the physical theatre work of companies such as Frantic Assembly are seeking to create spectacles that are in some physical sense 'true and genuine' (Bouissac, 2012: 199). The intensity, immediacy and multiplicity of sensory signals within these physical performances confirms the physical reality of the event, while also working to defer the audience's ability to understand the event intellectually or predict its outcome.

Circus (historically and in its more contemporary incarnations) and physical theatre are both driven by a desire for newness and innovation. There is a need (and indeed a necessity) to produce new work, or what Bouissac refers to as 'novelties' (2012: 202). The rhetoric of newness is deeply embedded within these areas of practice – part of the way that they market and promote themselves and part of the physical language and physical culture within which these forms operate. The sense of novelty is, of course, compounded by the extent to which other qualities such as difference, otherness, the use of unusual spaces, relationship to the audience, levels of danger and risk, and even the nomadic processes of touring are presented and made present in the work.

Finally, it is worth noting how the practices and issues raised in this chapter come together within the overarching topic of touch. Touch brings in to play not just the sensitivity of the body, its densities and weight, but also its awareness of the world around it. Touch is ordinary and everyday, but it also provides moments of intense connection, heightened awareness and even, at the worst, moments of oppression and abuse. Touch is about finding how a movement feels and not just how it looks. Within training, touch can help with corrections, alignment, precision, communication, awareness, teaching new movements, picking out details. In both movement performance and movement training it is hard to opt out of touch. For the physical performer, touch represents the border point for a range of excursions beyond what is accepted as normal practice – touching people you don't know, being lifted, potentially intimate physical contact, carrying others, and pushing/pulling. Touch brings risk and danger down to a personal level – a level in which the performer/

student has to deal with possibly feeling uncomfortable and awkward and has to negotiate new expectations around their body and what of it they share (Bannon, 2012: 10). Within physical theatre and circus, it would be odd not to touch; touch is integral to these fields of performance practice, and central to safe practice. Touch brings immediacy to the experience of performance for the performer and vicariously for the spectator. When we talk about being (emotionally) touched by a performance, we are recognizing how touch generates a very particular and immediate emotional reaction. For the student and for the performer, touch gives immediate feedback. Within circus and physical theatre, touch also happens across the whole body and not just the hands. This means that the quality of touch becomes very important. The performer/student learns how to touch; but they must surely also learn how to recognize and respond to cultural and social differences in attitudes to touch. Touch cannot be understood as solely sensory and without cultural significance. As events following the Harvey Weinstein case have demonstrated, touch has become an issue of ethics and informed consent, 'an arena immersed in politics, power, authority and cultural difference' (Bannon, 2012: 21). As this chapter has argued, this means that circus and physical theatre need to consider elements such as touch as intimately linked to how we understand ourselves as sociopolitical subject in the world. As Bannon suggests, this must mean that within these fields we do not assume that familiarity with danger, risk, physicality, contact and proximity negates the need for a kind of relational ethics – an approach to physical work that is both pragmatic and situational, acknowledging context and taking responsibility (Bannon, 2012: 24).

Within the work of Frantic Assembly, for example, as well as across the wider field of UK physical theatre, we can see that as the touch of dance becomes part of the situation of theatre making, it acquires a meaning that it does not have in most conventional text-based theatre. As has been noted earlier, within mainstream theatre companies are increasingly recognizing that intimate scenes require dedicated and specialist direction in order to ensure such work is underpinned by ethical awareness and care for self, and that the power and pleasure that can operate around touch are not abused. For Bannon, this means recognizing the need for a new sense of the self – a sense of self that is embodied, potentially empowering, aware and ethically and politically engaged – even in the very extremes of movement activity. In this manner, movement and dance are enabled to have a role in the process of creating the self (Bannon, 2012: 25).

If, in the physical work of practitioners such as Grotowski, DV8 and Volcano, intense physical activity exhausts and/or disrupts the rational activities of the mind, enabling the body to take over as the core site for sensory awareness and for creativity, then it is also necessary to maintain and not abandon a clear and shared sense of ethical practice within that movement field. Ideally, there should be no points of tension between learning movement for creative performance and learning movement to understand and transform the self. As Bannon puts it,

> It is through our own rhythms that we are inserted into the complexity of the world that we inhabit. This 'totality of possibilities', moves between an inside feeling of individual experience and the complex realm of negotiation and compromise generated through reciprocal engagement with others. The others that we brush past as we move through space, that we come into contact with in conversation, that we enter negotiation with in the practicalities of living socially. (Bannon, 2012: 28)

It is, in effect, at the boundaries of physical activity such as circus and physical theatre that we discover how central movement and physicality can be to determining what it means to be an embodied subject and what it means to create from that place, as well as what it might mean to be alienated from that sense of wholeness and engagement with the world around us. Performing and learning at these boundaries is an important part of how we resist the unlearning of touch. Touch is all about relationships, yet more recently we have become more aware of its associations with 'pain, abuse, authority and control' (Bannon, 2012: 33). Can we perform this crisis of touch in such a way that we can address it and heal it? If not, are we ready to live in a world in which touch becomes marginalized as a mode of communication and sharing? Inter/cross/trans-disciplinary work has value perhaps specifically because it is creating the space to make evident to us how touch, danger, physicality and risk operate, as well as how they might be best employed in order to interrogate what it means to be embodied.

Notes

1. Generation X can broadly be described as the demographic cohort that came after the so-called Baby Boomers. In this sense, it would include those people born in the period from the mid-1960s until the early 1980s.
2. Both Steven Hoggett and Scott Graham performed in Volcano's production of *Manifesto*.
3. Frantic's production of *Othello* (2008, 2014, 2015) was set in a West Yorkshire pub and amid the racial tensions of contemporary Britain.
4. Paul, François and Albert Fratellini were a clown trio who had remarkable success in Paris at the Circus Medrano after the First World War.
5. This is an act that involves acrobatics on a vertically suspended rope.

5 Movement and the Cultural Context

The speed with which globalization has taken place towards the end of the twentieth century and the start of the twenty-first means that cultural practices such as theatre and performance have become a site of considerable cross-cultural activity, controversy, discrimination, transmission and exchange. The transmission and exchange of culturally diverse movement practices has accelerated in relation to the speed and ease of human migration, the increased recognition of the rights of all those historically viewed within Western cultures as 'other' (women, LGBT,[1] disabled and non-white), and more recently in relation to the transmission of new ideas and practices via new digital media. Theatre and performance students in the UK may well now have access to training in African dance, Japanese Noh Theatre, various martial arts (for example tai chi chuan, aikido, karate, judo and capoeira), Japanese Suzuki training and Peking Opera as well as a host of other physical training regimes from all corners of the globe, both near and far. These will map more or less comfortably on to their sense of their own, possibly equally culturally complex and diverse, physical/movement heritage. Nonetheless, the UK conservatoire student, whatever their own background, still generally experiences all this diversity within the context of an overarching well-established movement practice that is broadly based on concepts of neutrality and efficiency shaped by white, middle-class, Western notions of desirable qualities for movement (see Evans, 2009: 14–68). This access and exchange also takes place at a professional level, where technology, social change and improved ease of travel have meant that performers are increasingly required and/or able to engage with movement practices from a range of different cultural contexts. At Coventry University, a recent project has explored the use of digital technology in order to create a telepresence environment, in which students in Coventry and in Tampere, Finland, can work together as if in a shared creative space – learning games, songs and dances, as well as rehearsing together.[2] The technology enables skills and techniques to be shared, on what is assumed as a level playing field; what it does not of itself reveal or interrogate is the power structures operating within, between and among these kinds of exchanges and technologies. For that to happen, additional critical awareness and reflection is required on the part of both the students and the teachers. At the same time, students who now are able to 'move' with increasing ease across and between geographical, national, political and cultural boundaries can experience significant tensions in relation to their sense of their own cultural identity and their own embodied cultural-physical heritage. Increased diversity, mobility and access have meant that for some students there is a struggle to find coherence within the diverse and eclectic influences on the construction of their sense of physical self. Of course, changes in access do not, in and of themselves, remove the operation of privilege, discrimination and prejudice.

Technology and cognitive science could be understood as conceptual approaches to performance that seek ultimately to reduce the body and movement to sets of digital or neurological data and instruction. If the body and movement is only viewed in this way this will tend towards marginalizing their cultural significance. The danger is that science and technology permit and facilitate engagement in culturally 'other' approaches to movement without requiring the kinds of cultural awareness that might be necessary to avoid hegemonic appropriation and the privileging of white male non-disabled embodied experience. Technology has also led to the rapid and almost borderless transmission of movement practices. Does the speed and ease of transmission of practice indicate the development of a globalized body, a body that is able to absorb any range and type of practice? Does the reduction of movement to neurological impulses further enable and encourage the idea of a globalized and essentialized 'pan-human' approach to performance and the body? Who does any such essentialized and globalized body belong to? For whom is it typically available or achievable? What kinds of bodies are typically prioritized in this kind of global body economy? These questions become particularly pertinent in relation to decisions such as the casting of Scarlett Johansson in the role of a Japanese cyborg in *Ghost in the Shell* (2017), or the proposed casting of Joseph Fiennes in the role of Michael Jackson in *Urban Myths* (2017). It is much harder to find evidence of Asian actors being cast as White Caucasian characters.[3]

This chapter will look at the challenges and potentials that these tensions open up for the performer, the student and the educator/trainer. It will examine the experiences of a selection of performers and theatre makers across areas of movement practice, and explore how these experiences are shaping movement performance and training. Emma Cox writes that 'Bodies on stage [...] actualize stories with a voice, accent, skin and history' (2014: 4); this chapter seeks to examine not just how the process of actualization works, but what effects of power are occurring in that process and how they might be resisted. I have chosen within this chapter not to examine the work of Grotowski, Barba and Zarrilli in detail. For the interested reader, there is a wealth of material on these practitioners already available elsewhere.[4] This is not in any way to dismiss their significance in relation to this area of practice, but rather because within the limited space available I prefer to focus on practices that have penetrated more extensively into the theatre and performance industries in general – looking at why they have penetrated in the way that they have, what they offer (and don't offer), and to examine performance and training practice that is more generally available to the average theatregoer.

Cultural Difference and Movement Practice

In my article for the 'Politics' special issue of the *Theatre Dance and Performance Training Journal* (Evans, 2014), which I will draw on extensively below, I argue that it is possible to recognize the diaspora of diverse, embodied, non-Western cultural practices as a feature of modern colonialism and late twentieth and early twenty-first century global capitalism. This diversity, coupled with the ease of global transmission, might suggest that we can all now be considered diasporic bodies – our embodied cultural histories increasingly dislocated from their various 'points of origin', whether geographical, cultural or historical. Histories of practice, in this sense, are becoming less linear and more networked. We literally carry our movement studio with us – we are, at least in theory, able to practise whatever movement we like whenever we find our bodies in places that enable movement. At the same time, this global and immediate access to various practices is not without its own impact on our bodies; historical and cultural movement practices accumulate and accrete upon us, moving with us and adhering to our sense of self. As human beings, we move through, or are moved through, different practices; many of us less and less able, in a complex, fluid, digitized and globalized world, to rest within one set of practices for long. Emma Cox speaks of 'the contact zone between those who arrive and those who lay claim to ownership or custodianship' (2014: 5) in relation to theatre and migration – the same tensions surely exist in relation to those practices that arrive within a culture and the subsequent political acts of claiming/retaining ownership and in relation to what that action of 'claiming ownership' might mean. For some people this is a difficult and troubling experience – seeing what they consider as their own culture treated as just another set of practices available for acquisition. Clearly a challenge for artists and students is how to move between movement practices in a manner that does not become a process of appropriation or infiltration of the cultural practices of others.

Our dispersed, diverse, dynamic bodies are evolving in relation to a context that is itself in flux. Our bodies, throughout our lives, have to settle into new cultural environments, along with the coming-into-being and the letting-go of other practices that that involves. Though deeply conditioned within our own, often complex, cultural contexts, we are all also increasingly active in our struggles for agency, and aware of the need to be so. I contend elsewhere (Evans, 2009: 143–175; and in Chapter 3) that a rigorous, even unruly, playfulness can offer ways of undermining and questioning the effects of Foucauldian power/knowledge on our bodies and our selves. This playfulness might mean that rather than absorbing, incorporating or commodifying practices from other cultures, we can engage with them in a way that maintains an appropriately critical relationship while still recognizing the immediacy, sensuality and seductiveness of the moment of en/action. I can playfully explore how to move between, for instance, tai chi and my own movement practice using the dynamics of physical action to locate points of migration back and forth. Through playfulness and reflection all practices can (to some extent at least) become 'other' while still remaining embodied in our work. We can, thus, 'meet' with other cultural practices in a playful process that can recognize and facilitate a more equal exchange.

As I attend workshops on movement practices from different cultures, nations and traditions, I am mindful of Cláudia Nascimento's questioning (2008: 49) of the basis on which we assume a correlation between practice and region (or history, class, gender or ability) that attributes a particular region's cultural practices exclusively to its indigenous peoples. If we are peoples of complex ethnic, national, political and cultural histories, then recognizing and engaging with diverse cultural practices becomes part of recognizing our own cultural complexity. In this sense, this is an inevitable process that needs to be understood as having its own history. Though this relationship between physical practice and cultural identity has been driven by particular politicized agendas in the past, to assume that it is always so is to essentialize the relationship between our bodies, our cultures, our politics and our nativities.[5] If this were the case, then 'the long process of embodiment' (Nascimento, 2008: 52) would not be able to transform 'seemingly "foreign" exercises into a familiar and "owned" practice' (ibid.); nor would change be possible. Citizenship is in this sense performatively embodied. Nascimento suggests, following Barba, that a long process of training creates a particular professional identity for the student/actor, 'a second nature that forever affects not only her way of performing but also of relating to the world offstage' (2008: 54). The ability of the actor to 'simultaneously [embody] different cultural elements' is, she suggests, what enables the actor to 'actively [question] socially prescribed boundaries, making visible how unstable they are' (Nascimento, 2008: 53). She effectively suggests that it is through learning the practices of other cultures that we better understand how cultures operate on our own bodies and that we are enabled potentially to critique that operation. The logical conclusion of this argument is that 'staying still' is not an option: the best way for us as performers to resist cultural hegemony in our practice is by engaging with other cultural practices in a manner that maintains dignity and difference, enables awareness, and promotes a sense of selfhood. In doing so, we inevitably locate ourselves in, indeed create for ourselves, a different *habitus* – that of the performer. Barba suggests that performers and trainers are then able to take ownership of that space and 'through continuous work to individualize their own area, seeking what for them is essential and trying to force others to respect this diversity' (1986: 194).

If the performer or student is not simply to ingest the cultural practices of the teacher or director, or of the professional environment within which they are working, then they must be given space to reflect on and contextualize the practice(s) that they *are* engaging with. They need to be able to understand the social and cultural history of these practices, and to place the practices they learn and/or adopt in relation to the practices that are part of their own cultural identity and history. For Foucault (1999), 'The truth about the disciple emerges from a personal relation which he [*sic*] establishes with himself'. Foucault suggests that the attitude the subject should take towards him- or herself might be that of the technician 'who – from time to time – stops working, examines what he [*sic*] is doing, reminds himself of the rule of his art, and compares these rules with what he has achieved so far' (1999). The emphasis for Foucault is on critical but caring reflection. In this way, the movement practitioner can take control of the ways in which what they do inscribes upon their body. In doing so, they not only develop their technique but also understand the effects of that technique – on themselves, on their discipline and on others.

In our society, there is often a dominant and largely naturalized assumption that the relationship involved in training or directing the actor is one of instruction rather than discussion and negotiation. However, if the paradigm of 'director/ teacher as instructor' is too dominant then it risks reducing the student/actor's sense of agency; the paradigm simply becomes part of the system and process through which the actor/performer is professionalized and through which their body can become trained to be professionally 'biddable' and malleable (Evans, 2009: 120–142). This set of relationships is closely aligned to the capitalist ideologies that underpin UK and American mainstream theatre industry practice; the actor is not there to contribute to the critical discussion of how to realize a meaningful performance of the play, they are there to do what they are told to do as part of achieving the director's vision for the play. The actor's creative contribution may be less constrained within companies that devise their performances through group or ensemble practices; nonetheless, few long-term UK ensembles exist within which actors might be able confidently to contribute to the making of theatre in ways that might challenge and/or undermine dominant ideological assumptions. Even if actors are employed on a fixed term basis as part of a devising ensemble, there is still a possibility that they will ultimately defer to the views and opinions of those who are employing them.

An effective director/teacher can, instead, enable a form of Socratic dialogue, or a set of provocations and invitations, that enable the actor/student to realize and examine their assumptions regarding their embodied cultural identity in ways that are affirming, provocative and enabling. As Paulo Freire states (1996: 71), such dialogue is only possible with humility and an openness to the contribution of others. Returning the student in a reflective way to movement practices that are foundational in respect of their own cultural identities, rather than moving them swiftly and uncritically towards established professional practices that embody certain cultural attitudes to movement, can provide an empowering point of reference for them.[6] In Freire's terms, neutral mask work can, for instance, be used to help the student identify 'limit-situations' (1996: 80) within the training environment. These 'limit-situations' are points at which the student does not feel able to do something which they have every right to expect to be able to do – to occupy space, to project through space, to be physically present. As Freire states: 'Once perceived by individuals as fetters, as obstacles to their liberation, these situations stand out in relief from the background, revealing their true nature as concrete dimensions of a given reality' (1996: 80). These situations are not simply personal 'problems' for the student, but the effect of what Freire calls 'generative themes' (1996: 78).

Generative themes are a way of understanding the nature and action of epochal historical themes; they are a conceptual tool that represents the 'ideas, values, concepts, and hopes, as well as the obstacles which impede the people's full humanization' (1996: 82). In my 2014 article, I suggest using the notion of foundational practices to unpick the relationship between actually embodied activity and Freire's 'generative themes'. The actor/student then better understands the relationship between movement practice, personal history and social history, and understands it as a relationship that is creative and generative. Although the actor/student might in this way experience their body as strange, they are not required to dislocate from the lived experience of their body. In this way, the role of the director/teacher can change from that of the provider of a 'foundational practice' to that of a facilitator for the discovery and interrogation of the actor/student's own 'foundational practice'. For the director/teacher, such an approach demands a high level of reflection and cultural awareness and also the creation of an environment in which the actor/student can 'tell the truth' about their experiences; acting, in Socratic terms, as a *parrhesiastes*.[7] Such processes are important in ensuring that the value systems underpinning theatre practice are in meaningful relation to the lived experience of actors and student actors. As Robert Gordon states:

> Acting teachers who are [...] serious in the aim of cultivating their students' wholeness of body, mind, and feelings are in danger of arbitrarily imposing an ideology at the most fundamental level of identity formation. Wholeness or balance are in practice words that conceal a speaker's complex of unconsciously determined feelings and prejudices that are never free of personal and social values. (2006: 127)

Although Augusto Boal goes some way towards addressing such issues in his writings (see Boal, 1995), he does not directly address the training of the actor's body and their movement practice but instead approaches movement through theatre games. Even somatic practices, such as the Feldenkrais Method and the Alexander Technique, which seek to enable the student to question habitual movement patterns, do not necessarily do so in ways that open up awareness of the cultural values and social forces acting upon the student's body. Alexander's notion of 'inhibition'[8] and Feldenkrais' of 'reversibility'[9] could provide interesting starting points from which to investigate a critical and politically empowering re-education of the body, and Boal's disjunctive techniques may offer ways in which movement is able to participate in redefining how power operates on the body; both will require further research and development to be fully effective rehearsal room strategies for this purpose.

Failure to address the responsibility to engage with the cultural and political context of their work can, in Freire's terms, dehumanize the actor/student and objectify them and their experience, removing from them the possibility of real agency, as they are constructed within the ideological frame of the director/teacher's sense of truth and authenticity which they are not encouraged to challenge or question overtly. How, then, might a culturally aware approach to movement work in practice? How do those engaging with movement-based performance navigate the complexities of cultural difference and the experience of different cultural practices? The next section of this chapter will analyse the practice of Kristine Landon-Smith[10] as an example of a practitioner actively seeking to explore ways to empower the actor and to challenge how cultural differences are responded to within the context of the UK theatre industry.

Empowering the Ethnically Diverse Actor through Movement

Kristine's own movement heritage draws on childhood experiences of ballet and contemporary dance. She was brought up in Australia, and also experienced a physically active childhood – she ran a lot, swam in the sea, and enjoyed the outdoors. Her experience of conservatoire training echoed elements of this childhood experience, but, as with many acting schools, it also focused on developing a physical imagination. Her enthusiasm for and interest in movement led to her choreographing work on fellow students, reflecting her early experiences in dance. After a spell as a successful professional actor, she co-founded Tamasha. As she began working with Tamasha she found that the strong visual sense developed through her choreographic sensibility fed in to her intracultural work with the company:

> I like making shapes that work, or pictures, and I'm very precise about those things, certainly I think I am very quick to put an actor in a position which seems to suit their body or give them comfort, or give them freedom, or give them openness. So that is quite a natural process for me, but it is linked to this idea of, if something feels right I'll think that normally it also looks aesthetically pleasing. (Landon-Smith, 2012)

But importantly, she also realized that for her and within the performance work that she wanted to make, embodied practice (the way an actor uses their body) is an important part of their cultural identity: 'I think the actor as a whole person has to engage their whole person, and cultural identity is part of their whole person' (Landon-Smith, 2012). This approach problematizes conventional notions of neutrality, and in particular European notions of physical neutrality such as those developed by Jacques Copeau and Jacques Lecoq: 'I just don't find that interesting [...] "leave your problems outside the door, leave yourself outside the door, come in and be neutral", I think that is very old-fashioned now and I don't think it's helpful' (Landon-Smith, 2012). Such an attitude opens up to critique the conventional idea of the 'neutral' within actor training and questions whether too often it becomes a shorthand for White British or White Caucasian – a movement version of Received Pronunciation (RP). As Lliane Loots writes:

> Like sexual identity, racial identity embodies the flesh and is thus ever present, no matter if an attempt is made to assume neutrality; as many postcolonial critics [...] would argue, 'neutrality' always assumes the centre hegemony of a white middle-class male and is thus a violence on the (female) body of colour, which does not embody these powerful discourses of the centre. (2010: 109)

Landon-Smith finds that conventional notions of the neutral do not echo with her own experience or with that of the diverse actors with whom she works:

> I have had so many conversations with actors who have said 'Do you know what, it now occurs to me that I've been second-guessing what is the neutral, and I've been performing as if I was a White British person and I'm not. I'm a British-Vietnamese person'. (Landon-Smith, 2012)

In this context, Landon-Smith has developed her own approach to movement, physicality and performance. Building on her understanding of the actor's body and what they do with their body, she sees movement as something that is central to liberating the embodied cultural identity of the actor. There has to date been no attempt at a thorough and comprehensive analysis of the ways in which key practitioners have attempted (or not) to address the issue of cultural diversity. For the most part, the issue has been avoided through recourse to humanist, modernist or scientific principles. The Grotowski/Barba approach is to focus on the pre-expressive elements of performance; Lecoq's practice is centred on the neutral mask and the analysis of movement; Laban's work addresses dynamic elements of movement in relation to abstract concepts of time, weight and direction. What Landon-Smith does very effectively is to create a link between the normal professional work of actors and their cultural heritage, their cultural identity and embodied cultural knowledges:

> [W]hen I set up early exercises or improvisations for an actor, how I ask them to sit or where I ask them to sit or the space they have between themselves or the physical framework is absolutely key to the success of the improvisation [...] Sometimes, I can see an actor who is just going to be able to do the most incredible improvisation around two people in an Indian village in the heat, sitting extremely still and not moving. Even if they are of Indian origin and they have never been to India. You know sometimes you can sense that they just would know how to do that. (Landon-Smith, 2012)

Such a statement could be misunderstood as proposing some kind of embodied cultural stereotype. There is an implication that the body of someone of Indian ethnic descent would instinctively know how to adopt a certain position in a certain context. Nascimento warns us that:

> Such perception is based on romantic assumptions and stereotypes about non-Western performers; in many ways, it is informed by the spectator's expectation that race and cultural knowledge are necessarily and inherently linked, and the uninformed notion that Asian culture is 'pure' and 'natural' among its artists. (2008: 38)

Landon-Smith's approach makes best sense if it is understood not as a proposal for some kind of cultural stereotype or genetic heritage, but rather as a recognition that embodied culture might sustain its own practices and attitudes for a significant period outside of the socio-economic and geographical conditions that created it. In which case, erasing or ignoring such cultural affects makes no more sense than oversimplifying them. In fact, such a description of the ways in which embodied cultural heritage functions could equally explain the invisibility of the 'neutral' White British body within Western society – it sustains itself without attention, even seeking to replicate itself, through the operation of colonialism, in the bodies of those not conventionally understood as within its boundaries. The aim therefore should not be simply to place the displaced body back within its embodied cultural origins – whatever those might be taken to be, and whoever might take it on themselves to decide what those were – but to enable the culturally migrated body to investigate the ways in which different states of embodiment speak to the complexities of their cultural identity. Landon-Smith recalls:

> [I]t's strong for me, the physical empowerment you give to people if you are allowing them to use their cultural identity. For example, recently I went to the

National Institute of Dramatic Arts in Sydney; I was directing a production of 'Port' by Simon Stephens,[11] set in Stockport, and I had a Thai boy in my company who had been to an international school in Bangkok and then he came to Australia. He was absolutely stuck, stilted. I got him to improvise as one of the street sellers, sitting on their haunches, as a starting point and he said to me 'What on earth has this got to do with "Port"? How am I ever going to get to "Port"?' And he was wonderful in it, because he'd never been given that freedom, so he'd never found the artistic power that resided in his cultural context and just squatting gave him this power; he didn't have to think about it intellectually, the physical shape just shot him off in that direction. (Landon-Smith, 2012)

Within this anecdote, it is possible to see evidence of the challenges presented to the ethnically diverse performer or student by a global cultural economy within which Western practices tend to be economically dominant. Cultural identity has also of course become less simplistically and rigidly defined; people's sense of their own and others' cultural identity is more complex. Our individual and communal cultural power is represented by the extent to which we can move with economic ease and freedom, and the extent to which we feel comfortable in any new contexts within which we find ourselves. For Landon-Smith, an important challenge arises as soon as we recognize that tension; our cultural identities are always changing and evolving: 'how do we work with them and how do we not fix them in an essentialized past?' (2012). Recognizing this complexity as a source of creative energy is at the heart of Landon-Smith's practice:

I met this great woman actually at Central the other day on the MA Voice course and she is looking at intra-cultural practice in voice, and not the neutral voice. She is of Korean origin, adopted with White American parents, so she's absolutely grown up with her adoptive parents, she didn't know her mother. And she recently met her birth mother and she now does this monologue which she wrote about her mother and performs it as her mother. She has had no experience of this Korean background as of yet but she finds this artistic power in this cultural context. I find this so fascinating because I have seen it so many times with my own actors. (Landon-Smith, 2012)

Provided that one can resist the essentializing impulse to say that this voice student's artistic power comes from simply 're-becoming' Korean in some sense, then it is possible to recognize how much else is happening here, to understand how much there is wrapped up in saying that (some)one is Korean, or to say that (some)one is American, or, of course, to say that (some)one is American Korean. Enacting and embodying different cultural identities and practices reveals to us their performative nature and hence their social construction. It reveals the intersectionality between our different identities, and the subtle inter-relationships between those identities within our lives and within our creative practices. It reveals to us the profound ways in which this performative process and its results relate to how we *feel* about ourselves and how we create and sustain notions of ownership over our cultural practices. For Landon-Smith, this means that she firmly situates her practice as *intra*cultural and aligned with the work of Rustom Bharucha rather than the universalizing and humanist approach of the kind of *inter*culturalism proposed by practitioners such as Peter Brook: 'I guess I am framing my work in that sort of place where one is always engaging with difference as opposed to disavowing it, particularly in a training environment' (Landon-Smith, 2012). In addition to the points raised by Landon-Smith there is clearly an imperative to apply such processes as rigorously as possible to white actors – this should not be seen as a process that is only applied to those whose ethnic or racial heritage is non-white. White middle-class non-disabled cultural identity must not be constructed as the norm; and the relative comfort such actors might feel as 'owners' of their physical/cultural heritage must not be simply taken for granted, but acknowledged as a privileged position. Simply finding their physicality as a white actor may not be in itself a difficult process, it is culturally open and available to them. What is challenging is how they then identify that physicality as something that is constructed and therefore open to interrogation and analysis. In a form of reversal of Landon-Smith's process, white actors may need to establish a distance from their movement practice, and a recognition of their own possible intersectionality, that enables them to understand its cultural implications and make critical decisions about how it is best employed.

This approach to movement inevitably presents certain challenges to conventional practice within the theatre industry. It proposes changes to the kinds of movement that diverse performers are enabled to bring in to audition, rehearsal and performance. The actor is conventionally not supposed to bring their embodied cultural heritage on stage, except in so far as it can be contained within certain parameters which prescribe its effects – it must fit within accepted understandings of the presentation of dramatic character, for instance.

Post-war migration means our rehearsal rooms are now full of diasporic identities … the suggestion that we have to therefore grapple with these webs of identities in our rehearsal rooms isn't even a suggestion to so many people. Often, you are having this parallel conversation and people have no idea what you're talking about, so it is not even at the resistance level, you're at the pioneering level where there is always going to be resistance because it is new. (Landon-Smith, 2012)

There have been some instances in which productions have sought to transpose plays into atypical cultural contexts – such as the RSC's productions of *Much Ado About Nothing* (2012), located in India, and of *Julius Caesar* (2012) and *Hamlet* (2016), both located in contemporary Africa. But these were not intracultural productions in the sense that it was not cultural complexity and diversity that was being presented, but rather a transposition or relocation of a play into a new set of cultural practices all of which had, or were given, some degree of unity and 'otherness'. This transposition is then primarily presented as casting a new light on Shakespeare's genius.[12] It is important to recognize that the 2012 production of *Julius Caesar* offered opportunities for a significant number of black actors to join the RSC and present one of the major texts in the canon through the lens of African culture. The movement work within the production drew on Black African cultural heritage[13] and the overall concept of the production meant that these movement practices were not presented as exotic/other within the frame of the production as a whole. The challenge for the movement director, Diane Alison-Mitchell, was to create a movement language that was recognizably African, but not specific to any one African cultural heritage, while attempting to avoid some kind of cultural homogenization. She relates how much of the movement work she did with the company was about tapping in to 'the cast's individual rhythmic sensibilities from their own heritages' (2017: 150), an approach that echoes some of the issues and practices raised above by Landon-Smith. She also refers to the importance of play within this kind of movement journey for the actors: 'the need for the actors to respect a particular physical language while having a spirit of playfulness and rhythmic spontaneity with their bodies' (2017: 149). However, with only one group of actors cast in this way within a much larger company and led by a white director, it is hard to know how and in what ways the impact of the project extended within the company as a whole and was sustained beyond this production.

At the same time that *Julius Caesar* was produced, the RSC also produced *The Orphan of Zhao*, an adaptation of a classic Chinese legend. This production was presented as part of the company's 2012–2013 *A World Elsewhere* season – the very name indicating a notion of otherness and difference that was not sensitive to the British East Asian community. In this instance, despite the Chinese setting, only three East Asian actors were cast, and all three were limited to minor roles in the production.[14] This created considerable uproar within the East Asian acting community, and resulted in heated debate about the RSC's casting policy and its cultural attitudes (Trueman, 2012). The casting of white actors in Chinese roles in a play set in China, given the acknowledged shortage of roles for East Asian actors, speaks of a universalized notion of human identity that ignores the political history of such appropriation and the lack of opportunities for East Asian actors to play white roles. Rogers and Thorpe (2014) examine the complexities of this production in detail, exploring in particular the accusations of 'yellowface'[15] and the realities of the RSC's approach to 'colour-blind' casting.[16] As Thorpe argues, this production presents whiteness as the 'normative racial force' (2014: 438). It is important to recognize, as Fusco suggests, that: 'Racial identities are not only black, Latino, Asian, native American and so on; they are also white. To ignore white ethnicity is to redouble its hegemony by naturalizing it' (1998: 72). In both of these RSC productions, to a greater or lesser extent, the presence of non-white bodies was at once broadly positive but also highlighted the cultural histories, meanings and resonances that were not effectively dealt with by the way those bodies were positioned within the company as a whole and by the extent to which they were allowed (or not) to represent their own histories, experiences and practices. The appointment of Will Tuckett as the movement director for *The Orphan of Zhao*, someone whose main previous experience was as Guest Principal Character Artist at the Royal Ballet Company, was also not an appointment that sent out messages of inclusion or of a commitment to diversity and Chinese cultural heritage. Inclusion on its own is not enough, especially if race as an issue is then disregarded and seen to have 'no semiotic value on stage' (Ayanna Thompson in Rogers, 2014: 454). It also oversimplifies notions of race, culture and ethnicity to 'root' culture solely according to region and place, 'in spite of the fact that more often than not contemporary nations are peopled by various ethnic groups who in turn exchange and engage in multiple cultural practices' (Nascimento, 2008: 49).

Such an approach to ethnic and racial cultural difference, of course, also resonates with the issues that arise through social, economic and class difference. In so far as Landon-Smith is developing an approach that seeks to help the actor access a physicality that works for them and their sense of creative agency, the same principles can apply to other sets of differences. She talks about working in the round, whatever the configuration of the theatre space – this offers the actor a sense of space that is 360 degree and that respects every dynamic and direction of their physicality. It allows the actor to let go of some of the theatrical conventions that effectively hold their bodies within a set of traditional white, middle-class, Western theatre paradigms. This works to support the actors, but also to create theatrical stage pictures that are challenging and that unsettle notions of conventional bodies in conventional stage spaces.

> I am always looking first to the actor and what can make that actor happy … that's my instinct. I will say 'OK, you need to sit like this, you need to be rougher, etc.'. And that sort of 'you need to be like this', I guess in my mind, sort of almost brings them to where they really are situated and so, the class pretensions that they may be putting on without even realizing it also get stripped away. Then you and they together find exactly where they're situated in terms of their ethnicity, and their class and their gender. (Landon-Smith, 2012)

All this of course amounts to a very challenging and quite sophisticated role for the director and/or movement practitioner: 'It is enormously sophisticated but my feeling is that it is the responsibility of the director to work with the actor in that way' (Landon-Smith, 2012). The director has to make decisions about what guidance or advice might help the actor to find a physicality that is of use to them and that is not oppressive nor heavy-handed. There can be multiple cultural identities at play, both within a company and within each individual actor, that need to be recognized and engaged with. At the same time, the actor has to be aware of 'the discourses, methods and traditions that have come down' (Landon-Smith, 2012), but then also not to work always within or towards those discourses. The actor or student has first to find themselves and then establish 'their own discourse within a range of discourses' (Landon-Smith, 2012).

As Nascimento (2008) suggests, the actor has not only a cultural identity composed from the various influences exerted upon them through their upbringing, they also have a cultural identity as an actor/performer. This cultural identity as an actor should also be recognized as socially, politically and culturally constructed. Within the theatre industry, it can oppress the other cultural identities that might be present and/or available for the performer. This can result in tensions for the actor, within which they can feel that acting is not a comfortable and affirming space for them.

> Somebody said something interesting about this the other day […] she said, 'If you have been trained, you are always going to see the trained actor and are not going to be able to see the person', and I must say, I think I only ever work with the cultural identity of the person. I don't really work with character either. So, I work with the actor and the pleasure to play something, whether that is to play a character called Juliet, a character in a white dress, a happy or sad character, etc.; that's what I work with. (Landon-Smith, 2012)

Landon-Smith proposes that the challenge is about renegotiating the starting place for the actor, the cultural and personal position from which they choose to begin to work. This is something that she works on from the very start of each session – getting rid of choices that have been imposed upon the actor, that have come from outside the actor's cultural context(s) but which are perceived within the professional theatre context as being somehow 'necessary'. These are the kinds of choices shaped by the perceived need to do Shakespeare in a certain way, to perform as an actor in a certain way, or to present a character in a certain way.

All actors can become adept at crossing cultural borders and exploring other cultural identities; it is in many senses part of the job – exploring and (re)presenting other kinds of cultural experience. For actors from culturally diverse, non-white, female and/or disabled backgrounds, this is of course something that they may well already have had to experience in multiple contexts, not always of their choosing or within their own control. There is always a challenge to ensure that the process of creating theatre performance is empowering, enlightening and respectful. Jerri Daboo notes how '[t]he teaching of practices which may be initially perceived as "other" or "from the margins" can serve potentially to make transparent some of the inherent systems and approaches which have become established in teaching more "mainstream" or familiar subjects' (2009: 121). However, that is not always the case; such investigations can also be naive and exploitable or exploitative. Landon-Smith comments on how actors can be driven by their professional insecurities to engage with approaches that they may see as a means to get 'better' as an actor, but which also are in tension with their own cultural identity – 'they are subconsciously creating a cultural identity which is not always conducive to working well' (Landon-Smith, 2012).

Actors in the UK are increasingly confronted by a complex and diverse mix of acting approaches, each of which makes (sometimes exclusive) claims to assist the actor to be more present or more convincing. Eclectic choices of approach (at worst a kind of 'pick-and-mix' of methods and techniques) can be seen as a response by the actor to economies that demand high degrees of flexibility and place strong value on innovation. At its best this can allow the actor to develop a deep understanding of different embodied cultural practices that enable and empower them as a performer and enrich their appreciation of the physical and performative representation of difference. As Jerri Daboo suggests, the student requires 'a re-training of the habitual patterns of the body to accommodate postures, movement, breathing patterns and ideas which are often initially unfamiliar [...] In this way, learning becomes an experiential process, rather than a quantifiable achievement of factual information' (2009: 124). At its worst the actor can become a cultural *flâneur*, sometimes with all the negative cultural undertones such a phrase implies – ignorant of the underlying ideologies behind each practice and with only a superficial understanding of the movement practices involved. This is a significant challenge for the institutions seeking to train actors and performers – how to enable the student to work from their own cultural identity and to find a starting place that has some personal resonance and meaning for them as a cultural subject. Despite the fact that forms of movement and performance from different cultures provide a rich environment within which to address issues of acting technique, embodiment, appropriation and (post)colonialism, institutions delivering actor training still tend to marginalize these practices. The process that Landon-Smith describes should enable the performer's creativity to flourish, because the process at least starts from where they are as a cultural subject and does not require them to locate themselves in a 'foreign' place, nor does it make assumptions about their knowledge of cultural practices. Her approach need not preclude the exploration of skills, techniques and methods from other cultural heritages, it simply means that the intention of such an exploration is to become more critically aware. The individual's cultural identity as an actor is thus recognized as not neutral but always culturally inflected by the particular place(s) that the performer starts from.

Race, Ethnicity and Movement

Access to the stage for ethnically diverse students/performers is still restricted. The gatekeepers for access are the funders, venue managers, teachers and workshop facilitators, the conservatoires and universities, and all those in decision-making positions in similar theatre organizations. In the UK, there have been increasing moves to identify the ethnic balance of such gatekeepers and to recognize the impact for general access that better, fairer representation should bring. The actor Tanya Moodie recently stated in an article in the *Sunday Times Culture* magazine, 'I don't tell necessarily black stories. I tell human stories. I don't act in a black way. I just happen to have brown skin' (Nicol, 2016: 10). But how true can this be? Of course, we want to be able to tell each other stories that transcend our differences, but does that mean that acting has to try to be culturally neutral?

It is now over 25 years since Adrian Lester played Rosalind in Cheek by Jowl's landmark 1991 all-male production of Shakespeare's *As You Like It* and

15 years since the same actor played the lead role in the National Theatre's 2003 production of *Henry V*. In 2015, the RSC cast a black actor, Lucian Msamati, as Iago in a production of *Othello* – a move which challenged traditional perspectives, particularly in relation to Othello's treatment by his deputy. Rufus Norris (Director of the National Theatre) has publicly affirmed: 'It's part of our duty to reflect and speak to the nation and the city we're in' (Nicol, 2016: 10), but outside London, according to Dawn Walton of Eclipse Theatre (Nicol, 2016: 11), there is less evidence of diverse and inclusive theatre practice. The Act for Change lobby group, co-founded by Danny Lee Wynter and Stephanie Street, organized a 'Diversity in Training for the Industry' event on 18 October 2016. The project included a survey of conservatoires and university drama courses that showed that although gender is broadly represented across institutions and courses, ethnic diversity is not represented and disability is rarely represented.[17] The issue of colour-blind casting is complex and controversial, as has been seen in relation to the RSC's production of *The Orphan of Zhao* (Rogers, 2014; Rogers & Thorpe, 2014). Ultimately, colour-blind casting can only ever be about ratios, contracts and salaries, as in reality colour is not invisible within our societies, and the aim should therefore be to recognize that fact and not hide from it. What does need resolving is which bodies do what on stage, so that race is acknowledged and addressed within the production processes, the creation of the performances and the structures of the companies that present those performances.

Natalie Simpson, a mixed race (White European and Black African) actor, reflected in a blog she wrote for the RSC on the way in which she would often be asked about her experiences as a black actor, while her experiences as a white actor were ignored (Simpson, 2016). She also discussed how the context in which her colour is understood can change so much – 'I have therefore lived my life as a chameleon, my skin colour distorted by the lens through which I am viewed' (Simpson, 2016). She describes her identity as one construct among many, but also as something that operates to define her path through tightly defined professional contexts. Within the context of her casting as a black, Asian and minority ethnic (BAME) actor at the RSC, she considers that 'I am made to understand that one half of me is being pushed to the forefront because it is the half that needs more attention' (Simpson, 2016). She talks about the ways in which access to the acting profession seemed to her to imply erasing aspects of her black cultural identity (hair, language, accent). She also writes about how different people make different projections of identity on to her – a situation that relates simultaneously to the nature of acting and to the reality of being a black person within the UK.

Kean and Larsen, in their recent report on diversity for the Andrew Lloyd Webber Foundation, state that 'if the theatre does not become more diverse it risks becoming irrelevant' (Kean & Larsen, 2016: 3). They report: 'A sense of isolation builds early for BAME theatre professionals' (Kean & Larsen, 2016: 3). BAME actors as a result are tending to turn to the USA or to set up their own companies; this, together with the failure of the conservatoires, in Kean and Larsen's view, to take in enough BAME students, 'has led to a shortage of actors suitable for the roles' (Kean & Larsen, 2016: 3). Financing students from disadvantaged backgrounds should be a priority if this situation is to be addressed in the UK; but the answer must also lie in what is taught and how within the various training contexts. While the theatre industry still considers that the white middle classes dominate theatre audiences there will be limited motivation to change decisions on casting, plays, performance styles and company ethos. According to Kean and Larsen, white actors and directors are perceived by BAME actors as part of the problem, their buy-in is 'superficial, based on liberal philanthropy' (Kean & Larsen, 2016: 9). They quote Hazel Holder, who states that she 'felt isolated because people assumed that my journey was exactly the same as theirs and it wasn't' (Kean & Larsen, 2016: 10). How many BAME movement teachers and directors are there within the industry, how much encouragement does our society and its systems provide for BAME practitioners to aspire to and achieve their career goals? 'Look at the training centres: where is the diversity in staffing or the curriculum?' (Celia Greenwood in Kean & Larsen, 2016: 14). Policies and projects have been put in place, but projects are often just that – of limited duration and limited impact.

The UK conservatoires are not blind to the problems facing BAME acting students and applicants, as evidenced by the Higher Education Academy report on the experience of BAME students at Royal Central School of Speech and Drama (McNamara & Coomber, 2012). However, it remains difficult for their institutional practices and approaches to acting to change – they are strongly connected to and deeply embedded in approaches to theatre that have considerable cultural power and weight:

> If there is a problem in wider theatre and film making with institutional racism and an erasure of BME actors, this will affect the study of drama and theatre if opportunities are not always present for BME actors or BME actors are less visible. (McNamara & Coomber, 2012: 25)

There is an underlying humanism that informs most of these training regimes, and that is deeply committed to a concept of shared humanity as a starting place for training. There may therefore sometimes be resistance to the idea that difference might have significances that cannot be easily subsumed into an overarching training regime for all.

Movement practices seem to have a knack of crossing cultural borders and being picked up within the host culture, often initially within youth subcultures (for example the migration of *parkour* practices out of the Paris suburbs in the 1990s). But what makes movement practices mobile and adaptable also makes them open to exploitation by dominant host cultures. Indian and East Asian martial arts, such as tai chi and yoga, have, for instance, been integrated into Western theatre practice through the work of scholars and practitioners such as Konstantin Stanislavsky, Jerzy Grotowski, Eugenio Barba, Richard Schechner and Phillip Zarrilli. It is important to understand these practices in relation to their wider cultural and ideological context (see Kapsali, 2013). Although such movement practices can be seen as practices that link together religion, self-development, performance and health, they can also feed notions of the teacher as master, and the notion of an ideal physical state (Kapsali, 2013: 80). Typically, such movement practices are used in the West to create high symbolic value for the teachers and the practices – requirements for intensive study, practice, dedication and even spiritual awareness. At the same time, they can be used to downplay the social role of movement practice and to mystify concepts of presence and being in the now.

The changes required are not as daunting and extreme as might be thought. As Landon-Smith's work suggests, starting from the actual lived experience of the diverse students and actors already within the industry would be a hugely positive step and one that it should be very easy to enable.

Disability, Performance and the Body

Disability typically functions as what Kuppers calls a 'master sign' (2003: 54) – disabled people are viewed as disabled before any other set of cultural criteria (gender, age, ethnicity). This means that disability can dominate the scenic space and the discourses within it; at the same time it also potentially gives the disabled performer a particular artistic power and presence. Disability is not generally studied as an important set of socio-political conditions within which acting and movement might take place. There have been few attempts within actor training practice to look at how disabled and non-disabled actors or students might meaningfully study how best to understand and then theatrically represent each other's life-world or actively to support prospective disabled students to consider training for a professional career.[18] Equally there have not been many attempts to create working environments within which the embodied experiences and capabilities of both disabled and non-disabled participants are both suitably and equitably engaged. At least projects such as Ramps on the Moon, a network of six regional UK theatres committed to creating a step-change in the inclusion of deaf and disabled performers, are creating contexts within which such explorations might take place.[19] How might conceptions of disability have to change within leading theatre organizations in order for initiatives such as Ramps on the Moon to have lasting impact? We need to conceive of disability as relating to the body's social presence, rather than its physical presence – thus allowing discriminatory categories to become less fixed. Acting need not be about verisimilitude, it need not take accurate naturalistic representation as a given. Instead it could emphasize continuing transformation and the recognition of the journey over the starting and finish points.

Disabled students/actors can transform themselves from their own individual starting point, in a manner similar to Landon-Smith's intracultural practice. The concept of the neutral body is, in a similar way, also challenged by disabled students' socially constructed 'otherness'. We should acknowledge that the act of transformation and our conception of what an actor does are also socially constructed. Transformation is not neutral, either physically or politically. Take, for example, the disabled actor who transforms him/herself into a non-disabled person/character. What is happening in this instance? What are the criteria for the success of such a transformation? What are the political implications of such a transformation? Is the disabled actor's understanding of neutrality any more or less complete than that of a non-disabled actor? Is their realization of neutrality compromised by their disability or made more immediate? The disabled actor may understand more directly and in a more politically sophisticated manner the way in which neutrality acts not as a goal but as a concept and a reference point. The neutral body no longer makes sense as an anatomical achievement, or even worse as a form of upright posture linked with good upbringing and sound moral fibre, but it does make sense as a way of recognizing the conditions under which each body transforms and the place(s) from which that body gains its transformative power. From the perspective of the disabled actor, the neutral body cannot be apolitical. The historical associations around the neutral body as object/outcome (rather than process) promote the idea of the upright and aligned body as a noble, universal referent. However, performing as non-disabled equally cannot be a neutral activity, since it is everywhere rehearsed: in somatic therapy classes, in rehabilitation centres, and in numerous contexts within our societies (Sandahl & Auslander, 2005: 3) and is so strongly associated with social, economic and cultural power. The disabled body, in fact, not only signals its difference, it also signals the difference of the non-disabled – in Butlerian terms, queering the non-disabled subject.

This distinction between non-disabled and disabled, and between who can represent what, is important; power is apportioned on the basis of it. Actors self-select on the basis of this distinction, pre-deciding whether they can be an actor or not on the basis of their body's ability to match a socially constructed model of the actor. Dominant forces within the industry require actors to move and stand like actors, to look like actors, to have bodies that signify conventional industry standards of beauty, athleticism, sexual allure and charisma. That is to say that they are expected to be able to demonstrate physical abilities that are established as commercially useful and that fit the way bodies are configured within the fictive environment of the production/performance.

What if the actor does not need to transform against such fixed industry criteria? What if transformation is about play, about the complicity between the actor and the audience and about the audience's willingness to go on an imaginative journey with the actor? Transformation is something that we *do* with our bodies, that takes us from one place to another, from one way of being to another. Each place is contingent and constructed; each place is already located. The process of play is the journey between – it is both liberating and constrained: liberating in its ability to allow us to make connections that jump social and rational constrictions, constrained in that its parameters and processes are already marked on the very bodies that playfully strive to escape them. As Bulmer states:

> Apart from assessment and curriculum issues – well, the word 'process' keeps coming up. It is used constantly in discussions of training as if it were sacrosanct. Yet in the outside world everyone who works as an artist has a different process.
>
> And excellent is another problematic word – I do not believe we should be talking about an excellent voice type or an excellent body type – in an educational environment we should not simply be looking for what are deemed to be current acceptable types within the profession. (Bulmer in Dacre and Bulmer, 2009: 137)

The meaning of disability therefore most often lies within its context (Conroy, 2009: 2). Play enables and provides freedom within that context (*paidia*), while also acknowledging and challenging the existence of that context (*ludus*).[20] Play may be best positioned to enable bodies of difference, those bodies which dominant cultures might not normally acknowledge or empower, such as the disabled body, to take the stage. Through play it should be possible for a wide range of bodies to become part of the physical language of performance, disrupting the logic that underpins the dominant physical norms and revealing a world in which such norms are all equally 'in play'. The disabled body offers to play with the normalized body, challenging its stability as reality and as concept, suggesting a different set of priorities and requiring a journey away from convention. This is facilitated by a focus away from the body as a fixed entity and towards movement as a fluid process in which we can all transform ourselves. Furthermore, allowing ourselves to focus on movement rather than notions of the body means that, as Kuppers states, 'it does not necessarily matter if one extends an arm, finger, or chin in order to place oneself into a spatial form' (2003: 130). Movement's fluidity can both communicate meanings and open up their uncertainties; the playful moving body is especially potent in this regard – constantly disrupting, dissolving and revealing meanings, and at the same time taking an attitude towards the body that asserts the body's contingent status. This may be why some disabled dance practitioners are attracted to contact improvisation as a form – allowing, as it does, for the emphasis to be on fluidity, the moment of improvisation, and responsiveness to the movement of the partner, and as such widening 'the range and definition of acceptable dancing bodies' (Henderson & Ostrander, 2010: 44).

Graeae Theatre Company – Disabled Bodies in Performance

The body experiences the world in relation to time, space and objects – to various others, both animate and inanimate. These experiences impact upon our body/mind and its construction. More so than for text work or voice study, movement work involves a change of consciousness; we start to experience our bodies differently, in the same way that one might during intensive or prolonged exercise. Time's effect on the mind is conventionally marked by memory (or its demise). Time's effect on the body is, however, marked by decreasing capacity (age and/or tiredness) or increasing capacity (maturity and/or training). The body's relationship to space is of course a key element of movement practice. Space defines the body's movement – movement is only possible in relation to other points in space – and also creates the social environment within which movement begins to signify and create meaning. The body is both object and subject – as a physical entity each body is part of a matrix of physical objects within which our own bodies exist. At the same time, we are the observing subjects who identify the objects around us and identify ourselves in relation to the objects around us. This is further complicated by our awareness of other people as both bodily objects and other subjects.

These distinctions become relevant as we come to consider how and to what extent various bodies are understood as bodies and/or as subjects (or non-subjects). When people are treated as (only) bodies they are (at least in part) objectified and their existence as subjects is (at least in part) denied. The disabled body in performance is an example of this. For many years disabled bodies were either absent from the stage or used to represent or signify mental deformity (*Richard III*) or abnormality and the object of disgust and derision (*The Elephant Man*, 1977) – in almost all instances they are bodies that are looked at as 'objects'. In more recent times, disabled bodies have entered the stage in their own right, as subjects and creative participants. Companies have been formed in order not only to provide performance opportunities for disabled performers, but also in order to celebrate the disabled body in its own right and to present performances that view the disabled body from the perspective of disabled people.

Graeae Theatre Company is perhaps one of the best-known examples in the UK of a company that has sought to address the opportunities available to disabled performers and the wider public perception of disability and disabled theatre performance. The company was founded in 1980 by Nabil Shaban and Richard Tomlinson, who had met at Hereward College in Coventry. One of their significant productions was an adaptation of Ben Jonson's play *Volpone*, entitled *Flesh Fly*, which toured the UK in 1996.

> This was a confrontational and challenging adaptation which made the audience face up to the constructions of ability [*sic*] and disability in *Volpone*. This was particularly the case in the many moments where broad slapstick was deployed by the performers: for example, in the very funny, very physically vigorous administering of an enema to Volpone, played by Nabil Shaban, the founder of Graeae. Shaban's first entrance was also one of the most memorable moments of the production. The audience saw what looked like a small bundle of rags carried onstage; suddenly the bundle burst into life, the face and torso of Shaban emerged, and the audience laughed but were quite clearly shocked. (Schafer, 1997: 113)

Play in this context both enables the performers' bodies to be used in different ways and enables the expectations of the audiences to be challenged, dissolved and transformed. In this instance, play represented an attitude towards the performance of a classic text - an attitude that was disruptive, rejecting a set of conventional logics which determine what kinds of actors play what kinds of parts, how bodies are portrayed, and how a character might be, for instance, foxlike.[21]

In 2004, Graeae collaborated with Paines Plough[22] and Frantic Assembly to produce a new play by Glyn Cousins, entitled *On Blindness*. The play explored what blind people could 'see' and what sighted people could not, but it also explored a number of other aspects of disability. A certain degree of physical fitness, stamina, complicity, awareness and coordination is, as we have seen in the previous chapter, encouraged and developed within Frantic's approach to physical theatre. Although Frantic have certainly been clear that they see none of this as an obstacle for disabled or non-disabled male and female performers of any ethnicity to engage in their work, the collaboration with Frantic Assembly brought a very specific set of challenges both for the Graeae performers and the Frantic Assembly performers. Frantic had created a reputation for a particular kind of high-octane movement style. They had not worked with disabled performers before and the disabled performers had not worked with this kind of movement before. The idea for the project had great potential, but the end performance struggled to deliver against the expectations. The attempt to integrate movement, dance and signing was only partially successful, possibly because the element of play was harder to maintain. The dance work did not have the exuberance that was typical of Frantic's own work, the signing introduced an element of signification that made the movement work less resonant (by locating meaning so directly in fixed gestures), and the different physical qualities and embodied experiences of the performers, as a result, were not fully explored or integrated. However, along with *Tiny Dynamite*, *On Blindness* marked a significant shift for Frantic, away from an athletic and raw physicality towards something more reflective and tender.

What is important to note from this case study is that play is not just about transformation; it is also about challenging something quite profound about how we understand our embodiment and our humanity. Although the industry praises non-disabled performers who transform themselves into convincing portrayals of disabled people (for example Daniel Day Lewis in *My Left Foot* (1989), for which he won the 1989 Academy Award for Best Actor in a Leading Role), these actors are not necessarily enabling us to understand the social construction of notions of disability if the focus is on their technical virtuosity and professional commitment. The real challenge for playful movement work is to achieve a transformation which is not simply virtuosic, worthy and well-meaning, but which also reveals and challenges our conceptions and expectations on a more profound level.

The Valley of Astonishment

Many of the key points in this chapter can be explored through an examination of a 2014 performance by Peter Brook's Paris-based International Centre for Theatrical Creation, entitled *The Valley of Astonishment*. This simple but intricate and subtle show examines various neurological conditions and their effects upon people. How these conditions are viewed by others is an integral part of this theatrical exploration. The piece is performed by three actors: Marcello Magni (who was also a founder member of Complicité), Jared McNeill and Kathryn Hunter (also an early member of Complicité, and who is herself disabled, the result of a car accident during her youth). They each perform a variety of characters – people who have neurological or physiological conditions as well as those studying such conditions. The set is very simple, a square of blue surface material, several chairs, a table and a coat stand. The actors are accompanied by two musicians, who play alongside and interact with the actors' performances.

The play tackles a range of conditions, including synaesthesia, memory ability, loss of limb, loss of proprioception, and seeing names as colours. In all of these cases, the subject experiences a connection between different senses that do not usually work in tandem or association. Each of the cases examines a different person for whom one set of sensory experiences interacts so as to enhance or replace another. This resonates with one of the central images referred to at the start of the performance – the mythical bird, the phoenix. In legend, the phoenix dies in flames but is reborn from the fading embers of its own demise. For the characters in the play, one set of sensory experiences brings new life to another. The phoenix is also of course an image of transformation and change that speaks to the very nature of acting – the being that remakes itself anew, transforming itself as an act of creative destruction. The considered and analytical feel to the staging of the play, scenes frequently set within the context of a medical institution, the use of disabled and non-disabled performers, all help to establish an eloquent tension between the social and the personal experiences explored. The metatheatrical elements in the production invite consideration of the ways in which society enforces forms of performance of disability and disabled experience on disabled people over which they do not always have control, but which may potentially enable ownership and identity to be reclaimed.

Among the most prominent sections of *The Valley of Astonishment* are those that tell the story of a woman who has an exceptional memory capability, played by Kathryn Hunter. This woman is able to store an exceptionally large number of memories by visualization, creating images that 'hold' the memories for her. This process is an extreme example of the very process of acting, in which the actor uses multiple associations between experiences, objects, feelings and events in order to maintain a vivid experience as a potent memory, capable of recapture and reinvigoration. Tellingly, the character in the play who has this condition is advised that a career 'on stage' is the best place for her, where she can make a living out of this (dis)ability. If an actor's ability to play through the body could be understood as related in some form to the condition of synaesthesia, then the very way in which the body/mind of the actor can be taught to engage with the world is potentially thrown into a new light. Actors no longer need to 'lose themselves' in another character or world, but rather they can transform themselves and their environments through playing with the effects of the dynamic sensory qualities of the world. The very simplicity of the set then becomes part of the way in which the audience is drawn into this same form of association. They see the simple set and yet at the same time, through the quality of the actors' playing, they also see the offices, stages, laboratories in which the stories take place. In their own way, they make the same neurological associations that the character uses – a way of walking and gesturing creates the experience of watching a person on stage, a way of sitting and talking creates an office space.

In a subsequent section, Marcello Magni portrays a character who suffers from a loss of proprioception. Unable to move unless he is watching his movements, he demonstrates how he works to disguise his disability/condition – hiding the effort it takes, he studiously imitates/performs the everyday gestures and movements that might make his movement look 'normal'. Normality, or conventional movement, in this way becomes performed, learnt and presented and, indeed, revealed as such. We are aware of its everyday qualities, but at the same time his performance alienates us from these movements as we become aware of the effort required/taken for granted. This section of the performance 'plays' with this effect, for example the character falls as he demonstrates losing sight of his movements in a blackout and we gasp, knowing that we are watching an actor playing at being helpless in a darkness that does not actually exist. This playfulness reaffirms the humanity behind the condition – without belittling it and without any false pity. We are also aware of the ways in which this theatrical image echoes the actor's fundamental conundrum, that their actions lack theatrical significance unless watched by an audience.

In his next section, Magni plays a one-armed magician, performing card tricks with members of the audience. The tricks act as a form of theatrical metaphor – we are drawn into a form of compliance with the act of pretence.

We see what we cannot see and cannot see what we should see – we are drawn into complicity with the magician, just as we are with the actor who plays the magician. He is followed on to the stage in the next scene by Kathryn Hunter's memory act – making a theatrical connection between our acceptance of the actor/magician's sleight of hand and our acceptance of her ability to associate memories and experiences. Memory becomes an act – both a form of physical action (she describes how she journeys through her sequence of memories as if describing a real experience) and a performance act, even an act of magic.

Throughout all of this, the playful nature of the style of presentation and performance constantly prompts us to ask ourselves: what attitude should actors have to portraying people who have such unusual conditions? What attitude should we have to watching such conditions be performed? Towards the end of the show, Kathryn Hunter's character speaks poignantly about the painful flipside of her condition – the inability to forget. She is faced with the challenge of learning to forget. This challenge is at the heart of the dilemma for the playful actor – how to let go of what has been written on the body in order to engage with bodily inscription in a more resistive and reflexive way, how to forget the rules while still working within or against them. Hunter's character describes how she remembers sequences of words by creating associations with journeys from her childhood house and the streets surrounding it. Memory is portrayed as beginning from a sense of self; childhood experience is presented as core to this process. Memory and a sense of self are intimately intertwined in this image. The actor is also required to start from a sense of self and to create journeys outwards from that core, linking new sets of personal experiences into the sequences required by the text, the audience, or the director. How easy is it to delete or erase these journeys once they are completed? How desirable is it to be able to do so? When does a particular ability become a disability and vice versa? How much of a struggle is it for actors to remake themselves anew each time? What are the implications for all of us in terms of how memories (patterns of behaviour) are written on to the body, and how they might become hindrances and need to be unwritten?

At the performance of *The Valley of Astonishment* at Warwick Arts Centre, Coventry, on Friday 13 June 2014, two events occurred which threatened to interrupt the theatrical event. At the start of the performance, during a speech by one of the actors, a disabled audience member appeared to become distressed and began to vocalize their discomfort. At first there was the possibility for the audience that this was an intentional part of the performance; it soon became evident that this was not the case. The actor (Jared McNeill) visibly acknowledged the presence of this person, the sound that they were making, and their discomfort, but without breaking from his performance. His relationship with all aspects of the performance meant that he was able to engage with the elements at play in that moment, and to acknowledge it and very subtly let the audience know that it was being included and accepted. The skills required in order to achieve this are not conventional performance skills, nor are they simply a matter of confidence and experience; instead I would suggest that what is required is an openness to all the bodies that might constitute an audience, as well as a playful attitude towards performance and towards what it means to be in the same space with other people and sharing a story. Later in the performance, during Marcello Magni's magic act, a member of the audience is asked on stage to participate in one of the tricks. On this night, the audience member concerned misunderstood the instructions from Marcello and steadfastly refused to respond to the cues he was given. The audience initially enjoyed this misunderstanding, but eventually felt some awkwardness and embarrassment. They wanted the audience member to recognize and accept what was proposed by the performer so that the trick might work and the performance event progress. Marcello recognized the difficulty that he was in; he was required playfully to adjust the predetermined trajectory of the scene in order that a resolution might be achieved which did not belittle or disrespect the audience member. It was also clear that he needed to acknowledge the expectations and reactions of the audience in order to achieve this. As he was already asking the audience to use their imaginations and playfully to engage with his own representation of a one-armed card magician, this was less of a step than might be imagined. Not only was the 'real' acknowledged and integrated through the absorption of the stubborn or reluctant audience member, but the 'real' also momentarily became both playful and played with through Marcello's ability to draw this event into the performance as a whole. Far from the 'game' of theatre being broken, in this respect it was enhanced and enriched.

It can be seen, therefore, that for disabled people, 'reality is viscerally created through bodies that are in a constant state of re-experience and re-interpretation' (Scott, 2012: 101). Disabled people narrate from a place of hyper-awareness of the body's role in the creation of their identity. This is a hyper-awareness that society places upon them, but that also brings potential power and presence to their performance work. Kuppers argues that '[m]any disabled people, if their differences are visible or not, have to perform their disability, perform their stories' (Kuppers & Marcus, 2009: 143). They are regularly reminded of the ways in which social pressures on our bodies construct important parts of our notions of self. It is painfully ironic, therefore, that while 'non-disabled people can prove the "mastery" of their craft by "acting disabled"' (Kuppers, 2001: 29), this is denied for many disabled actors who are generally perceived within the industry as not being able to enact their own disability – disability being conceived of as inability, authenticity linked only to their identity within their own disability (Kuppers, 2017: 77). The dramaturgical trope of overcoming physical adversity can end up only speaking to the medical model of disability. Instead, dependence and mutual support needs to be seen as just as valuable as individualism and personal bravery (Lewis, 2016: 307). Disability makes evident the reality that we all move in different ways; that we, our embodied selves, what we do and can do in performance, are not simply interchangeable (Lewis, 2016: 312) – yet without universalizing the body, it reminds us of the real source of our equality, 'in a web of interdependence' (Lewis, 2016: 313).

Gender

Theorization around gender and the body has been very well covered over the last 30 years (see, for example: Butler (1993); Grosz (1994); Orbach (2010); Young (1990)). Over the last decade there has also been research into the relationship of such theory to movement performance and pedagogy (see, for example, Evans (2009) and Mitchell (2013)). In this section I want to examine how some of the movement practices already discussed in this book can be considered in relation to gender. Acknowledging Judith Butler's work on the performative nature of gender, this section will consider how different movement practices function to enact gender on the bodies that engage with them – but it will also examine how they can, do already, or might in the future, challenge notions of gender, performance and movement.

I have already mentioned ways in which neutral mask work, such as that employed at the Lecoq School in Paris and in many other leading training institutions, cannot avoid the cultural differences that are currently recognized as distinguishing different bodies. Just as the most well-known neutral masks, such as those designed for Lecoq by Amleto and Donato Sartori, are visibly Caucasian, so too are they visibly gendered. There are male and female masks – the female mask is slightly smaller and more softly contoured than the male mask – and at the Lecoq School students are discouraged from wearing the mask that is inappropriate for their sex. The emphasis within neutral mask training is on simplifying and paring away – some of the complications of contemporary gender theory are perceived as unnecessarily distracting in this context. Given that animals, colours, materials and the like are explored through work based on the neutral mask, it seems strange that gender is not also explored in the same way (for example, women exploring the movement of men and vice versa, or explorations of what straight, transgendered, gay or lesbian movement might be from any one of a number of gendered perspectives). Throughout the training at the Lecoq School, considerations such as gender, race, class and politics are not ignored, but in terms of the teaching and the tasks set for students they are deferred until after graduation. The training emphasizes the development of foundational skills and practices which the student may choose to use after leaving the school to explore complex cultural issues. As a successful pedagogue, perhaps Lecoq did not see the need to question the political beliefs of his students or to provoke debates that could not be easily resolved within the classroom. Nonetheless, it seems increasingly desirable to explore how what are now well-established practices, such as neutral mask training, might not only enhance the students' ability to explore and express gender issues, but might even provide a valuable practice through which to begin such an investigation. Being masculine or feminine, or male or female, gay, lesbian, bisexual or transgendered is not about the body, anatomy, and movement and gesture alone, it is also about the lived experience of such a body within its social context. Lecoq was, perhaps understandably, sensitive to the need to allow students to work out some of these issues in relation to their own physical lives in their own time and at their own pace. Neutral mask work can, however, help the student to explore how social constructions have worked on their own bodies, and might also operate as a process that may help resist such social construction in their work. It is all about the relationship that the student has with the mask – if the mask represents only the student's biological identity then it will be limited in what it enables the student to explore.

Gender and Grotowski

One of the other important influences on UK physical theatre practice over the last 50 years has been work associated with Jerzy Grotowski (his own work, and the work of those associated with him such as Odin Teatret, Gardzienice and Song of the Goat). The intense nature of these approaches has allowed a certain mythology to develop around the work, particularly during the 1970s, 1980s and the early 1990s. The mystique was further enhanced by the decision of most of these companies/projects to locate themselves away from urban civilization and within tight-knit community groupings. This has limited and delayed the impact of these practitioners within UK theatre practice – no mainstream company has engaged with Grotowski-based practice since the RSC's production of *US* in 1966 (the preparation process for which directly involved Grotowski and some of his actors) and Katie Mitchell's work at RSC in the 1990s (drawing on her experience with Gardzienice in 1990). Prior to the Odin Teatret residency in London in April 2014, the last visit to the UK by the entire Odin company was to Coventry in 1994. Gardzienice's work is reasonably well documented within the UK; however, opportunities to train with them or to experience their performances are very limited. Those wishing to train in the work of Song of the Goat can now do so at Rose Bruford College, where Gabriel Gawin (one of the early members of the company) runs an MFA/MA course in Actor and Performer Training, based on working methods developed with the company.

Virginie Magnat reminds us that '[a]lthough the strenuous physical training emblematic of Grotowski's approach is not gender specific, it has historically been associated with a masculine conception of the performer disseminated through scarce yet iconic archival film footage and photographs' (2016: 222–223). These Polish companies have often been led by male directors, but this is not exclusively the case. Anna Zubrzycka, who worked initially with Gardzienice, was co-founder of Song of the Goat with Grzegorz Bral. There is clearly importance in the existence of such female role models. This tradition of training and theatre making is physically and emotionally demanding and it is important that this is not seen as defining the work as essentially male/masculine in nature. As Magnat suggests,

> acquiring confidence in one's abilities to direct one's own life is politically significant for women, especially in the case of artists placed in a particularly precarious position by a profession in which both women and experimental performance practice tend to be marginalized and receive little support. (2016: 230)

This particular tradition of physical training and performance also focuses on the combination of movement and song. This gives it an emphasis unique in UK theatre practice outside of musical/music theatre. This relationship is largely explored through songs from folk traditions and cultures around Europe, an aspect that, while it brings powerful resonances with European folk culture, has perhaps also tended to limit the wider audience appeal for such work within the UK, where such traditions are now less recognized than they might have been during the mid-twentieth century folk music revival.

The emphasis within the Grotowski tradition of training and performance on the pre-expressive, the deeply embodied creative roots of performance, and on the personal psychophysical journey of the actor, all operate to place this work within a very specific social, cultural and political context, which Barba has described as the Third Theatre. In placing the actor/performer within a cultural context that identifies around the ontology of performance, the very nature of being a performer, this work seeks to carve out a unique place for the performer's skills and psychophysical technique that raises the significance of what the actor does. The danger is that it does so through a process that in some important respects also removes the actor/performer from aspects of everyday life and their social, cultural and political context. Grotowski's emphasis on 'unlearning' and the use of the *via negativa* can be historically situated within the context of the movement within the 1960s towards '[l]earning not to fabricate, to act purely from instinct' (La Frenais, 1986: 18), and as part of a vision for technique as something that would eventually consume itself in the flames of the actor's creativity. The almost monastic dedication required to achieve this level of performance mastery is most probably a key factor that has limited its wider appeal and maintained perception of it as male-orientated.

Frantic and Gender: The Courage to Be Soft

Similarly, one question that arises from any discussion about the wider social significance of Frantic Assembly's work is the extent to which the movement dramaturgy of such companies is gendered, and the specific ways in which gender is constructed within such work. These kinds of choreographic and compositional practices draw on a mixed heritage: Pina Bausch's interrogation of the gendered significance of movements and gestures; Eurocrash's bold construction of the female dancer's body as muscular, robust and powerful;[23] Lloyd Newson's examination of the physicality of masculinity, homosexuality and difference, especially when taken to extremes; but also, traditions of sport, exercise, martial arts, and the gendered activity concealed within conventional late twentieth-century dance and theatre practice. Undoubtedly, women who have been part of companies such as DV8 (Wendy Houston), Volcano (Fern Smith) and Frantic Assembly (Cait Davis, Georgina Lamb and Vicki Manderson) have all demonstrated impressive physicality and inspiring levels of commitment. All three companies have also not shied away from exploring gay sexual identity as a theme or narrative element within their work. Victoria Lewis points to a strand of feminist devised theatre making that seeks to blend feminist body politics with 'physical strength and financial and emotional independence' (2016: 305). She links this to cultural phenomena such as the appearance of female action heroines and various fitness crazes. The role of the woman within physical theatre practice in particular is still conflicted in relation to these aspects – where does physical strength and risk-taking start to masculinize the female body rather than simply empower it? Practitioners such as Lloyd Newson, Nigel Charnock, Liam Steel and Steven Hoggett have also helped establish a significant gay presence within the contemporary physical theatre sector, blending the marginal in to the mainstream in ways that critique, resist and erode heterosexual privilege and normalization.

The opportunities for female and male, gay and straight performers to engage in physical theatre on more equal terms has meant that all participants have been challenged to extend their physicality confidently into the world around them and to resist the constraints they may have experienced through their gendered socialization (for instance, as described by Iris Young in her 1990 article 'Throwing Like a Girl'). Frantic's workshop approach deliberately rejects assumptions that the female participants cannot engage in the same way as their male colleagues. While this is potentially empowering, there is also a need to be aware of the perils of assuming any form of universality of physiognomy or of ignoring the social significances that can still be attached to certain exercises and movement challenges. To what extent are period pains, post-partum changes to the body, concerns about weight, issues around intimate touch, or physical contact with sensitive body parts addressed prior to or during workshop activities? To what extent do the exercises used to develop skills and practices in Frantic's workshops embody masculine physicality, masculine body practices and masculine attitudes to the body? Raising these issues is not to imply that companies such as Frantic are insensitive to or ignorant of such considerations, far from it – however, within the context of this kind of work, there is often an implicit imperative to get on with the physical activity and to ask questions, challenge assumptions or raise issues afterwards. Sometimes there are social or professional pressures that work against the airing of any of these issues, which might be seen as embarrassing and/or too sensitive to be discussed in mixed gender groups, or as inappropriately personal within professional work contexts. In this sense, if the process is not carefully and reflexively monitored and managed, the female, homosexual or transgendered body can certainly be physically empowered but can also be subsumed within a patriarchal dramaturgy at the same time. At least there is an opportunity within work such as Frantic's, and processes such as those that they use, to separate the muscular from the masculine and reappropriate the former for women and other genders, so as to be configured and understood in relation to their own bodies. It has become more socially acceptable for a woman, for instance, to develop traditionally male attributes of strength, stamina and muscle tone, though debate continues as to whether such (re)constructions of the female body are subversive or regressive. Judith Butler warns that '[t]he female body that is freed from the shackles of the paternal law may well prove to be yet another incarnation of that law, posing as subversive but operating in the service of that law's self-amplification and proliferation' (Butler in Albright, 1997: 31).

If physical theatre, such as the work of Frantic Assembly, has appropriated a particular set of practices from the world of New Dance, it has done so as part of a wider societal and cultural change that has seen a more diverse range of people taking centre stage – bodies that, in the context of this chapter, are younger, older, more working class, more ethnically diverse, that identify with different gender types, and with different backgrounds and different levels of dis/ability. As Nadine Holdsworth argues:

> The social construction of gender and the gendered meanings associated with dance play a pivotal role in influencing young people's involvement in dance as, according to Doug Risner, 'the Western European paradigm situates dance as primarily a "female" art form' (2009, 58). From an early age, many young girls are encouraged to pursue dance as a gender-appropriate activity, whereas it is something largely avoided by boys, who are rapidly learning and synthesizing appropriate male behaviour, which generally means 'avoiding all that is feminine, homosexual or unmasculine to any degree' (62). (2013: 170)

Similar paradigms exist around dance and ethnicity and around dance and disability. In everyday social situations men dancing, moving and performing physically seem to act in a way that either emphasizes muscularity, danger and risk, or emphasizes campness, desire and vulnerability – a balance between supposed opposites that is eloquently presented in DV8's 1995 production of *Enter Achilles*. How do these tensions relate to the challenges facing the female performer within physical performance practice? After the work of Black Mime Women's Troupe, Three Women Mime, Suzy Willson and the Clod Ensemble, Cunning Stunts and Foursight Theatre company, how well known are the other, newer examples of contemporary, feminist physical theatre, and what opportunities are being made available for them? What impact should these challenges have on male physical theatre practitioners? How can women moving in physical theatre best be (re)established as a place from which to (re) create gender identity?

In the case of Frantic, the solutions that they have found, while not resolving all of the issues raised above, do attempt to offer something for both female and male participants, and for participants of different sexualities. They have found ways for men's movement and physicality to be explored and performed as gentle, graceful, pleasing, expressive, intimate, vulnerable, eloquent, playful, as well as being, when required, strong, powerful and skilful – qualities that have deeply informed their work on projects such as *Ignition*, their long-term, free, national training programme for young men aged 16–20, and *Fatherland*, their 2017–2018 show exploring the complexities of contemporary fatherhood. And they have found ways for women's movement to be explored as strong, confident, occupying and owning space, dynamically projecting through space, yet without denying their physicality as women. As the company increasingly works with older female actors (*Lovesong* (2011) and *Things I Know To Be True* (2016)) some of this dynamic is changing further and the movement vocabulary has become enriched by what older female performers can do – the kinds of attitudes and abilities that their experiences of their older bodies bring in to the rehearsal room. It is not just about the physical skills that the performers or workshop participants acquire; it must surely also be about the value ascribed to those skills.

Holdsworth (2013: 170) also warns that, for young men, the display of physical prowess is often also connected to gaining status among other men or to attracting sexual partners; it may be only tangentially related to self-expression, releasing and expressing emotions through movement, caring for the body or acknowledging the pleasure and beauty of rhythmic and expressive movement. To critique this defensive masculinity, she quotes Risner, who asserts that 'boys who dance, unlike their male peers in athletics and team sports, are participating in an activity that already casts social suspicion on their masculinity and heterosexuality' (Risner in Holdsworth, 2013: 170). Risner's form of words suggests a general social assumption that dancing is inherently feminine, and that sport is inherently masculine. Can such fixed positions around the social forms within which bodies move hold in contemporary British culture and performance? These social changes are perhaps something that dance-based physical theatre has been quickest to identify and find ways of expressing. Frantic have very specifically addressed the training of young men through dance and movement as part of their long-running 'Ignition' programme.[24]

They also address stereotypical gendered behaviour indirectly in shows such as *Hymns* (1999, 2000 and 2005).

> *Hymns* [...] was a very obvious assault on the stereotype because we used the stereotype, embraced the stereotype. It wasn't about men suddenly becoming beautifully eloquent in their words in a situation where they weren't used to being. We used all the bluster and strength and masculinity of those guys but the play wasn't about that. It was about the construction you create around them and how that doesn't protect them in the long term at all actually, it leads to their demise. (Graham, 2015)

A year or two after the first performances of *Hymns*, Graham and Hoggett explored a subtler, gentler and more emotionally nuanced physicality in *Tiny Dynamite* (2001 and 2003), where they worked again with Vicky Featherstone and Paines Plough. The characters in this piece 'were capable of a tenderness; and that was something that we were adamant that we wanted to put across, that this show shouldn't have the physical lustre and bravado of a physical theatre company' (Graham, 2015). Featherstone was an important guide for the company at this moment of transition and change.

This tension between the club-energy physicality of Frantic's 1990s work and the subtlety and vulnerability of a lot of their work in the 2000s is what enables their performance practices to resonate around the social pressures that harden people's assumptions about gender. It is this dynamic relationship between what male bodies do, why they do it and how they might do it differently that Frantic seek to 'unfix' so that audiences can 'see through the cracks of the veneer and [...] get a glimpse of something else, get an understanding of something that's underneath' (Graham, 2015). In their early work, pushing the body to the limits of its capabilities was a way in which the experience of the body could become less stable (Evans, 1999: 137). Steven Hoggett has spoken about the way that within Frantic's 1995 production of *Klub*, 'all six characters hurdled the perimeters of gender stereotypes in both appearance and action to create an environment where sexuality flowed so freely from one state to another that it defied prejudice and labelling' (Hoggett in Evans, 1999: 141). The key issue here, something that is at the heart of this chapter and pertinent to several of the arguments in this book, is that crossing disciplinary borders also brings into play the cultural forces (good and bad) effective within those other fields. Holdsworth discusses how:

> As [Ramsay] Burt writes, 'dance is an area through which, as embodied beings, we negotiate the social and cultural discourses through which gender and

sexuality is maintained' (2009, 150). Therefore, if the social and cultural discourse on masculinity is evolving then this will be played out in and through dance as much as elsewhere. (Holdsworth, 2013: 171)

She refers to evidence of changes in male engagement with dance, citing cultural events such as the success of the film *Billy Elliot* (2000), and the participation of rugby player Matt Dawson and cricketer Darren Gough in the BBC programme *Strictly Come Dancing*. However, just because men dance does not in itself mean that they are renegotiating the power structures around their bodies, gestures, actions and movements. It could even be argued that men are moving into physical practices traditionally associated with women primarily because they are now seeing social, cultural and economic benefit in doing so. The danger is that young men are 'met halfway' as they start to engage with their physicality and confront their attitudes towards physical expression, allowing them to retain attitudes that should actually be challenged. The movement vocabulary of such introductory sessions must therefore guard against allowing the emphasis to move too easily towards competitiveness and physical skill over process, collaboration and expressivity.

Despite these reservations, it is important to recognize that contemporary physical theatre and also New Circus very often function to undermine, parody or displace the traditional gendered practices associated with forms such as circus, classical dance, classical theatre, and the conventional dramaturgies of these forms (for example, 'dramatic suspense' and 'triumphal climaxes' (Bouissac, 2012: 170)). Physical theatre, contact improvisation and New Circus have challenged the conventional gender roles of performers within conventional forms such as mainstream theatre, commercial circus and acrobatics, and classical dance. Close physical contact in such forms was traditionally staged as a romantic heterosexual display between male and female performers; as we have seen in Chapter 4, physical contact can be capable of signifying so much more. To some extent, the alternative forms of physical performance that have emerged in the late twentieth century deliberately forsook claims to respectability in order to achieve and maintain this kind of equality and inclusivity. Traditional circus and classical dance tended to display the woman as an 'object' that was physically manipulated by the man; physical theatre and contact improvisation deliberately reject such gender dynamics. The bond between performers moving together and supporting each other is not necessarily desexualized nor disassociated with pleasure and excitement, it is recognized as a valuable element in and of itself in the creation and/or construction of a relationship with the audience.

Conclusion: Chapter 5

Women strongly desire fair opportunity to develop their creative abilities and to express their own ideas. Contemporary physical theatre, in all its forms, has the potential to provide double empowerment for all those whose performance work has not been privileged in the past: the empowerment of the expressive and energized body, and the empowerment of finding a creative voice of their own. As we have seen, everyday behaviour is implicitly challenged within these movement practices as well as the limitations of what is physically possible; in this way, physical theatre and New Circus practices can provide spaces within which it may be possible to reveal and interrogate social constructions of gender.

Movement practices can offer empowerment through exorcising fear of the physical – changing the performer's attitude towards their own body, the bodies of others and the ways in which bodies interact. The next step will be to remove the political, cultural and social fears, anxieties and restrictions that can circulate around physical practices. A recent Arts Council England report revealed that 17 per cent of the workforce within National Portfolio Organizations are BAME, 4 per cent self-define as disabled, 55 per cent are female, 29 per cent are aged between 20 and 34. In 2015–2016, 11 per cent of all strategic funds and were awarded to BAME-led organizations and 3 per cent to disability-led organizations (Arts Council England, 2016). In a company of the size and prestige of the RSC, the report records that 57 per cent are female, 8 per cent are BAME, and 2 per cent are disabled. It is interesting to compare this to an organization such as Rich Mix in London, which focuses on diversity and inclusion, within which 50 per cent of staff are female, 37 per cent identify as BAME, and 1 per cent identify as disabled. Arts Council England has stated that, 'In the 2018–22 investment round, all National Portfolio Organizations will be required to demonstrate how they contribute to the Creative Case for Diversity' (Arts Council England, 2016); however, there is a massive impediment to achieving cultural equality in relation to performing, training and making theatre within movement practices and physical theatre making while the institutional and organizational structures do not visibly support such change.

'Normal' bodies have, within Western cultures, conventionally and historically been defined as male, non-disabled, heterosexual and white. An effect of this cultural hegemony has been the entwining of female, black, queer and disabled within the patriarchal hierarchy. Disability, as a trope, has been used to stigmatize not only the bodies of those conventionally categorized as disabled, but also, historically, the bodies of women, gays, lesbians, transsexuals, the working class, and people of non-white ethnic origin – representing physicalities that might 'taint' what was viewed as the dominant gene pool as less than 'normal'. Physical theatre and movement work now needs to challenge 'masculine strength and autonomy' (Lewis, 2016: 304), and to prioritize and privilege other (gendered/classed/aged/disabled) strengths, our physical interdependence, the richness of our diverse physical heritages and the empowerment that comes from finding our own physical 'voice'.

Royona Mitra, in her book on Akram Khan (2015), identifies six themes that inform the ways in which she sees Khan as successfully interrogating 'his own multiple and fragmented selves through his art' (2015: 154). She starts with the importance of a 'fundamental spirit of *auto-ethnography*' (ibid.); within which she identifies the importance of basing enquiry within the 'lived corporealities' of the practitioners and the spectators. From this position, she asserts the logical consequence that '*bodily language*' should then be prioritized as a means of communication. For the contemporary social subject, awareness of their multiple cultural reference points suggests the importance of '*multistitiality*'; identity thus oscillates 'between different and changing affiliations and thereby [remains] dynamic and permanently unfixed' (ibid.). Mitra identifies Khan's success as allowing a 'privileged *mobility*' (ibid.) and consequent access to 'interactions with different places, people and cultures on a global scale' (2015: 155). These qualities come together to enable what Mitra calls 'a constant *queering of normativity*', an aesthetic through which everything can be perceived as 'unfamiliar and othered' (ibid.). This creates an interculturalism that enables the dismantling of 'the simplistic and mutually exclusive nature of the us-them binary' (ibid.). Drawing together the strands of this chapter, and reflecting on Mitra's six themes for a new interculturalism outlined above, it should be possible to make a case for an approach to performance making, performing and training, that can:

- recognize and start from the lived experience of the body, and what our bodies do;
- challenge society's attempts to identify us and categorize us in relation to our bodies and to prioritize the experiences of some bodies over others;
- start from a place that recognizes that how we perform our 'selves' changes all the time and can be changed *by* us and not just *for* us;
- unfix what is fixed, allowing fluidity and mutability into our concepts of self;
- accept mobility and welcome what it brings;

- help us to understand what it means to have cultural histories of movement practices, and the responsibilities that go with those histories;
- keep making the normal strange, and keep making the strange normal;
- recognize de-stability as a creative and playful space to be in.

Mitra, talking about Khan's performances, recommends to us the value of:

> engendering through [our] art an important shift from perceiving artworks as objects that reveal critical issues about the world [we] inhabit, to enabling audiences [and performers and makers] to consider ways in which they can participate in and potentially transform the boundaries through which they interact with and negotiate this world. (2015: 167)

The real and continuing challenge, therefore, is to develop rehearsal, devising, training and performing practices that actively address and critically engage with equality, diversity and racism within the field of movement and physical performance. As well as encouraging critical reflection and theorization, this must also include developing practices that do not relegate BAME, LGBT or disabled performers', theatre makers' and students' experiences to the sidelines, or objectify their movement practices and experiences for the benefit of the white, heterosexual, male, non-disabled subject.

Notes

1. LGBT is a commonly used acronym for 'lesbian, gay, bisexual and transsexual'.
2. For details, see http://telepresenceintheatre.coventry.domains.
3. Rogers and Thorpe list a few British East Asian actors who have played conventionally white parts in Shakespeare plays, including David Lee-Jones, Benedict Wong and Daniel York (2014: 434).
4. See, for example: Grotowski (1975); Schechner & Wolford (2001); Barba (1994); Turner (2004); Watson (1995); Zarrilli (2008).
5. The danger of essentializing this relationship is perhaps most evident in parts of the history of early modern dance, such as the reaction to the work of Josephine Baker in Paris in the 1920s and National Socialism's use of gymnastics and dance to promote German ethnic identity in 1930s Germany (Burt, 1998).
6. The movement director and choreographer Diane Alison-Mitchell refers to the ways in which 'the language of African dance(s) frequently acts as a foundational lens through which I encounter other dance forms and movement' (2017: 147).
7. *Parrhesiastes* is an Ancient Greek term, which Foucault suggests can be understood as meaning 'one who speaks truth to power'.

8. McEvenue offers a useful description of Alexander's concept of inhibition in relation to acting (2001: 14–18).

9. By reversibility, Feldenkrais means the ability to stop, start and reverse an action or gesture. This is only possible if a level of conscious awareness is achieved in relation to the body and its functioning (Beringer, 2010: 99).

10. Kristine Landon-Smith co-founded Tamasha Theatre Company in 1989 with actor/writer Sudha Bhuchar. The company focused on producing previously marginalized Asian plays and performance work, including the premiere of Ayub Khan Din's play *East is East* (1996), which was nominated for an Olivier award.

11. Stephens, S. (2002) *Port*, London: Methuen Drama.

12. See Michael Billington's review of this production of *Julius Caesar* (Billington, 2012).

13. The cast and creatives included actors from a range of Black and African cultures. The heritages represented included: Nigerian, Ghanaian, Ugandan, Zimbabwean, Jamaican, Brazilian, Trinidadian and Barbadian (Alison-Mitchell, 2017: 150).

14. The cast included 'three Asian actors, three mixed race actors, ten Caucasian actors and one Arab actor' according to a letter to British Equity from the RSC (Rogers & Thorpe, 2014: 431). Those parts that the East Asian heritage actors did play ('dogs and maids') were also deeply problematic (Chen, 2012). The term 'East Asian' also needs to be problematized; offering, as it does, to collapse cultural experiences across a number of regional, national and ethnic boundaries.

15. Yellowface is historically understood as the practice of casting white actors in East Asian roles, normally also implying a stereotypical representation of such ethnic identity (see Rogers, 2014: 452–453).

16. The RSC's failure to cast East Asian actors in any productions of non-East Asian texts in the same season clearly demonstrates the inadequacies of its 'colour-blind' casting policy at the time. In fact, Greg Doran was quoted as stating that there was 'no way I was going to do this with an exclusively Chinese cast that would then go through to those other plays' (Rogers, 2014: 455), thus indicating how the RSC's casting policy was clearly reinforcing existing power relationships within the industry.

17. For details see: https://issuu.com/theactforchangeproject/docs/training_event_presentation. A review undertaken by *The Stage* in 2018 also revealed that of major drama conservatoire surveyed, only 1 per cent of graduates declared a physical impairment, compared to the wider population in which, according to 2016 figures, 11 per cent declared mobility impairment, 3 per cent visual impairment and 3 per cent hearing impairment (Masso, 2018).

18. In 2012 RADA established a programme of free workshops for young people with impairments. The sessions were taught by senior staff and included sign-language interpreters and support workers.

19. A good example might be the 2016 production of *The Government Inspector* by Birmingham Repertory Theatre in association with Ramps on the Moon. Movement direction was provided by Ayse Tashkiran (Senior Lecturer at Royal Central School of Speech and Drama).

20. This distinction is borrowed from Roger Caillois' analysis of play. For a discussion of its relevance to theatrical play, see Kendrick (2011).
21. Volpone means 'sly fox' in Italian. Jonson's play is set in Italy.
22. At this time, the artistic director of Paines Plough was Vicky Featherstone. She had previously worked with Frantic Assembly on the co-production of Abi Morgan's play *Tiny Dynamite* (2001). Featherstone has subsequently been artistic director of the National Theatre of Scotland and of the Royal Court Theatre.
23. See, for instance, the work of Québécois contemporary dance company La La La Human Steps, and in particular of their lead dancer Louise Lecavalier.
24. A programme designed for young men aged 16–20. For details, see: www.franticassembly.co.uk/ignition.

6 Movement and Digitized Performance

One of the new challenges facing performers in the twenty-first century is the increasing digitization of the field of performance. Although more and more conservatoires and universities offer courses that train actors in the skills required to meet the needs of the film, online gaming and television industries, there is very little written so far on the ways in which movement training, direction and performance can respond to the challenges of performing within screen-based media. Trevor Rawlins (2014: 1) argues that 'screen-based media have become the dominant working environment for the professional actor'. He cites Cynthia Barron and Sharon Carnicke's statement that: 'Live performance has been associated with legitimacy, complexity, and authenticity, while screen performance has often been viewed as something other than true acting' (2008: 11), but suggests that there has been, over the years, a significant shift in cultural status. As recently as ten years ago, actor trainers were still maintaining that theatre training remained a sound basis for working in the film industry (Churcher, 2003; Benedetti, 2006); the technical challenges of acting for film, television and digital media mean that this claim is increasingly only partially true.

This chapter will present a critical investigation of movement-based work in screen performance fields. This will range from the work of movement directors in the 1980s, who aimed to achieve specific effects for films through a combination of puppetry, costume and physicality, to the more recent challenges of CGI-enhanced movement and performance capture[1] within films such as *The Lord of the Rings Trilogy* (2001–2003), the recent reboot of the *Planet of the Apes* franchise (2017), and the newest *Stars Wars* franchise (2015–2019). Within all of these fields of screen-based performance practice, what the performer does on set and what the audience sees on screen are directly or indirectly linked but visually very different. Conventional training struggles to respond to the challenges that come with digitally enabled weightlessness, with radical physical transformation and enhancement, with performing in virtual environments (such as online games environments), or with the possibilities that digital media provide for the dissemination and delivery of physical training. This chapter will examine how digital environments present performance challenges that question how we currently understand the body's potential and its ability to signify and create meaning, and that challenge conventional perceptions of the actor's role within the production process. In line with the central themes of this book, this chapter will explore the changing cultural and economic status of the actor and their movement work within this field. It will do so most specifically in relation to the developments in digital performance capture, while acknowledging the changes that have led to where we are now. It accepts the proposal that motion and performance capture are 'legitimate form[s] of performance in the digital era' (Allison, 2011: 325), but seeks to examine the wider significance of such a claim. It will finish by considering how this relates to live theatre performance practice.

Digital technology has enabled the rapid and widespread sharing of performance and performance training practices, creating new economies and ecologies of performance in the process. This ranges from the proliferation of live and recorded streaming of performances (for example National Theatre Live and RSC Live) to the sharing of exercises and movement routines via YouTube. Professor Jonathan Pitches (University of Leeds) has designed and delivered a MOOC[2] through the online platform FutureLearn that has enabled several thousand participants to study, practise and share examples of Meyerhold's biomechanical *études*.[3] *Parkour* practitioners share exercises and routines via YouTube and other social media platforms – destabilizing traditional notions of training and of the training centre.[4] Such projects rely upon the digital capture of movements and gestures and then a process of editing or reconstitution into appropriate digital media for transmission and/or dissemination. These processes have also created the possibility for digital elements to be integrated into live performance – either on a simple level (the projection of digitally-created video material on to appropriate surfaces within the stage scene) or in more complex ways (interactive hologrammatic projections of movement-captured performances – such as the presentation of Ariel in a recent RSC production of *The Tempest* (2016) created in collaboration with Intel[5]). The focus for this book is on the challenges and the changes in movement practice that this creates for the contemporary actor, their significances and their impact on the actor's sense of self (personal and professional), as well as the wider cultural implications.

Motion Capture, Movement and Performance

What is motion capture? In contemporary motion capture (MoCap) for film and online games, cameras connect with 3D animation software so as to triangulate the position of the actor's body parts, identified by a series of markers attached to the performer's body on an otherwise non-descript close-fitting body suit. This MoCap suit renders the performer 'naked' enough to be digitally scanned – the motion capture cameras need the markers in much the same way that a normal camera needs light. The markers create a 'point cloud' from which the animators can build a 'digital skeleton', which is then attached to 'the computer-generated character's skeleton' (McClelland, 2018: 32). Although this is a very new field within film production, it is part of a wider field of practice that has a very long history.

Darren Tunstall reminds us that motion capture is part of a long tradition of movement documentation and analysis (2012: 3). Since the earliest times, people have sought to find ways of capturing movement (etching, painting, sketching, photographing, filming, videoing and 3D scanning). Before the twentieth century, movement capture relied upon memory and oral/written testimony, or on the frozen images created by artists and illustrators, such as those in John Bulwer's *Chirologia* (1644). Movement in such contexts would inevitably be associated with whatever lasting powerful images might be retained by the observer – perhaps a reason for the strength and boldness of the gestures we see recorded in this way. A number of developments in the late nineteenth and early twentieth centuries saw the emergence of more sophisticated analyses of the movements of the body and more elaborate and complex ways of recording them. In my book on movement training for the modern actor (Evans, 2009), I describe the development of a number of influential approaches to movement analysis – including the work of François Delsarte (1811–1871) and Rudolf Laban (1879–1958). Laban, building on his principles for the analysis of movement, devised a form of notation which enabled the general nature of movements and of choreography to be written down. By its nature, it captured a simplified version of the movements – it was unable to encapsulate all the movements of every part of the body, the facial expression of the performer, or the particular emotional intention. However, rapid improvements in early photographic technology allowed pioneers such as Étienne-Jules Marey (1830–1904) and Eadweard Muybridge (1830–1904) to provide detailed records of human and animal movement based on multiple frame rapid capture technology. Film and video technology have since then become entirely integral to how we record, view and interrogate human movement. Originally, the role of movement capture was to document and record something that had appeared transitory and ephemeral – either for scientific ends (sports science and ergonomics have made extensive use of motion capture) or for aesthetic ends (it is closely connected to the early days of cinema). The more (apparently) complete the capture of movement became, the more able it has been to stand in for, or even replace, the live performance itself.

Digital technology has enabled a step-change in the processes of the capture and reproduction of movement, framed within the changing parameters of the technologically possible and the economically viable. What was initially known as motion capture technology has enabled a number of new possibilities. Drawing on Tunstall (2012) we can identify these as the capture and viewing of movement from any angle and as a three-dimensional output, and the streaming of this capture as digital data that can then be manipulated and/or used to configure and manipulate digital avatars. Motion capture is a collaborative process; it requires working with others who have expertise in the digital technologies involved. Like film, it only captures what is presented to it – unlike film, what it captures is more multi-dimensional, and can be endlessly repurposed and quickly discarded or recreated during the process.

'Me' and 'Not Me' – Performer and Avatar

Tunstall reports that students reviewing their movement work after a process of movement capture experienced a strong sense that what they were viewing was both 'me' and 'not me' at the same time (2012: 9). Motion capture gathers and presents data that can be read as containing the student's own movement 'signature', but that is also abstracted (initially into white dots) and therefore distanced. The performer experiences themselves as a puppeteer whose puppet is themselves – they make the abstract series of dots move, they can interpret that movement as theirs, and yet it is no longer theirs at the same time. In the professional context, this is often contractually the case as well. The motion capture performer whose movement is recorded for a video game or a film may get no direct credit for their work and only be listed as one of many motion capture performers. The performance may instead be contractually owned by the actor whose voice (and possibly face) are used, rather than by the actor who has provided the movement and the rest of the body. This contractual relationship can be seen as representative of the cultural, social and economic status of movement and the body in relation to the face and the voice.

In such instances, where the actor is employed to become a form of body-mask for the voice of another actor, they also become silenced; disembodied only to be reconstituted digitally as the body that appears to bring forth another's voice. The identity of the motion capture (or MoCap) actor, unvoiced, untethered to the character that they have created, becomes professionally and creatively fluid, disembodied, silent, but profoundly expressive – perhaps in the way that bodies always seem capable of and/or socially destined towards, and in ways that might appeal to a generation for which multiple identity and gender constructs have become more normal. Causey (2016) writes about the gender tourism of the early version of the online virtual environment, *Second Life*, in which the avatars were not voiced. The lack of a direct connection to the sense of a gendered self that voice creates for the players allowed the early *Second Life* gamers to adopt genders and physicalities that they might not normally adopt in their everyday lives. Equally, the MoCap actor can potentially explore the opportunity to be whatever they want to be as long as the (absent) voice does not reveal possible details of their cultural identity. However, this same process simultaneously operates to distance the silent MoCap actor from celebrating their actual cultural identity and confronting the effects of its social construction and industrial/commercial reconstitution.

Another way in which this distancing takes place is through the selectivity of the motion capture process. Depending on the sophistication of the equipment, the technology will abstract the movement into core gestures and actions. Those parts of the body not marked for capture will be irrelevant to the final output. When exploring the use of motion capture within the context of actor training exercises (such as the neutral mask exercises of Jacques Lecoq), Tunstall noticed that students, on their own initiative, used motion capture to refine the efficiency with which they performed the exercises, effectively removing movements not related to the core demands of the exercise. One effect of motion capture, then, is the conscious shaping and simplifying of movements by the actors. Again, in the professional context of motion capture for film, the performer is required only to provide those actions, movements and gestures that the project requires – the ability to simplify and edit the performance during rehearsal and digital capture then becomes a valuable skill to have.

This might suggest that there is something inherent in the use of digital technology that demands enhanced levels of control over movement, and that this efficiency is operating culturally to shape our ideas of the digital body and of the postdigital human. Tunstall refers to the 'capacity to signal to others that one has conscious control of one's intentionality' (Tunstall, 2012: 17). This sort of capacity has traditionally been useful for the performer and something that professional training has sought to develop. But the digitization of movement capture means that this control may become heightened for the performer over time. Control of the body would then become particularly important for the performer, but at the same time such control can now be exerted technologically at a micro level; the raising of hair on the back of the neck, the flicker of an eyelid, the twitch of a finger, can be created not by the actor, but by the digital animator. Digital technology, used in this way, erases dysfunctionality and removes or displaces the 'play' of the body, its unruliness. The significance of this erasure lies in the effect it has on the performer's body – what is not valued, what is discarded, what is invisible because it is not captured and the relation of that which is erased to the performer's personal and professional sense of self. Mihailova (2016: 42–46) suggests that this is one of the reasons that actors actively promote the importance of their own role within the motion capture process.[6] Tunstall reflects: 'Without these subjective behavioural signals it hardly matters to the world how rich my inner life happens to be: unless I show I am competent at regulating them, the world will tend to label me as dysfunctional' (Tunstall, 2012: 18). This effect works both ways; remove those signals and, over time, what is left of our sense of inner life? Do we run the risk of becoming that which we have created to mimic us?

Movement Direction in Pre-Digital Film Production

At the turn of this century, most of the established figures working in movement direction and movement capture, particularly in the film industry, trained and/or developed their initial careers outside motion capture. The movement director Peter Elliott is an example of someone who has experienced movement work for films both prior to and after the advent of digital technologies. Peter trained as an actor, but was always into sports and physical activities. His first film work came when he was hired to play one of the apes in the film *Greystoke: The Legend of Tarzan, Lord of the Apes* (1984). When he was first hired to work on the film in 1978, there wasn't such a thing as a movement director for films; there were only dance choreographers and stunt directors. The process of development for the film reflected the technology and the economics of the film industry at that time. Initial work on the rehearsals and costumes took place in separate locations (London and Los Angeles), until the producers realized that that process wasn't creating good enough results. Peter was flown out to LA:

> I was meant to be there for a week. I did a test film, they adjusted the costume to fit me and [...] they suddenly decided that they weren't as ready to go as they thought. So, they asked if I'd stay on and do the R&D [...] I took on that project and did a lot of research work and also got involved in how to build the costume. (Elliott, 2012)

The film suffered some delays in the production process, meaning that overall Peter had two years of research and development activity, including periods of close observation at a primate centre, enabling the development of an advanced knowledge of ape and primate movement. Early ideas from the producers included the mixing of performers with real chimps – a blending of the real and the performed that revealed a particular and erroneous set of assumptions about how the two might complement each other.

Peter worked as a performer and movement director for the film *Quest for Fire* (1981), before the filming was finally completed for *Greystoke*, and then went on to work on *Gorillas in the Mist* (1988). He recalls that:

> movement was very different then. It used to be 'Let's find a stuntman or a dancer and put them in a costume' (obviously, they weren't doing motion capture then), put them in front of the camera and say 'do it' and then wonder why it wasn't any good. (Elliott, 2012)

Peter combined mime skills, close observation and physical agility with a Method approach to acting, involving in-depth study. His approach, although developed for work on film, is essentially based on the analysis of movement and character, and adapted to cope with technology that was based on 'strings and rubber' (Elliott, 2012). While some costumes work still exists – for example Doug Jones, who plays the unnamed fish-man in *The Shape of Water* (2017), wears a costume made from rubber, foam and latex – the advent of motion capture and CGI has brought some different challenges.

Casting for movement in film has its own dynamics. For Elliott, casting decisions inevitably depend on the nature of the project, but generally he expresses a preference for physical actors over stunt-performers or dancers. When costume was a central component, the casting would have to focus on the physical size, shape and morphology of the actor, both individually in relation to the part they were playing and in relation to any groups that they would have to work with. With motion capture, there is much more freedom, 'because you're driving an avatar or you're driving a character which has its own dimensions and its own proportions and you just have to attach the person to the character' (Elliott, 2012). Until recently, the lack of professional training opportunities meant that reputation was developed on the job, the skills were understood as niche, and, certainly in so far as they were initially associated with non-speaking or minor roles, were perceived professionally as low status. This perception is unfair, as performers working in this area are often very well-trained and in addition come with a variety of life experiences and specialist skills, such as mime, martial arts (for example capoeira and karate), dance, specific acrobatic skills and *parkour*. Since the late 2000s, opportunities have emerged to train specifically in movement direction and movement capture work, but although this is useful in terms of professionalizing the field and facilitating the passing on of experience, is something significant lost? Elliott points out that in the past, 'people [...] have had to make up the difference, people have used mime skills, Lecoq skills and stunt skills and they have tried to make up the gaps' (Elliott, 2012). This has brought a wide range of skills and experiences in to play. For him, it also meant developing a personal methodology rather than inheriting one from a teacher or director: 'it has all been made up ad-hoc in the past but it's now becoming more of a formalized skill' (Elliott, 2012).

Elliott's process typically might start with observation: 'we start with observation and start with the basic motor mechanism skills: walking, running, sitting, standing' (Elliott, 2012). It will then progress to working from the inside out: 'I use improvisation, I use that a lot, so what I tend to do then is start them living it, being it, improvising it, looking at the relationships, looking at the politics' (Elliott, 2012). This is a detailed process, potentially expensive in production terms, and one that is different from the typical process for conventional character acting on film, in which 'you do a read through, maybe a basic block-through and the first time you really do it is the first time in front of the camera' (Elliott, 2012). For the kind of movement work required to create animals or fantastic creatures, Elliott suggests that such a standard approach will be insufficient and a false economy. He instead prefers a careful, collaborative and technologically enabled process, designed to generate a highly professional end result.

The technological and artistic processes involved take place within a wider cultural context which shapes expectations of and attitudes towards this kind of work. The development of the technology and the advances in CGI mean that audiences are becoming used to higher and higher degrees of visual verisimilitude alongside more and more fantastical scenarios. It is perhaps to be expected that expectations and attitudes will continue to evolve in line with the technological advances, and in play with the desire for an art that is so sophisticated that the game is to spot what, if anything, is 'real'.

A Body that Isn't A Body

The technological developments during the last decade mean that in terms of digitized movement work within the cinematic context, 'you can now do anything. You don't have to be restricted by the physical restrictions' (Elliott, 2012). In 2012, Elliott remarked that:

> If you've got something the right size and morphology you can put a human being in a costume. You can still do it because financially the costumes, although sometimes costly (the costumes for *Gorillas in the Mist* cost five million dollars), it still would be cheaper than trying to do it as a visual effect. (Elliott, 2012)

He also points out the advantages of filming performance work within the same space, recognizing the value of the live interactions that he argues are not possible when performers are working in different studios, at different times and against mono-colour backdrops. Nonetheless, continual refinement of the technology means that already, towards the other end of the decade, it is possible to use digital capture outside the studio environment and to produce quick animation that will enable directors and performers to get an early view of their impact within a shot. In terms of economic impact, the liveness that Elliott argues for has become less important than the sophisticated and sometimes visually stunning effects now available through digital movement capture and manipulation.

In the Star Wars movie *Rogue One* (2016), two characters are created through the use of what is called a digital face pipeline by visual effects company Industrial Light & Magic. In a scene very near the end of the movie, a digital version of the face of the actor Carrie Fisher (1956–2016) as the young Princess Leia is imposed upon the image of a different actor, Ingvild Deila. The face and voice are created to exactly replicate the young Carrie Fisher, they are 'carried' (pardon the pun) by the body and movement of another person. In another scene, the same process is used to impose the face and voice of the now-deceased actor Peter Cushing (1913–1994) on to the body of another actor, Guy Henry. In this case, where the character in question (Grand Moff Tarkin) is on screen for significantly more time, not only is the facial image, created from a life mask made of Cushing in the 1980s, mapped onto Guy Henry's body, but the animators also work to integrate the digital capture of Henry's performance with what they can repurpose from Cushing's original performance in the earlier *Star Wars* films. At this point, the work arguably belongs to three sets of artists: Guy Henry, Peter Cushing and the animators;

however, what the audience see is Peter Cushing/Grand Moff Tarkin, or at least a highly credible representation of him. Guy Henry models as closely as he can to the movements of Cushing from the original Star Wars film (*Star Wars* (1977); now referred to as *Star Wars: Episode IV – A New Hope*), but ultimately neither he, nor his movements, are directly 'seen' by the audience. He does not represent Cushing/Tarkin, he has in effect become part of the pipeline process that enables Cushing/Tarkin to be (re)created for this film. Though Henry may be providing part of the basic building blocks for the performance, what he creates does not ontologically define the performance, except in the sense that any of his movements can remain identifiably his. If the audience notices anything, they might notice ways in which his movement performance and its manipulation is insufficient and does not adequately rec-reate Cushing/Tarkin,[7] denoting, in this case, a kind of professional failure.

In *Rogue One*, Henry's performance is captured, only to be erased of every-thing that made it 'his performance' – it is a digitally enhanced act of imper-sonation, so effective as virtually to remove Henry's presence within the film. What is imposed on the digital body lifted from Henry's performance is a very close visual approximation of Peter Cushing. In a strange mirroring of events elsewhere within the *Star Wars* plotlines (for example the transforma-tion of Anakin Skywalker into Darth Vader), the body is reconstructed, tech-nologized and rendered into the control of others to the purpose of the film's overall project. Within MoCap, simply put, someone becomes something that becomes someone. Software absorbs the movement information provided by the performer in an act of possession (the body is absorbed, contained, trans-formed), during which the software itself remains elusive and virtual to the MoCap performer. MoCap performers are constantly putting themselves in the process of 'becoming technological/digital/virtual' (Causey, 2016: 208). As much as the software captures their bodies, they also willingly extend their own bodies in to the technology around them – more and more so as the tech-nology enables them to see this process as it happens.

The director and possibly also the movement director also have input into the motion capture process; however, the overall coherence of the perfor-mance, and of the movement work in particular, relies on the creative skills of several people, some of whom may never meet. In the MoCap production process, the individual performer (as opposed to the character that they help create) eventually becomes invisible; it is the movement qualities of the perfor-mance itself, transformed into a digital artefact, that instead is all that is visible to those watching the film.[8] Furthermore, as Elliott points out, at this level of digital manipulation 'it means that all interaction is preconceived' (2012).

Instead of actors being enabled to develop a scene as they work on it – adapting lines, improvising, changing moves – everything has to operate to facilitate the technical processes. This will usually mean sticking to the script and to any pre-visualization, so that when the technicians and animators come to edit the various elements together the process is less costly.

Performance quality, within this context, is about effective creative collaboration, mutual understanding of each other's roles and responsibilities, and a recognition of the various elements that everyone is working with. As all kinds of effects and enhancements become possible, and as CGI becomes ever more photo-realistic, it is not clear where this takes movement and performance. The technology will at a basic level become cheaper and easier to use, while at the upper end it will become highly sophisticated but very expensive ($200 million is not an unusual budget for a high-cost film). Quality, therefore, also relates to the economics of the production process and either the ease with which errors can be discarded or the importance of efficient responses to instruction.

Risk, Presence and the Virtual Body

Despite the control that digital manipulation of movement creates within contemporary films, is there still room for what we might conventionally recognize as risk, danger and physical presence? Can these be created in other ways and what might the effect of such a process be on the actor's work? To some extent, the sensation for the audience of risk and danger can be enhanced through CGI. Falls can look more dramatic, wounds can be deeper and/or more drastic, effort and pain can be exaggerated. At the same time, paradoxically, the digital processes actually work to make the actor safer and the creative process (including rehearsal and filming) less risky. Elliott describes how some amazing stunts are now done on green screen:[9]

> To watch as an audience, the risk element looks higher and bigger but actually as a performer I think it gets smaller and smaller in a way (health and safety, insurance etc.) and the endless possibility of the different ways of compositing the shot means that there isn't the necessity to push those risk elements anymore. There are easier ways of doing it. (Elliott, 2012)

As the settings and backdrops for films become increasingly bold and visually extreme, so the performer also needs to develop and utilize a heightened physicality and a strong imaginative sense in order to align with the fictive world presented.

[Y]ou might find yourself working in a street that only exists up to ten feet tall or even less sometimes and the rest is CG. In fact, there is more CG work than anyone realizes going in to set building and all of that. (Elliott, 2012)

The skills and techniques of the MoCap actor develop in relation to these changes within the film industry, while simultaneously participating in the cultural shifts that drive them. Presence and risk are not as they used to be within a film production process – but they are still available. They are just constructed differently, and shaped by the new technologies available and by our changing understanding of danger and charisma. The appearance of risk in filmed performance is always undermined by the nature of the medium, as the event is always taking place in the past and we are watching its representation. In video games, immediacy is created through the presentation of choice and interaction, coupled with the increase in processing speeds for visual effects within the games, and risk through 'rules' that present the possibility of instant failure. Unable, at least for now, to tap in to more interactive forms of immediacy, motion capture within films has had to fall back on increased degrees of 'reality' for more and more fantastical characters, environments and storylines – almost as if it doubts its own efficacy.

Where does this leave the body of the performer? It might be tempting to see the MoCap actor as a cyborg,[10] connected to technology through the nodules attached to the motion capture suits and through the dots marked on faces. Like the cyborg, the virtual characters created by the MoCap actor and the animator are both 'entities and metaphors, living beings and narrative constructions' (Hayles in Giannachi, 2004: 48). But within motion capture, the real is dominated by the virtual/metaphoric/constructed. The performer's body is in a sense enhanced by its technological connections, just as much as it is also revealed (at least partially). The MoCap body is not leaky or unpredictable – it can be considered a cyborg body in the sense that technology functions to remove its porosity, abjection and plasticity in favour of definition and clarity, economy and efficiency. Within the MoCap process, the body is digitally disassembled and reassembled through the technology and software; it is (re)coded as a set of digital signals. Laura Bissell suggests that the body that is being coded is still complex and sometimes ambiguous (2013: 262); but the degree of that complexity and ambiguity is no longer within the control of the performer. MoCap enables a particular fusion and interplay between technology and the body. The body can be rendered as grotesque or efficient, heroic or despicable, dangerous or predictable, through the combined efforts of the performer and the animation team; but it is always rendered. The fusion and interplay is not neutral, not without its own power dynamics and not without its own politics. All of that socio-political and cultural context that lies within the industrial process is then projected into the field of performance through that process and represented within the economic realities of the MoCap performer's professional life. Of course, this is an effect that has always happened within the film industry – every actor's performance comes to the audience through the projected gaze of the director and cinematographer, through the editor's selection and the music composer's setting of mood and atmosphere. Yet within that set of multiple relationships, the skills of the performer have historically played an important part, regardless of the size of the actor's role.

Motion Capture and Video Games

The actor's body has historically been defined by its recognizable features. The MoCap performer's body is always, initially and clearly defined by the positioning of its marker nodules, and then subsequently and definitively by the animator's choices. This interconnectivity between actor and animator is even more clearly evident in video game production. The video game creators and animators provide the player with an extensive choice of movement options, all of which have been performed initially by the MoCap performer. Each of these movement options is a unit within the overall game narrative and the network of choices offered to the player. The video game, however, removes the ultimate control of the character/avatar further away from the MoCap actor, beyond the animator, into the hands of the viewer/player. This powerful change in dynamics works in tandem with the overlapping of audience and player markets, to further limit and constrain the ways in which the performer can conceive of what takes place within the process as a creative collaboration. The MoCap actor's body becomes a shared body, inhabited directly or vicariously by the will of the director/animator and the player/viewer. The actor's movements become detached from their own body through the MoCap process and are used to create a form of life which the performer can only partially, and in a limited contractual sense, own. In making MoCap work, the actor is directed by the client/animator; this relationship then resonates with the process in the game in which the player/viewer directs the avatar's movements. Culturally this creates a set of expectations that could explain why an audience might be more concerned about the skill with which familiar *Star Wars* characters are (re)created than about the skill of the performers creating the basis for the digital artefact

that becomes that character. The notion of 'ownership' of the body's image
– always of course a complex issue within the field of performance, where
the actor is often employed and contracted to perform as instructed by
another – is thus thrown into starker relief than before. The MoCap actor's
body becomes a marker in space – signifying the presence of something that
they are not. Thus, the MoCap actor, their body and their movement work
become drawn in to ever deeper and murkier issues around identity, presence,
authenticity, subjectivity and experience (Goodman, 2007: 107). Games are
often spin-offs from films, meaning that the movement of the characters is
another stage removed. The MoCap actor is faced with trying to recreate
the movement of an existing character, movement that may itself have
been generated and created in part through a MoCap process. Experienced
MoCap performer Gareth Taylor[11] recalls how, 'I had to do Voldemort, be
Snape;[12] all of these characters already had bodies and ways of moving and so
I had to research by watching the film and how they move' (Taylor, 2015).
Body shape, movement and timing (the tempo, rhythms and dynamics of
movement) all become very important for the performer, but they are being
employed to blur the boundaries between their own physicality and that of
another actor's portrayal of a fictitious character.

Goodman (2007) reminds us that the world of MoCap performance is not
neutral. She points out that the game avatar is typically engaged in action
(running, jumping, flying, fighting, shooting); and she suggests that it is
constructed as masculine through these actions, through the efficient definition of its boundaries and through the lack of abjection. In addition, the
MoCap suit and the headsets currently required for facial mapping typically
make physical intimacy (for example hugging, holding and kissing) difficult,
awkward, limited or impossible. Typical physical interactions in these video
game contexts (as well as in some films using motion capture) tend to be
based on combat, conflict, exertion and pursuit. The game avatar and the
digitally created film character have to always be in motion or anticipating
motion. The virtual body's presence is defined by movement or the immi-
nence of movement. Even when it stops moving through space, the breath
must still be visible as a movement within the body, the face or other body
muscles must twitch or flex, or the hairs must bristle, in order to make the
digital representation appear lifelike. The MoCap performer requires, for
instance, an Idle or Base Pose: 'a video game animation term, denoting the
range of positions the actor performs that will be placed at the beginning
and end of an action sequence' (Jennings-Grant, 2017); such poses need to
retain a sense of action and readiness if they are to link effectively with the

activities that frame them or which they frame. This pose, together with the T-stance,[13] act as the punctuation of the MoCap action that makes it readable and editable by the animators and programmers.

Consumers of video games and films are sold CGI and MoCap performances on the basis of the incredible effects that are now possible. The desire this creates, for an unfulfillable set of potentialities for the body, might even indicate that CGI is an ultimate form of assistive technology. In fuelling an unachievable desire for superhuman capabilities, it is rendering us all into a form of disability – something that we unconsciously project on to ourselves and our bodies. It can, fictively, create disability where there is none, and repair it where it exists. In doing so, it can offer a reconfiguration of our perceptions of disability, but it also represents disability not as a form of experience of the body within a set of specific social contexts, but as a technological problem to be solved. The experience of the video game player and to a lesser extent of the film viewer in part operates to confirm the appropriation of the MoCap performer's body, and as such the appropriation of any body. The more obscure or anonymous the MoCap actor becomes in the production process, the less their personality is allowed or enabled to be evident and present, the more the process becomes like that of the pornographer – enabling the body to be disassembled into the desired parts and reconstituted within the needs of the film producers to titillate, arouse, entice, astound and/or shock. As with pornography, bodies can become enhanced to ridiculous proportions, effectively constructing as inadequate what might previously have been conceived of as normal. As with all cinema, the audience can also become complicit in this process if we accept this kind of attitude to the body, rather than calling it out when we see it.

What MoCap performance does, within the contexts of video games or films, is to participate in the performative creation of the spaces and shapes of our desires and dreams. The cultural and gendered limitations of those spaces and practices then operate, together with the conscious or unconscious predilections of those controlling and designing the end product, to structure our imaginations, dreams and desires in ways that we need to be aware of. In this way, MoCap may work to subjugate us to discriminatory notions of the body which are no longer in our control. Within the digital processing of movement capture, certain ways of using the body become key to success; consequently, it becomes important to be aware of the extent to which certain body types may also become prioritized and access to engagement with these technologies limited to bodies determined as, in MoCap terms, desirable and/or efficient.

The MoCap Space and the Performer: Space, Scale and Size

Despite the elaborate scenery and settings that CGI can now create for the final product, the MoCap studio (or 'volume' as it is called in the industry) is typically a bare and empty space, with a range of digital capture equipment around the edges. There is little or nothing in the way of sets, props, make-up or lighting. The primary and ultimate focus is on the movement of the body. Although the MoCap volume can be a 'huge open space for fun and play and imagination to happen', it is also somewhere where 'self-consciousness doesn't really have a place […] there is nothing there, it's a blank space. It is all down to you and your imagination' (Bolet, 2015).

The MoCap studio space will typically have a number of reference cameras positioned around the space. In a manner not dissimilar from the use of video in contemporary rehearsal practice, this reference footage allows review of work created throughout the session. At the same time, it is made abundantly clear that the camera is omnipresent, everything is captured. The MoCap actor is embraced and encompassed by the technology in a very literal sense. Gareth Taylor states: 'In terms of performance you don't know where "the" camera is going to be necessarily' (Taylor, 2015). Taylor reflects on his own experience of the spaces in which MoCap performance work takes place:

> You are often in a huge volume of space that's incredibly, brightly lit, and you are wearing lycra, and the only things you have is tape on the ground. It's just such an alienating experience as an actor and there isn't another field where you need an imagination as strong as you do for motion capture. Your internal life and everything beyond that has to be exceptional, exceptionally strong. (Taylor, 2015)

This description of the MoCap volume is somewhat reminiscent of the early days of physical theatre and the 'poor theatre' aesthetics of Jerzy Grotowski or the spatial qualities of Jacques Lecoq's School in Paris. Lecoq's neutral mask work, requiring the student to improvise while wearing an expressionless leather mask, was designed to help the student to experience the stripping away of unnecessary detail and the location of the body within imaginary spaces that the actor then makes present for the audience and themselves through movement. For Lecoq, the neutral body is a starting point from which the actor can create whole theatrical worlds; the actor is a poet who writes with their own body. In motion capture, this sense of three-dimensional creation within space is technologically realized.

One space, through the use of movement applied within a CGI-enabled environment, can become many spaces or any space. This means, however, that location and the particularities and histories of spaces becomes less and less important within the production process: 'the most profound shift to occur in the Twenty-first Century will be the shift from a place oriented to a more "placeless" society' (Goodman, 2007: 115). If, as de Certeau suggests, 'space is a practiced place' (in Cox, 2014: 4), then we can recognize the spaces created through MoCap as created not only by the animators and illustration artists, but also by the actions, movements and gestures of the MoCap performers. The cultural context of the space and place becomes detached unless the movement of the performers recreates it within the performance work. It will take effort from all involved in the motion capture process to ensure a recognition of the ways in which movement and space interact around each other's social construction.

Motion capture is not just about the technology; for Taylor it is very definitely about moving in space: 'I am looking […] at how you can use the body and the space, so mine is much more of a Lecoq approach to motion capture' (Taylor, 2015). This is further complicated by the fact that space in the MoCap studio is multi-directional. Motion capture for video games involves probably the most mechanistic approach to movement and space:

> you will have a few days where they will basically just want you to bash out every single move that those characters in the games are going to make, what the controller can make them do as a player. It is extremely repetitive […] because everything you do you have to do straight on, forty-five, ninety degrees, one hundred and eighty, three hundred and sixty, both ways. (Taylor, 2015)

Within the MoCap performance environments, gestures and movements need to read as bigger than naturalistic film-acting conventions would normally allow. Gareth Taylor recalls that:

> One of the first conversations I have with the Director through the lead animator when I get in the room is what size performance are we looking at? For me that answers almost every other question that I have about the project. (Taylor, 2015)

The scale of the performance is, of course, not simply set by the aesthetic decisions of the director and animators, it also relates to the technicalities of what the equipment can effectively read, process and then replicate.

The relatively small size of the gaming screen (computer/tablet/phone screen size) means that small movements can get lost amid the rush of energetic activity and the tension built in to the experience for the gamer. In film, smaller movements can be captured effectively and can work well on a large screen; however, the increased emphasis given to these movements (breathing, facial twitches, small reactions) creates a dramatic focus on them that accentuates their significance, generating a certain recognizable style of digital film performance that can seem slightly mannered (for instance Andy Serkis' performance as Supreme Leader Snoke in *Star Wars: The Last Jedi*).

Small changes in posture, walk and physical dynamics are not just movement technicalities. These kinds of changes, developed at a scale that reads for the audience, often represent more profound shifts in narrative structure, character complexity and wider social shifts in attitude and taste. Taylor's comments about the changing ways in which hero figures are portrayed in these kinds of games reveal how these changes relate to the work of the MoCap performer:

> There are a lot of archetypes in computer games [...]. The amount of heroes I have had to play, or the amount of villains, they are becoming way, way more interesting now and the hero character has changed and is probably changing again [...]. The hero when I started was very much upright, very open, [...] that kind of 'anything is possible', positive character. And then the hero changed through *Assassin's Creed* [2007], and games like that, where it became this much more mysterious, hunched, 'I-am-good-but-I-blur-the-line'. And the walk became much more ... there was much more collapse and there was something brooding about it. (Taylor, 2015)

No doubt the use of an enhanced physicality within MoCap contributes to the professional perspective that this style of performance, compared to the naturalistic acting that has dominated film performance over the last 70 years, is somehow less authentic, less real and less important. Nonetheless, the narratives revealed above indicate a strong sense of professionalism, technical expertise and willingness to collaborate that do much to affirm the importance and value of MoCap as a form of performance.

Improvisation and Play

The technical parameters of the MoCap process might seem to make play and improvisation unlikely. However, the reality is that a certain amount of play and improvisation can be encouraged, enabled, and even required in order to achieve the desired kinds of physical transformation. The starting point is with the performer's understanding of how their body communicates in this new digital context. Only when that has been mastered can the performer find the movement skills and understanding that might enable physical transformation. Gareth Taylor relates his own training at the Lecoq School to the training he provides for MoCap performers: 'we start with neutral mask, because we have to see how the body looks naturally before it gets adjusted. To find the neutrality, who are you? What are you physically? And what does that tell?' (Taylor, 2015).

Just as in the wider film industry, opportunities for improvisation and play depend on the project and the director. But for specific effects and for many game scenarios the work has to be very precise: 'There are so many things you have to do within a certain period of time, someone is counting down from ten until you have to go and do something else' (Taylor, 2015). Only when you have worked in the field for a long time, been involved in a project over a significant period, does flexibility start to become possible:

> you start to build a trust with the Director and with the lead animator and then they allow more improvisation because they trust you. You have to earn that trust before you get the freedom to play around with character and improvisation. (Taylor, 2015)

MoCap performance is often about offering up for capture a quick and focused outline of the movements of a given character; and, given the time and the additional creative work that will also take place on the data before the end product is viewed, it is not surprising that the movement work sometimes is only required to be generic, broad brush strokes. Where actors are often trained to be detailed, thorough and specific in their work, MoCap offers a set of parameters which push the performance towards what might be considered the melodramatic – large gestures, strong (even stereotypical) characterization: 'it really tests your skills as an actor because every impulse in your body screams not to be general, to be specific' (Taylor, 2015). The avatar created from the MoCap actor's performance cannot experience pain or any of the other human emotions in the way that the MoCap actor themselves can. Instead, it enacts the symptoms of these emotions, in the same way that Coquelin's actor[14] does. There is a degree of technicality in portraying emotions in such a process; this technicality, although partly a response to the demands of the technology, also relates to the requirement for a heightened performance style – the signs of the required emotions have to be more evident than they are in conventional naturalistic acting if they are to be captured by the digital technology.

There is no direct exposure to performance in front of a normal audience; the people to please are the animators and director – this gives some freedom, if time allows, for trying things out. There can be a lot of on-the-spot decision making and improvisation simply because MoCap actors often may not know before they arrive at the studio what the script is or who they are playing, and because experiment in the MoCap volume is cheaper than experiment through digital manipulation.

From MoCap to PeCap: Changing Perceptions of What Acting Is

We are, at the end of this decade, at a point of change – from MoCap to PeCap (performance capture). This is a moment that may also be seen to represent an attempt by the human subject to reoccupy a space that had been largely given over to the digital, the avatar and the cyborg. The move towards performance capture is arguably driven by a consumer desire for character representation that provides a more recognizable level of genuine human behaviour than the motion capture technology on its own was able to create. Initially motion capture technology only captured the physical movements of the actor's body. Advances in technology have enabled the additional and simultaneous capture of facial expression and voice, giving far more importance to the actor's ability to convey subtle or powerful emotions and thought processes within the digital capture process. This has meant that the MoCap actor, who has conventionally been professionally anonymous, if not invisible, has become increasingly prominent in the film-making process. The legal status of MoCap and PeCap work has had to change quite rapidly to keep pace with the evolution of the technology and the growing number of performers working in this field. It is only fairly recently that American Equity has started to recognize motion capture work, and UK Equity has still not fully done so. Not many MoCap actors have the profile of Andy Serkis; he is important as an example of an actor almost entirely recognized for the creation through performance capture of a number of notable film characters.[15] In 2017, BoxOfficeMojo.com ranked Serkis in the top 30 actors by ticket sales (Sulcas, 2017). He has, almost single-handedly, transformed the professional and public perception of performance capture. Nonetheless, although Serkis' name is becoming increasingly well-known, the nature of his work of course means that his face is probably unfamiliar to most of the film-going public.

Watching the end product of PeCap on screen, it becomes more difficult to easily distinguish between the art of the actor and of the special effects animators. This complexity has led to a level of controversy. Twentieth Century Fox has suggested that Serkis should have been nominated for an Academy Award for his role in *War for the Planet of the Apes* and Serkis himself is adamant that 'Caesar and all the other computer generated characters I have ever played are driven by one thing and that is acting' (Serkis in Hiscock, 2014). Even the special effects supervisor for the *Apes* movies, Dan Lemmon, feels that:

> Andy Serkis is authoring the performance one hundred per cent [...] If you look at our before and after shots, you can see Caesar do exactly what Andy did – if that's not worthy of recognition for acting, then I don't know what is. (Dan Lemmon in McClelland, 2018: 33)

Serkis is thus reasserting the 'existential origin of the performer' (Allison, 2011: 326), and implicitly claiming the importance of psychology and human interpretation in creating an authentic performance. He suggests that it is the performance that is captured that creates the character and the drama within the film; the visual effects are more like a form of digital make-up. It is indeed true that the actor's performance has always been 'augmented' to some degree, whether by costumes, masks, lighting, sound, make-up, prosthetics, design or architecture. MoCap is positioned by Serkis as one more form of augmentation. His reference to animation as make-up makes some broad sense, but is far from the full picture. This is 'make-up' that bristles and moves, that has a life of its own (hairs standing on end, tails flicking, saliva frothing). There is a level of interplay between what the actor does and what the visual effects team do that indicates what posthumanists might refer to as an entanglement between the actor, the avatar and all of the other artists creating the effects. In creating the 'character' of Kong (*King Kong*, 2015), Serkis' movement data was substantially adapted by the animators in order to better match the physiology of a large male gorilla (Allison, 2011: 327). He also had to learn to 'play' the software, moving in ways that enabled it to recognize particular 'gorilla' movements.

The idea of the individual actor creating a role thus becomes problematized – PeCap performance of a character is not something that ultimately can be created by only one person. Furthermore, as we have seen earlier, the actor cannot create effectively without some knowledge of and engagement in/ with the technologies and creative practices that will be used to construct the character seen on screen. The actor's point of engagement with the technology is through motion, rhythm and space. As with the work on animal study in Chapter 3, this fluidity and sense of transformative play is central to the creative success of the performance and yet, at the same time, these qualities also destabilize notions of individual talent, the ownership of the character by the actor, and the identification of the actor with the role in the mind of the audience (and of the actor).

In Serkis' work, and indeed in that of the majority of PeCap performers within the film industry, the product and the processes are still anchored on and/or orientated towards modernist conceptions of character, psychology and authorship. The creation of Caesar in *War for the Planet of the Apes* is referred to by Serkis as a process of 'humanizing' the character (Serkis in Sulcas, 2017). This humanizing process is modernist in intent, prioritizing a conception of selfhood that aligns with the acting theories of Stanislavsky. Despite this, the more complex, collaborative and interdependent the processes of creating these CGI characters becomes, the more the humanist principles (individual creativity, personal psychological intention, discrete identity) commonly perceived as underpinning the industry within which they function are challenged and eroded.

The small field of MoCap practitioners and the lack, until the later part of this decade, of any serious training in motion capture movement work, has led to a self-help, DIY training culture that is a little bit reminiscent of early physical theatre and *parkour* training. Without training, the motion capture process could get slowed down by actors/performers not being used to the technical requirements and how to respond to them. To address this gap in the market and a perceived industry need, Taylor, together with his colleague Oliver Hollis-Leick, started a company called The MoCap Vaults, which offers training courses as well as an online repository of advice, training videos, interviews and information. Despite Serkis' success, and the workshops offered by MoCap Vaults and individual tutors such as Asha Jennings-Grant and Sarah Perry, routes in to the MoCap/PeCap profession are still largely ad hoc and not easy to navigate. Drama conservatoires are only gradually starting to recognize the possibility of motion or performance capture as a career path. Taylor was appointed as a movement tutor at the Academy of Live and Recorded Arts in 2016, having previously also taught at Rose Bruford College and Guildford School of Acting. For the most part, aspiring MoCap actors still have to approach the studios directly: 'because [the work] doesn't at present come through the normal casting channels so it is much more direct. [...] They often do days where they bring actors in. They act as their own casting directors usually' (Taylor, 2015). It is an area of the entertainment industry, like physical theatre and New Circus, where specialist movement skills are recognized, encouraged and valued. If you have trapeze, flying, acrobatic, *parkour*, juggling, martial arts or combat skills then motion capture is an area where work will be available. These features operate, however, to diminish the professional status of the MoCap/PeCap performer. This perhaps explains the determination of performers such as Serkis to align their work more closely with the more established field of film acting, a position supported by the Screen Actors Guild in the USA (Mihailova, 2016: 43).

Being Different Bodies

Motion capture helps capture the physical action, the key frame then builds, dissolves and transforms that action,[16] enabling the visualization of things that the physical body cannot do. The MoCap/PeCap performer contributes to this process through their ability to put together moves in games scenarios or sequences of action in line with the agreed qualities of the film character; in games production this can extend to the creation of tens of thousands of different moves. As a result, MoCap/PeCap can be 'very physical, physically demanding' (Bolet, 2015). The MoCap/PeCap actor may, throughout their career, play different ages, sizes, genders and races or ethnicities. They may even be playing three or four different characters within one film. The linearity of the performer's bodily identity and its representations of gender and difference is thus dissolved. The availability of such a range of opportunities may be artistically stimulating for the actor, but if not handled with critical awareness and sensitivity it runs the danger of replicating a system in which white male MoCap/PeCap actors[17] are able to colonize other subjectivities without real consideration of the responsibilities and implications of doing so. Clearly such opportunities also need to be available to women and to all other cultural groupings, and there should be continuous critical examination to ensure that white male privilege does not operate oppressively or as a dominant mode of experience within this field. In the Sony PS4 video game *Uncharted 4* (2016), white actor Laura Bailey plays a black character, Nadine Ross. At the time the performance was captured, the ethnicity and race of the character hadn't been decided; this created a situation in which a 'white' performance was at a later stage in the process converted to a 'black' performance through nothing other than the digital manipulation of skin colour, as if no other element of being black was relevant. The norm established here is not simply that colour doesn't matter in motion capture, it is that white can play black and that skin colour doesn't also relate to a wider set of life experiences. Thus that which is represented on screen may still adhere to repressive social norms – Carrasco points out that, too often, '"The cyber-body" expresses existing cultural values, negating the idea of postcorporeal male or female identity. As a consequence, social norms of beauty, fitness and health continue to inform these bodies' (2014: 43). There is some degree of inequality within the MoCap field at present; it is, after all, a subset of an industry that is notoriously unequal in what it offers women, people with disabilities, and black and minority ethnic people. According to Taylor (2015), there is recognition of this need within the MoCap world and a sense in which improvement is coming.

Certainly, the recent success of *Black Panther* (2018) has brought opportunities for greater diversity within what is represented, by whom, and in what ways through digital capture and CGI. Movement, including movement that is captured, cannot be solely understood as just the dynamics of motion, just how something moves. It must also relate to the social, cultural, political and economic experience(s) of individual bodies – what it means to be a woman, or black, or disabled or old, for example. There needs to be a recognition that movement is deeply constructed around the social, cultural and economic experiences of each body. It will not be acceptable if, between the MoCap/PeCap performers, the animators and the directors, these differences are ignored or erased. The challenge then is how MoCap and PeCap might adapt and develop to better capture those qualities and differences. In large part, this will of course also depend on why the industry makes games and films and who they are made for.

Digital Technologies and Live Theatre Performance

Not only have MoCap/PeCap performers often come from theatre backgrounds, sometimes they are also actively involved in live theatre practice that is engaging with these new technologies. Taylor refers to his role as a creative associate with Curious Directive:[18] 'We are interested in using motion capture on stage, so that's where I am starting to look at it from a creative angle' (Taylor, 2015). Curious Directive have been operating within the small-scale theatre sector since 2008. They have received funding that has enabled them to explore some of the emerging technology (for example an Oxford Samuel Beckett Theatre Trust research and development grant in 2012), nonetheless aware that the costs of good-quality animation limit what is currently possible on stage, even for companies of the scale of the RSC. Certainly, an important consideration for its future interaction with live theatre will be a richer and fuller understanding of the poetics of motion and performance capture. An understanding of the poetics of two fields is important to either resolving any disjuncture or to making it resonate with meaning. While mainstream theatre, such as the RSC, is focusing on high-end technology, for smaller companies one answer may be to acknowledge the technological and financial limitations, and to focus instead on the possibilities of using cheaper and more pervasive technologies (smartphones, simple location devices). It is feasible, with these simpler devices, for movement practitioners to play with and between different modalities, to explore capturing limited data sets that focus on individual limbs, specific movements or whole group motion. The development of perception neuron[19] technology, for instance, offers a motion capture system that is not reliant on visible markers – it can be worn under costumes and does not require an infrared lighting set-up. This kind of technology will offer more exciting possibilities as it develops and improves its stability. The rituals of digital calibration (a series of set postures that are currently required from the performer in order for the software to adapt to the data the performer is presenting) may even become part of the live performance rituals of the early twenty-first century. The physical demands of working with and between live and digitized performance may start to shape live performance practice in something like the same way that masks shaped the development of what was to become Commedia dell'Arte. Just as touching the mask breaks the illusion that it creates and reveals its presence, so the awkwardness of touch in the MoCap world (the manoeuvres required to accommodate headsets and the risk of obscuring markers) reveals both the limitations of the current technology and speaks to its particular mystique. The challenge that is yet to be fully resolved is the tension for the performer between the different levels of physicality required for live performance and for MoCap/PeCap. It is challenging to achieve both within the same performance, and as a result either the live performer or the avatar can look awkward, exaggerated or unconvincing. In addition, the visual currently dominates the audience's attention when screens are used in live performance contexts, possibly to the detriment of exploration of the ways in which sensation might also be meaningfully explored. All of these challenges can, however, also be viewed as opportunities. Being able within the performance space to see both the actor and the avatar could enable what we might refer to as the 'queering of the avatar'. If we understand queering as an action that 'disturbs, disrupts and centers – what is considered "normal" in order to explore possibilities outside of patriarchal, hierarchical and heteronormative discursive practices'

(Ruffalo in Mitra, 2015: 139), then we can see how perceiving both the actor and the avatar within the same performance event might enable tensions between the two, particularly around differences in the representation of gender, ethnicity, race, disability or age, to be made explicit and performative.

The elision between the real and the virtual will continue as the ability to capture live performance within synchronous theatrical environments increases and as the speed of digital data processing improves, enabling results to be visible very quickly and within the rehearsal or performance studio: 'if instead of imagining a huge forest you can be in a huge forest then your performance is going to be easier, you can focus on other things' (Taylor, 2015). Taylor describes a future that is almost with us now and which will probably only become more present: 'instead of reading the points that they mark on the body they are starting to mark your whole body in the space [...] They are also looking at GPS reading your body in the space' (Taylor, 2015).

What is being changed in the making of films, and perhaps within the wider notion of performance/acting, is the notion of fixed perspectives. MoCap/PeCap is designed around unfixing the single point of view of the audience or the camera and thus is capable of creating a multiple perspective that is closer to the experience of immersive theatre or virtual reality performance: 'it just takes time to get used to the rules, that there is no camera, it can be anywhere you like [...] It's a complete loss of any wall let alone the fourth wall' (Taylor, 2015). Likewise, in video games, the game is created by connecting together a complex collection of inter-related movement sequences. There is no centre, no 'primary axis of organisation' (Landow, 1997: 36–37). The lack of a fixed point of perspective within the studio camera array replicates the lack of a single perspective point for the actor and the viewer/player. Steven Spielberg reflects something of this change in his recent prediction that cinema will increasingly tailor itself to the individual viewer. He believes that 'we have to be prepared for entertainment coming at us in many different shapes and genres' (Spielberg in Pirelli, 2016). The impact of the interactivity available for consumers within the gaming industry will be very significant in the future of the cinema industry. Already Disney, Lucasfilm, ILMxLAB and The VOID are marketing a 'hyper-reality experience', based on the *Star Wars* film franchise, that offers a high-end, full sensory, immersive, virtual reality experience (www.thevoid.com/dimensions/starwars/secretsoftheempire).

Jennings-Grant (2017) presents motion capture as a challenge for the actor, a set of new techniques that they need to learn. The workshops and training now available, including the extensive and industry-recognized provision by The MoCap Vaults, indicate that MoCap is likely to become something more than that, and has indeed already started to reshape how performers move and use their bodies. The fixed points that movement practitioners such as Lecoq and Gaulier use within their training as part of the orientation and articulation of the body within the stage space are being superseded by the points around which changes happen within the movement sequences in online games, or the points around which visual effects rotate, such as in 'bullet time'.[20] Both deal with the ways in which motion is punctuated by stillness, yet in very different contexts.

Companies such as DV8 pioneered the use of video to record rehearsals and to assist in the devising process; they used it for several purposes:

> in order to recall improvised work from each rehearsal; to have access to improvised material for purposes of editing and shaping the final piece; and as a generative element, registering and recording unconscious movements which, in their revealing honesty, may be creatively vital. (Buckland, 1995: 373)

In the future motion capture may also be able to do much of this, in increasing detail and then made available through VR playback. And as Buckland suggests, 'The performers' sense of themselves as the source of material [may be] emphasized by the use of video as more than just a tool to recognize mistakes which would have to be corrected in a formal dance medium' (Buckland, 1995: 373). What Goodman calls 'the uses of the digital to capture the live' (2007: 110) will mean that future advances in MoCap will dissolve the boundaries between what is live and what is mediatized in provocative ways. They may also increasingly dissolve the boundaries between performer, audience and player. At the moment, in conventional gaming, the viewer/player does not move, except by the movement of a mouse or a finger. What if they were invited to move in more elaborate and engaging ways? It is possible to conceive of technologies similar to Microsoft Kinect that might enable the movement of the audience member/player to interact with the digitized performer in new and innovative ways, or haptic suits that enable the spectator to feel what the performer feels.

The theatre performer practises and trains to be in a state of becoming; they are typically creating, in the moment, the performance that is required for that set of circumstances. MoCap holds the moment and transforms it, and does so by reducing its complexity. The rising popularity of immersive theatre in the second decade of the twenty-first century reflects the interests of a generation raised on the experiences of online gaming and the limitations of the currently conceived digital body. Here is a form of theatre rich in interactivity and viewer/player control and collaboration, yet which currently is also more complex, visceral and immediate than that which is digitally mediated and experienced via a screen. Of course, the challenge that awaits is how it might be possible to combine both. How can live theatre offer a space within which motion capture can be used as part of the construction of performance – simultaneously enhancing the event and revealing the complexity created by the juxtaposition of the digital and the non-digital? It is in the field of theatre and performance that it might be possible to realize the subversive potential of motion capture, and its ability to be resistant to the forces seeking to utilize motion capture as a tool within a global capitalist industry.

Conclusion: Chapter 6

The MoCap actor is at once part of a vibrant community of performers, animators and film-makers, and yet also (at least as of 2018) remains concealed within the product that they are involved in creating. It might be tempting to think of the MoCap 'space' as 'no longer sexualized, racialized or naturalized but rather neutralized as figures of mixity, hybridity and interconnectiveness, turning transsexuality into a dominant posthuman *topos*' (Braidotti, 2013: 97); to see MoCap as a process that links the organic and the inorganic to create performances of identity and personality. Certainly MoCap/PeCap performances challenge conventional notions of individual control over our movement, our constructions of identity and our sense of self. As a final example, let us consider Arnold Schwarzenegger's 'body' in *Terminator: Salvation* (2009). This is a body that is actually a digital construct, modelled from a cast of his younger body. What Schwarzenegger did was to grant permission for the use of his likeness (Sperb, 2012: 384) – he willingly, and through a commercial transaction, surrendered his body so that it would become an entirely digital construct. Was what was then screened a performance – and if so, by whom? In what sense is an actor as conventionally conceived present in this process – does the animator then become actor, perhaps in the same sense that a video game player becomes an actor? The virtual or digital actor in this manner can achieve a semi-mythic status – a science-fiction idea that is literally becoming real in front of our eyes. As we look at such a construct, our sense of historical consciousness decays; the actor's body is no longer touched by time, just as Carrie Fisher as a young Princess Leia is digitally recreated in *Rogue One* (2016). Whereas movement directors such as Peter Elliott built non-human characters through detailed observation, working with sophisticated costume and puppet technology, and using physical performance skills, characters are now created through MoCap/PeCap technology that have no 'real world' referent and that are performed by actors digitally transformed into what they are not. This is no longer strange to us. Culturally we are used to a world in which we can (re)produce and manipulate images and content – we are no longer surprised when this happens around us, often we are delighted. Allison confirms that 'digital manipulation of the image is now so pervasive that digital effects are no longer "special"' (2011: 331). What we must ensure we consider in all of this is where the power and control lies. The MoCap/PeCap performer's body – commodified and transformed by the operation of global capitalism through the technology of the film industry – wishes and desires to see itself as empowered and pioneering; and yet is it any more or less docile or controlled than the body of any actor within the conventional entertainment industries?

Thus, within MoCap/PeCap, our everyday notions of embodied performance are deconstructed – what we see may be the digitally captured body of an actor who is dead mapped on to the body of an actor who is alive but whose identity we do not know. As Sperb (2012) points out, artifice is then revealed as everywhere. Equally, labour is concealed within the film spectacle – we do not see the work of the motion capture actor or the actual labour of the animator, we do not see the processes of collaboration, only their effects. The more MoCap and PeCap skills that actors learn, the less worth those skills are to them, as they are ultimately designed to make them less visible as an actor. The current trends for classes and workshops in MoCap acting, and for videos that reveal how motion capture effects are achieved, function to demystify the process of the performer. At the same time, digital technology is remystified in relation to performance – the animators are kept in the background, even less visible than the MoCap actors themselves, and their skills are little understood. As a result, what makes an award-winning performance in the digital film-making era consequently remains contentious; as Mihailova argues, 'the animators' labor is rarely acknowledged in contemporary conversations about motion and performance capture' (2016: 42), and as a result, motion capture is effectively redesignated as 'digital acting' (2016: 43). For a range of cultural and economic reasons, Mihailova suggests that it suits the film industry to maintain the human actor (ideally a marketable star) as the true source of creativity within the making of a film (2016: 44).

Capitalism seeks efficiency, economy, and decreasing cost against increasing income. Technologies such as MoCap and PeCap cannot help but operate within this economy, and in some ways, as we have seen, are very well suited to delivering against its demands. Yet within the race towards increasing digitization there is a persistent nostalgia for the human, as might be evidenced, for example, within the narratives of films such as *Blade Runner 2049* (2017). The closer MoCap performance gets to the physicality of human life, the more the technology struggles to capture it. Physical contact and touch are challenges for MoCap and PeCap – their multiple interactions and sensory intensity complicate the coordination of shots; data dissolves as markers overlap and get obscured. The portable technology of MoCap/PeCap – the marker points and the head cameras – continues to limit the ability to engage with something as simple and yet as complex as the kiss. The MoCap/PeCap body is thus, for now, always constructed and revealed as a MoCap/PeCap body. Live performance continues to offer important opportunities to represent things that MoCap/PeCap, as of now, still cannot. This will probably remain the case until digital technology manages to reformulate our notions of the touch and the kiss – a change that may not be as far away as we think. The challenge then is to fully understand and realize the particular poetics of performance capture within both live and recorded performance. In the future, MoCap and PeCap, within both these types of performance, may have to be far more visible, actively disruptive and provocative than they currently are. They will have to offer more than Serkis' digital make-up if they are not to go the way of so many technologies before them and become effectively invisible. Despite their high-end profile within the film industry, the ability, through low-level, low-cost technologies, to connect across countries, to challenge notions of identity, to reveal how technologies select and prioritize, and to enhance collaboration may yet be where their most interesting future lies.

Notes

1. CGI refers to computer-generated imagery, the use of digital graphics and animation packages to create special effects in films.
2. A MOOC is a massive open online course, in which participation is usually not limited by number and is accessible to all via the internet.
3. Full details can be found at: www.futurelearn.com/courses/physical-theatre.
4. A recent Google search for videos with the subject '*parkour* training' brought up over 520,000 results.
5. For more detail on this project see the RSC's video at: www.rsc.org.uk/the-tempest/gregory-doran-2016-production/video-creating-the-tempest.
6. Mihailova (2016) offers a detailed and rigorous interrogation of the gendered nature of motion and performance capture within the film industry. Her article

also includes perceptive critical analyses of the use of motion capture in a few key film productions.

7. If the reader wishes to explore this in more detail, there is a YouTube video that provides a comparison of the two performances (www.youtube.com/watch?v=KsuvXHGCVXE).

8. See Allison (2011) for an analysis of the ways in which films now create additional documentary material that specifically aims to make visible those who undertake this work, as if seeking to rehumanize the process. Another effect of this phenomenon has been to increase and deepen the entanglement of actor and technology – revealing the technology and how it works emphasizes the interdependency.

9. Many stunts are now 'performed' by digital stunt doubles, who are capable of changing imperceptibly back in to the human actor after the stunt is completed (Allison, 2011: 328).

10. Allison (2011: 326) indicates that prominent MoCap actors in the film industry are often referred to as 'synthespians' or 'cyberstars'.

11. Taylor started work as a MoCap performer within the video games industry. In addition to training as a gymnast in his youth and a one-year period of study at the Lecoq School (2007–2008), since the early 2000s Taylor has worked extensively for the motion capture company Centroid 3D.

12. Voldemort and Snape are characters in the *Harry Potter* film franchise.

13. In the T-stance the actor stands upright with arms out to the sides, resembling the letter T. This stance ensures that all the markers are readable by the cameras.

14. Benoît-Constant Coquelin (1841–1909) was a French actor, who wrote a treatise on acting (*L'Art et le comédien* (1880)), drawing on the theories of the philosopher Denis Diderot, that suggested that the true art of the actor lay in representing emotions and not in feeling them (see Coquelin, 1932).

15. His major PeCap roles to date include: Gollum in *The Lord of the Rings* trilogy (2001–2003), Kong in *King Kong* (2005), the ape Caesar in the rebooted *Planet of the Apes* franchise (2011–2017), and Supreme Leader Snoke in the *Star Wars* films *The Force Awakens* (2015) and *The Last Jedi* (2017).

16. Key frame in film-making is a process to define the start and end of a transition.

17. A search of The MoCap Vaults undertaken on 7 November 2017 revealed 30 MoCap vault trainees; of these, 14 are female and five are non-white.

18. Curious Directive were founded in 2008. Led by director Jack Lowe (also a graduate of the Lecoq School), they are an Arts Council-funded company based in Norwich that create performance events designed to explore the relationship between theatre and science.

19. This technology involves the use of active markers worn by the performer and connected wirelessly to the software. For details, see https://neuronmocap.com.

20. Bullet time is a special effect, also sometimes known as time-slice photography, in which motion is slowed down drastically, allowing the trajectory of some fast-moving object such as a bullet to be tracked. Some of the best-known examples can be seen in the film *The Matrix* (1999).

7 Conclusions

This book has attempted to reveal some of the challenges facing the moving body in performance within the twenty-first century, and to do so by examining contexts that are at once possibly quite well-known and at the same time often under-researched – mainstream theatre, aspects of actor training such as animal study, approaches to movement and cultural difference, forms of physical theatre and New Circus, and motion and performance capture. As a white, middle-class, non-disabled, heterosexual male academic, I am aware of the complexities of speaking to some of the issues I write about in this book from what I acknowledge is a privileged position – nonetheless, they need to be brought to the table and I offer them with humility and respect for all those already working in these fields.

We all experience the beating pulse of our everyday embodied existence in all of its rich unpredictability, variety, fragility and immediacy. As theatre makers, this richness is channelled through the meaning-making processes of theatre and its various forms, techniques and spaces. I have argued throughout this book that we all are required constantly to re-examine those processes to ensure that they are adequately responsive to the cultural diversity and socio-political challenges of our physical life. A theme throughout this book has been the journey that all theatre practitioners have to undertake to find, own and understand their own body and its potential for meaningful expression. We all share a need as performers to understand the foundations of our own movement practice and to start from our own stories – discovering how best to tell those stories, what forms of movement will best serve them, and how best to respond to the environments within which we wish to tell those stories. Throughout this book, I have argued for the necessity of recognizing both the socio-cultural context and the poetics of each form of movement practice in order to fully recognize its potential. I have attempted to interrogate what it means to perform animal, to perform circus or physical theatre, to perform difference or to perform through a digital avatar. Although form is a necessity within theatre, I would therefore take issue with forms and processes that do not allow or enable the student or actor to bring their own cultural movement experience and heritage into play in a way that both liberates them and releases their own creativity. Without experienced and sensitive direction, processes such as Viewpoints (Bogart & Landau, 2004) and Pulse (Gerstle, 2010) can impose a particular and dominant cultural aesthetic focused on what might appear to be abstract qualities of performance, rather than achieving the release of performer creativity that is intended and the level of cultural awareness required. Equally important is that these processes have to be extended into mainstream performance if real, profound and lasting change is to be achieved. The availability in the UK of specialist masters courses in movement teaching and direction provides opportunity and encouragement for the introduction of a wider awareness of different practices, different contexts and different cultures into mainstream theatre practice.

Emma Cox (2014) reminds us of de Certeau's argument that '[e]very story is a travel story – a spatial practice' (de Certeau, 2011: 115). The stories we tell with our bodies cannot escape the socio-political reality of where our bodies are from, and the spaces that we have taken them to. The stories told by the people interviewed for this book indicate the journeys that they have travelled and the cultural spaces that they have traversed. It is of real importance that as theatre practitioners we recognize the place from which our bodies start, their cultural locus and the technical abilities which situate them in that space. At its best, contemporary physical devising and theatre movement practice in the UK has created opportunities for diverse practitioners to explore diverse physicalities, playing both with and against conventions of movement practice. The challenge for the future is to create these opportunities outside of a safe creative space and within the wider, sometimes harsher socio-political reality of twenty-first century global society. There is some reason to be hopeful. As Landon-Smith reports,

> there are a handful of people who are starting to really rigorously question historical, traditional trainings [...] I do think those diasporic identities are starting to take some power in their own hands and they are starting to drive things [...] A lot of people's cultural hubs are completely not the establishment, and I think that is also going to really impact. (Landon-Smith, 2012)

The erosion of the kinds of collective practices within theatre that might best support the development of an inclusive approach to movement and physical theatre can in part be blamed on the strengthening of hierarchical structures within the industry and changes in arts funding policy over the last ten years, but Mermikides and Smart (2016) also suggest that the tension between the individual voice and the collective identity can end up compromising both if it is not handled with skill. The more collective the devising process, the greater the danger that the individual body may be subsumed or erased. How can this be avoided, in order to ensure that the patriarchal and/or colonial process is not simply replicated within and by the collective process? Individual bodies within the theatre-making process have to be empowered to reveal and sustain their own stories.

Over the last few years, there has been much more attention brought to bear on the treatment of different bodies within the performing arts industries, particularly in the UK and the USA. The *#MeToo* campaign that followed on from the revelations of unacceptably predatory behaviour by influential figures such as Harvey Weinstein has highlighted the exploitation of women. The lack of genuine opportunities and recognition for women and for black and minority ethnic people has also been raised and is being addressed with increasing determination for change. Telling rich and diverse stories about, and with, richly diverse bodies must be the best way forward. Theatre and performance remains a vital space in which to ask all sorts of questions about how we treat all kinds of bodies, including our own: 'The story of a body told through a body focuses the audience's attention on the body and the visceral experience of co-constituting identity with an audience situated, enabled, and constrained by embodiment and cultural discourse' (Scott, 2012: 102).

As performance work moves increasingly into digital environments, it is necessary to remember that 'the biological is no longer what it once was and that the logic of power will seek control of those new forms of life and their electronic partners' (Causey, 2016: 204). Chapter 6, on motion and performance capture, questions the ways in which power operates on the body and movement within the digital realm. We cannot assume that the ways in which we could previously perform movement will retain for us the same degree of control over our bodies and their expressive potential as they once did. As we move in to a postdigital and posthuman period, it may be that we actually feel less certain now than we have ever been about what it means to be embodied. The digital performance field seems to allow for the possibility of the removal of physical expression from the control of the performer as of the moment that they produce it. After that moment of capture, it is manipulated and re-presented. Causey, drawing on a cartographic metaphor borrowed from Jorge Luis Borges, suggests that, within the digital performance realm, 'the real world disappears leaving its trace in the maps of its previous existence' (Causey, 2016: 204). The original physical experience/performance of the MoCap performer is, in this same sense, something that, after digitization, can only be known through its digital traces. Although the performer's movement work is in some basic sense archived by the process of digitization, at the same time that experience becomes increasingly unattainable in its 'original' form. To this extent, we have, therefore, to ask whether motion capture reveals or hides any truths about our bodies beyond those which are purely a matter of dynamics and trajectories. And if it does encapsulate any truths, by whom and for whom are they provided? Performance capture as a newer concept seeks a kind of 'embeddedness' (Causey, 2016: 204–205) within which the performance is re-performed and re-scripted, but not veiled or obscured in the way that motion capture used to be – however, the dynamics of power ultimately still operate in the same way.

From a perspective situated inside Western, technological society, we find ourselves surrounded by multiple digital traces of our bodies – airport scans, hospital visualizations of illness, Microsoft Kinect consoles, CCTV images, for example – these are everyday traces that are naturalizing our experience of digital movement capture. These forms and digital artefacts inhabit cultural 'non-spaces' in which the body of the captured subject disappears and the avatar or digital trace becomes the point of linkage between the technology and the wider environment. It is interesting the number of videos on social media that reveal how motion capture works and openly outline for the viewer the stages of development from the movement work of the MoCap/PeCap performer to the finished artefact. Technology is employed to subvert its own illusions; it is used on one level to reassert the human within the machine while on another level it simultaneously makes more evident the power of the machine. Digital technology has enabled the visibility of movement practices for mass audiences, but has not necessarily made them any better understood – it is likely that more people understand the process of motion and performance capture than understand the specific movement skills and techniques employed by the performers whose movement is captured. So much physical theatre performance has now been archived through video recording and documentation and through motion and performance capture, and yet we don't seem to have the potential to interrogate and utilize any of this data. What might be possible in terms of accessing and analysing such an archive of movement, if it were feasible to create a movement, circus and physical theatre archive as rich, accessible and searchable as exists in the field of dance (for example Siobhan Davies Replay: The Choreographic Archive of Siobhan Davies Dance[1] or the Digital Dance Archives[2]) and/or in more limited form around the finished productions of particular companies (such as are available in Digital Theatre+[3] and the Routledge Performance Archive[4])? At the same time, by digitizing so much practice we sustain it in forms that don't allow for its visceral qualities and that cannot always capture its full context. Digital archiving, like digital movement capture, also does not necessarily reveal any distinctions between what is kept and what is discarded (and who decides which to do); who 'owns' such materials; and what processes and techniques are being preserved, in what state, and to what level of detail. Movement that is digitally captured is not de-sexualized, it does not lose its ethnic roots nor its location within frames of dis/ability. If they are not present, they have been erased or the viewer has decided not to see them. We should, all of us, as performance practitioners and scholars, question how that process works, who is excluded from it, and to whose benefit it is employed.

Finally, at the heart of this book there is an argument that the notion of play is vital, that it is play that enables us to be part of a world that is not defined solely by us and by our own constructions. Play reasserts diversity, change and unpredictability. As a conclusion to this argument, we might consider the extent to which we should resist technologies, in whatever form they exist, that seek to replace play with labour and work. Play is essentially transformative, in ways that ultimately technology still finds hard to replicate. When the French theatre pedagogue Philippe Gaulier, an expert in 'play', was asked what would be the effect on the student of attendance at his school, he wrote, 'The school will change you totally' (Gaulier, 2018). The change that Gaulier envisages is not simply the cumulative effect of new knowledge; instead it relates to the disruptive and transformational ability of play to release powerful and liberating creative energies.

Play changes our attitude towards the work that we do. One theme of this book has been about shifting the emphasis of enquiry away from a focus only on what is done and towards ways and modes of doing, and the social framework within which we act. Movement performance practice is then about more than particular sets of skills or somatic/kinaesthetic experiences; it is about how bodies create different meanings when they move in different ways and in different contexts. The story that a disabled circus or black physical theatre performer tells is never just a simple dramatic narrative, nor is it just about their professional skills: it is always also about their (social, cultural, political and personal) experience of their body. Bodily differences, which we should understand as socially constructed, bring to the audience's attention the tension between what is done and how it is done. Just as women have had to work against the expectations, misunderstandings and prejudices that circulate around what the female body can/should/might do, so the same also applies for the disabled performer, the LGBT performer, the black performer and the older performer.

Movement performance practice, New Circus and physical theatre may be exactly the places where these tensions, challenges and prejudices need to be worked out, as they are arenas in which cultural difference can be revealed and challenged in ways that can combine the visceral, the emotional, the psychological, the social and the political. The effects of movement practice that this book seeks to investigate have to be understood as not just about how different skill sets, practices, processes and structures can interact with each other, but also about how we can work across bodies, across embodied experiences, across the social experiences that shape our bodies and our attitudes towards other bodies. This will have implications for the infrastructures and resources that are provided for movement-based performance practice and training, wherever it occurs. Freelance aerial tutor and academic Tina Carter suggested in a 2013 conference paper that circus equipment is currently not usually designed with people with disabilities in mind. From her perspective, and in relation to teaching circus skills, accessible teaching and practice works best when it is based on setting tasks and not on dictating specific movements (Carter, 2013: 7). She reports that the disabled body can perform aerial routines that a non-disabled body cannot, but that this is not often realized and the potential of such performers is not often engaged with because assumptions are made at a much earlier stage about what is or is not possible for them (Carter, 2013: 9).

The same issues can be raised in relation to movement practices and physical theatre activities in general. If we start by assuming that the doing of the activity is the purpose, the solving of a wider problem through the medium of movement and not the demonstration of skills against a set of defined criteria, then we are starting from a much better place.

Theatre is not *about* theatre; it is about everything else, even when it *is* about theatre. In this respect, the training of actors' bodies should not just be about training actors in particular professional skills, it should be about training them to better understand, investigate, critique and present the world around them through movement. This means that movement training and movement practice should not focus solely on technical aspects but should, as its primary focus, enable students and actors, through movement, to engage critically with the world around them. For many movement tutors teaching within higher education or conservatoire institutions this is the challenge that they continually seek to address – how does movement training ensure that it does not simply and uncritically replicate existing constructions of the body?. This is a challenge made harder by the continuing invisibility of movement direction within theatre reviews, press releases for productions, and visual materials disseminated to publicise productions. Even while movement is everywhere visible on stage, its professional labour can still be obscured and dismissed elsewhere. If the problems of theatre are too far distant from the global, cultural, interpersonal and bio-technological problems facing our societies, then theatre will be seen as an irrelevant extravagance. Training for actors is hard enough to maintain against cuts to budgets for health, welfare, defence and justice. When economics has such a comprehensive hold on many areas of the arts, the performing body can too easily become little more than a commodity that is bought and sold, an afterthought in terms of its expressive and investigative potential. Viewing the body as capital counteracts our ability to pay attention to my/our/your/their various bodies. When we live in a time in which increasing numbers of people are sold as slaves, and in which migrant bodies become commodities exploited for their economic value, it is no longer acceptable to stand back and allow such commodification to take place. The attention that we pay to movement and embodiment needs to become in many ways more politicized, critically aware and interrogatory – this book aims to assert the importance of that process within the theatre.

Notes

1. Siobhan Davies Replay is available at: www.siobhandaviesreplay.com.
2. The Digital Dance Archives is available at: www.dance-archives.ac.uk.
3. Digital Theatre+ is available at: www.digitaltheatreplus.com/education.
4. The Routledge Performance Archive is available at: www.routledgeperformancearchive.com.

Bibliography

Agnew, M. & Landon-Smith, K. (2016) The whole of humanity: Voice and intracultural theatre practice, *Voice and Speech Review*, 10: 2–3, 169–178.

Albright, A. (1997) *Choreographing Difference: The Body and Identity in Contemporary Dance*, Hanover & London: Wesleyan University Press.

Alison-Mitchell, D. (2017) 'Dancing since strapped to their mothers' backs: Movement directing on the Royal Shakespeare Company's African *Julius Caesar*', in Jarrett-Macauley, D. (ed.), *Shakespeare, Race and Performance: The Diverse Bard*, London & New York: Routledge, 146–153.

Allain, P. (ed.) (2011) *Andrei Droznin's Physical Actor Training*, Abingdon & New York: Routledge.

Allison, T. (2011) More than a man in a monkey suit: Andy Serkis, motion capture, and digital realism, *Quarterly Review of Film and Video*, 28: 4, 325–341.

Arts Council England (2016) *Equality, Diversity and the Creative Case: A Data Report 2015–2016*, London: Arts Council England.

Babbage, F. (2010) 'Augusto Boal and the Theatre of the Oppressed', in Hodge, A. (ed.), *Actor Training* (2nd), London & New York: Routledge, 305–323.

Bannon, F. (2012) *Relational Ethics: Dance, Touch and Learning*, Lancaster: PALATINE.

Barba, E. (1986) *Beyond the Floating Islands*, New York: PAJ Publications.

Barba, E. (1994) *The Paper Canoe: Guide to Theatre Anthropology*, London & New York: Routledge.

Barker, C. (1977) *Theatre Games: A New Approach to Drama Training*, London: Methuen.

Barker, C. (1995) What training – for what theatre?, *New Theatre Quarterly*, XI: 42, 99–108.

Barker, J. (2012) 'Jos Houben talks about Lecoq, Complicité, Beckett & working with Peter Brook', *Culturebot*, 25 October 2012. Available online at: www.culturebot. org/2012/10/11643/jos-houben-talks-about-lecoq-complicite-beckett-working-with-peter-brook. Accessed on 13 October 2018.

Barron, C. & Carnicke, S. M. (2008) *Reframing Screen Performance*, Ann Arbor, MI: University of Michigan Press.

Beckett, F. (2005) *Laurence Olivier*, London: Haus Publishing.

Benedetti, J. (1982) *Stanislavski: An Introduction*, London: Methuen.

Benedetti, J. (1988) *Stanislavski: A Biography*, London: Methuen Drama.

Benedetti, R. (2006) *Action!: Professional Acting for Film and Television*, New York: Longman Publishing Group.

Beringer, E. (ed.) (2010) *Embodied Wisdom: The Collected Papers of Moshe Feldenkrais*, Berkeley, CA: North Atlantic Books.

Billington, M. (2012) 'Julius Caesar – review', *The Guardian*, Thursday 7 June 2012. Available online at: www.theguardian.com/stage/2012/jun/07/julius-caesar-review. Accessed on 13 October 2018.

Birkett, D. (2018) *Women in Circus* [video], London & Achill Island: Circus 250. Available online at: https://vimeo.com/258997312. Accessed on 13 October 2018.

Bishop, B. (2018) 'How The Shape of Water's visual effects turned a merman into a romantic lead', *The Verge*, 17 January 2018. Available online at: www.theverge.com/2018/1/17/16898382/the-shape-of-water-special-effects-vfx-cgi. Accessed on 13 October 2018.

Bissell, L. (2013) The female cyborg as grotesque in performance, *International Journal of Performance Arts and Digital Media*, 9: 2, 261–274.

Boal, A. (1979) *Theater of the Oppressed*, London: Pluto Press.

Boal, A. (1995) *The Rainbow of Desire: The Boal Method of Theatre and Therapy*, trans. Jackson, A., London & New York: Routledge.

Bogart, A. & Landau, T. (2004) *The Viewpoints Book: A Practical Guide to Viewpoints and Composition*, New York: Theatre Communications Group.

Bolet, J. (2015) 'Interview with Jeannie Bolet', *The MoCap Vault* (video). Available online at: www.facebook.com/themocapvaults/videos/interview-with-actor-jeannie-bolet/734972496622017. Accessed on 19 October 2018.

Bouissac, P. (2012) *Circus as Multimodal Discourse: Performance, Meaning and Ritual*, London: Bloomsbury.

Bradley, K. (2009) *Rudolf Laban*, London & New York: Routledge.

Braidotti, R. (2013) *The Posthuman*, Cambridge: Polity.

Brecht, B. (2015) *Brecht on Theatre* (4th), eds Silberman, M., Giles, S. & Kuhn, T., London: Methuen Drama.

Brissenden, A. (1981) *Shakespeare and the Dance*, Basingstoke: Palgrave Macmillan.

Buckland, F. (1995) Towards a language of the stage: The work of DV8 Physical Theatre, *New Theatre Quarterly*, 11: 44, 371–380.

Bull, J. (2004) 'The establishment of mainstream theatre, 1946–1979', in Kershaw, B. & Thomson, P. (eds), *The Cambridge History of British Theatre, Volume 3*, Cambridge: Cambridge University Press, 326–348.

Burt, R. (1998) *Alien Bodies: Representations of Modernity, 'Race' and Nation in Early Modern Dance*, London & New York: Routledge.

Butler, J. (1993) *Bodies that Matter: On the Discursive Limits of Sex*, London & New York: Routledge.

Caillois, R. (2001) *Man, Play and Games*, trans. Barash, M., Urbana & Chicago, IL: University of Illinois Press.

Callery, D. (2001) *Through the Body: A Practical Guide to Physical Theatre*, London: Nick Hern Books.

Carnicke, S. (1998) *Stanislavski in Focus*, London & New York: Routledge.

Carr, P., Dennis, R. & Hand, R. (2014) *Dancing With Inter-Disciplinarity: Strategies and Practices in Higher Education Dance, Drama and Music*, York: Higher Education Academy.

Carrasco, R. (2014) (Re)defining the gendered body in cyberspace: The virtual reality film, *Nordic Journal of Feminist and Gender Research*, 22: 1, 33–47.

Carter, T. (2013) 'Dis/abling' aerial transmission for small statured performers in London 2012's Paralympic Opening Ceremony', unpublished conference paper, TaPRA conference, Glasgow, September 2013.

Causey, M. (2016) 'The object of desire of the machine and the biopolitics of the posthuman', in Wilmer, S. E. & Žukauskaitė, A. (eds), *Resisting Biopolitics: Philosophical, Political and Performative Strategies*, London & New York: Routledge, 202–215.

Cave, R. (2015) Feldenkrais and actors: Working with the Royal Shakespeare Company, *Theatre, Dance and Performance Training*, 6: 2, 174–186.

Chen, A. (2012) 'Memo to the RSC: East Asians can be more than just dogs and maids', *Guardian*, 22 October 2012. Available online at: www.theguardian.com/commentisfree/2012/oct/22/royal-shakespeare-company-east-asians. Accessed on 13 October 2018.

Churcher, M. (2003) *Acting for Film: Truth 24 Frames a Second*, London: Virgin Books.

Cohen, L. (ed.) (2010) *The Lee Strasberg Notes*, London & New York: Routledge.

Conroy, C. (2009) Disability: Creative tensions between drama, theatre and disability arts, *Research in Drama Education: The Journal of Applied Theatre and Performance*, 14: 1, 1–14.

Conway, M. (2008) *Tea with Trish: The Movement Work of Trish Arnold* [DVD].

Copeau, J. (1990) *Copeau: Texts on Theatre*, trans. and ed. Rudlin, J. and Paul, N., London: Routledge.

Coquelin, B.-C. (1932) *The Art of the Actor*, trans. Fogerty, E., London: Allen & Unwin.

Cox, E. (2014) *Theatre & Migration*, London: Red Globe Press.

Daboo, J. (2009) To learn through the body: Teaching Asian forms of training and performance in higher education, *Studies in Theatre and Performance*, 29: 2, 121–131.

Dacre, K. & Bulmer, A. (2009) Into the scene and its impact on inclusive performance training, *Research in Drama Education: The Journal of Applied Theatre and Performance*, 14: 1, 133–139.

Darley, C. (2009) *The Space to Move: Essentials of Movement Training*, London: Nick Hern Books.

Davis, K. (ed.) (2009) *Embodied Practices: Feminist Perspectives on the Body*, Thousand Oaks, CA: Sage.

De Certeau, M. (2011) *The Practice of Everyday Life*, trans. Rendall, S., Berkeley, CA: University of California Press.

Deleuze, G. & Guattari, F. (1988) *A Thousand Plateaus: Capitalism and Schizophrenia*, London: The Athlone Press.

DramaUK (2012) *Accreditation Guide*, London: DramaUK.

Eldredge, S. & Huston, H. (1995) 'Actor training in the neutral mask', in Zarrilli, P. (ed.) *Acting (Re)Considered: Theories and Practices*, London & New York: Routledge, 121–128.

Ellingsworth, J. (2009) 'Interview: John-Paul Zaccarini', *Sideshow*. Available online at: http://sideshow-circusmagazine.com/magazine/interviews/interview-john-paul-zaccarini. Accessed on 17 April 2015.

Elliott, P. (2012) *Interview with Mark Evans*, unpublished. 30 January 2012.

Elswit, K. (2018) *Theatre & Dance*, London: Red Globe Press.

Evans, M. (1999) 'Looking good? – Perceptions of the body in the dance/Theatre of Volcano and Frantic Assembly', *Conference Proceedings, Momentum Conference*, Manchester Metropolitan University, Crewe: Manchester Metropolitan University, 135–146.

Evans, M. (2007) Another kind of writing: Reflective practice and creative journals in the performing arts, *Journal of Writing in Creative Practice*, 1: 1, 69–76.

Evans, M. (2009) *Movement Training for the Modern Actor*, London & New York: Routledge.

Evans, M. (2012a) Dancing with Socrates: Telling truths about the self, *Journal of Dance & Somatic Practices*, 3: 1&2, 117–125.

Evans, M. (2012b) The influence of sports on the actor training of Jacques Lecoq, *Theatre Dance and Performer Training*, 3: 2, 163–177.

Evans, M. (2014) Playing with history: Personal accounts of the political and cultural self in actor training through movement, *Theatre Dance and Performance Training*, 5: 2, 144–156.

Evans, M. (2015) 'The myth of Pierrot', in Chaffee, J. & Crick, O. (eds), *The Routledge Companion to Commedia dell'Arte*, London & New York: Routledge, 346–354.

Evans, M. (2018) *Jacques Copeau* (re-issue of 1st ed.), London & New York: Routledge.

Evans, M. & Kemp, R. (eds) (2016) *The Routledge Companion to Jacques Lecoq*, London & New York: Routledge.

Ewan, V. & Green, D. (2014) *Actor Movement: Expression of the Physical Being*, London: Bloomsbury.

Foucault, M. (1999) 'Discourse and truth: The problematization of parrhesia'. Available online at: http://foucault.info/documents/parrhesia/. Accessed on 20 October 2018.

Frank, A. W. (1995) *The Wounded Storyteller: Body, Illness and Ethics*, Chicago, IL: University of Chicago Press.

Freire, P. (1996) *Pedagogy of the Oppressed*, London: Penguin.

Frost, A. & Yarrow, R. (2015) *Improvisation in Drama, Theatre and Performance: History, Practice, Theory* (3rd), London: Red Globe Press.

Fusco, C. (1998) 'Fantasies of oppositionality', in Kester, G. H. (ed.), *Art, Activism, and Oppositionality: Essays from Afterimage*, Durham, NC: Duke University Press, 60–75.

Gaulier, P. (2006) *The Tormentor: Le jeu – light – theatre*, Paris: Filmiko.

Gaulier, P. (2018) *École Philippe Gaulier – Frequently Asked Questions*. Available online at: www.ecolephilippegaulier.com. Accessed on 13 October 2018.

Gerstle, T. (2010) 'Pulse: A physical approach to staging text', *In/Stead 3*. Available online at: www.insteadjournal.com/article/pulse-a-physical-approach-to-staging-text. Accessed on 13 October 2018.

Giannachi, G. (2004) *Virtual Theatre: An Introduction*, London & New York: Routledge.

Giannachi, G. & Luckhurst, M. (eds) (1999) *On Directing: Interviews with Directors*, London: Faber and Faber.

Giedion, S. (1948) *Mechanization Takes Command: A Contribution to Anonymous History*, Oxford: Oxford University Press.

Goodman, L. (2007) Performing self beyond the body: Replay culture replayed, *International Journal of Performance Arts and Digital Media*, 3: 2–3, 103–121.

Gordon, R. (2006) *The Purpose of Playing: Modern Acting Theories in Perspective*, Ann Arbor: University of Michigan Press.

Graham, S. (2015) *Interview with Mark Evans*, unpublished. 24 April 2015.

Graham, S. & Hoggett, S. (2012) *A Guide to Frantic Assembly for Students (aged 14+), Teachers & Arts Educationalists*, London: Frantic Assembly.

Graham, S. & Hoggett, S. (2014) *Frantic Assembly Book of Devising Theatre* (2nd), London & New York: Routledge.

Grosz, E. (1994) *Volatile Bodies: Towards a Corporeal Feminism*, London & New York: Routledge.

Grotowski, J. (1975) *Towards a Poor Theatre*, London: Eyre Methuen.

Haver, W. (1997) 'Queer research: or, how to practice invention to the brink of intelligibility', in Golding, S. (ed.), *Eight Technologies of Otherness*, London & New York: Routledge, 277–292.

Henderson, B. & Ostrander, N. (eds) (2010) *Understanding Disability Studies and Performance Studies*, London & New York: Routledge.

Hiscock, J. (2014) 'Andy Serkis interview: Audiences are moved by acting not effects', *The Telegraph*, 10 July 2014. Available online at: www.telegraph.co.uk/culture/film/film-news/10956372/Andy-Serkis-interview-Audiences-are-moved-by-acting-not-effects.html. Accessed on 13 October 2018.

Hodge, A. (ed.) (2010) *Actor Training* (2nd), London & New York: Routledge.

Hoggett, S. (2014) *Interview with Mark Evans*, unpublished. 10 November 2014.

Holdsworth, N. (2006) *Joan Littlewood*, London & New York: Routledge.

Holdsworth, N. (2013) Boys don't do dance, do they?, *Research in Drama Education: The Journal of Applied Theatre and Performance*, 18: 2, 168–178.

Huizinga, J. (1980) *Homo Ludens: A Study of the Play-Element in Culture*, London: Routledge & Kegan Paul.

Jennings-Grant, A. (2017) 'Movement training for motion capture performance', *Theatre Dance and Performance Training Blog*. Posted 28 July 2017. Available online at: http://theatredanceperformancetraining.org/2017/07/movement-training-for-motion-capture-performance. Accessed on 13 October 2018.

Johnston, C. (2006) *The Improvisation Game: Discovering the secrets of spontaneous performance*, London: Nick Hern Books.

Johnstone, K. (1979) *Impro: Improvisation and the Theatre*, London: Methuen.

Jousse, M. (2000) *The Anthropology of Geste and Rhythm: Studies in the Anthropological Laws of Human Expression and their Application in the Galilean Oral-Style Tradition* (2nd), edited and trans. Sienaert, E. & Conolly, J., Durban: Mantis Publishing.

Jousse, M. (2008) [1974–1978] *L'Anthropologie du Geste*, Paris: Gallimard.

Kapsali, M. (2013) Rethinking actor training: Training body, mind and ... ideological awareness, *Theatre Dance and Performance Training*, 4: 1, 73–86.

Kean, D. & Larsen, M. (eds) (2016) *Centre Stage: The Pipeline of BAME Talent*, London: Andrew Lloyd Webber Foundation. Available online at: http://andrewlloydwebberfoundation.com/downloads/centre-stage-the-pipeline-of-bame-talent.pdf. Accessed on 4 January 2018.

Keleman, S. (1999) *Myth and the Body: A Colloquy with Joseph Campbell*, Berkeley, CA: Center Press.

Kendrick, L. (2011) A *paidic* aesthetic: An analysis of games in the ludic pedagogy of Philippe Gaulier, *Theatre, Dance and Performance Training*, 2: 1, 72–85.

Krasner, D. (2012) *An Actor's Craft: The Art and Technique of Acting*, London: Red Globe Press.

Kumpulainen, S. (2012) From sweat and tears towards sweat and harmony, *Theatre Dance and Performance Training*, 3: 2, 229–241.

Kuppers, P. (2001) Deconstructing images: Performing disability, *Contemporary Theatre Review*, 11: 3–4, 5–40.

Kuppers, P. (2003) *Disability and Contemporary Performance: Bodies on Edge*, London & New York: Routledge.

Kuppers, P. (2017) *Theatre & Disability*, London: Red Globe Press.

Kuppers, P. & Marcus, N. (2009) Contact/disability performance. An essay constructed between Petra Kuppers and Neil Marcus, *Research in Drama Education: The Journal of Applied Theatre and Performance*, 14: 1, 141–155.

La Frenais, R. (1986) Learning to fly, *Performance*, 40: 18–31.

Laban, R. (1980) *The Mastery of Movement*, Plymouth: Northcote House.

Landon-Smith, K. (2009) 'Using, not ignoring, the cultural background of the performer'. Transcript of a masterclass at National Institute of Dramatic Art, Sydney, Australia, on 12 October 2009. Available online at: www.tamasha.org.uk/nida-masterclass. Accessed on 13 October 2018.

Landon-Smith, K. (2012) *Interview with Mark Evans*, unpublished. 30 January 2012.

Landow, G. P. (1997) *Hypertext 2.0: The Convergence of Contemporary Critical Theory and Technology*, Baltimore & London: John Hopkins University Press.

Lavers, K. & Burtt, J. (2017) BLAKflip and beyond: Aboriginal performers and contemporary circus in Australia, *New Theatre Quarterly*, 33: 4, 307–319.

Lecoq, J. (2000) *The Moving Body: Teaching Creative Theatre*, London: Methuen.

Lecoq, J. (2006) *Theatre of Movement and Gesture*, trans. Bradby, D., London: Routledge.

Leslie, S. (2012) *Interview with Mark Evans*, unpublished, 11 July 2012.

Lewis, V. (2016) 'Hands like starfish/Feet like moons: Disabled women's theatre collectives', in Syssoyeva, K. M. & Proudfit, S. (eds), *Women, Collective Creation, and Devised Performance*, Basingstoke: Palgrave Macmillan, 301–316.

Logan, B. (2010) 'Mark Rylance: Acting is just play. You have to look for the joyful thing', *The Independent on Sunday*, 4 July 2010. Available online at: http://independent.co.uk/news/people/profiles/mark-rylance-acting-is-just-play-you-have-to-look-for-the-joyful-thing-2017947.html. Accessed on 10 November 2014.

Loots, L. (2010) The body as history and memory: A gendered reflection on the choreographic 'embodiment' of creating on the socially constructed text of the South African body, *South African Theatre Journal*, 24: 1, 105–124.

Lutterbie, J. (2011) *Toward a General Theory of Acting: Cognitive Science and Performance*, Basingstoke: Palgrave Macmillan.

Macintosh, F. (ed.) (2012) *The Ancient Dancer in the Modern World*, Oxford: Oxford University Press.

Mackrell, J. (2007) 'Ultima Vez', review. *The Guardian*, 12 February 2007. Available online at: www.theguardian.com/stage/2007/feb/12/dance. Accessed on 13 October 2018.

Magnat, V. (2016) 'Women, transmission, and creative agency in the Grotowski diaspora', in Syssoyeva, K. M. & Proudfit, S. (eds), *Women, Collective Creation, and Devised Performance*, Basingstoke: Palgrave Macmillan, 221–235.

Masso, G. (2018) 'Disability in drama schools – study reveals extent of under-representation', *The Stage*, 11 July 2018. Available online at: www.thestage.co.uk/news/2018/disability-in-drama-schools-study-reveals-extent-of-under-representation. Accessed on 13 October 2018.

Matthews, J. (2011) *Training for Performance: A Meta-Disciplinary Account*, London: Methuen.

Mayhew, H. (1968) [1861] *London Labour and the London Poor – Volume 3. The London Street Folk (concluded)*, New York: Dover Publications.

McCaw, D. (2011) *The Laban Sourcebook*, London & New York: Routledge.

McClelland, D. (2018) 'And The Best Actor Goes To…', *Metro*, 23 February, 31–33.

McEvenue, K. (2001) *The Alexander Technique for Actors*, London: Methuen.

McNamara, C. & Coomber, N. (2012) *BME Student Experiences at Central School of Speech and Drama*, York: Higher Education Academy.

Meisner, N. (1992) 'Strange Fish', *Dance and Dancers*, July 1992, 10–13.

Merleau-Ponty, M. (2008) *The World of Perception*, London & New York: Routledge.

Merlin, B. (2001) *Beyond Stanislavski: The Psycho-Physical Approach to Actor Training*, London: Nick Hern Books.

Merlin, B. (2003) *Konstantin Stanislavsky*, London & New York: Routledge.

Mermikides, A. & Smart, J. (2016) 'Doing what comes naturally?: Women and devising in the UK today', in Syssoyeva, K. M. & Proudfit, S. (eds), *Women, Collective Creation, and Devised Performance*, Basingstoke: Palgrave Macmillan, 253–267.

Merrifield, N. (2014) 'More than 75% of actors earn less than £5k per year – survey', *The Stage*, 28 May 2014. Available online at: www.thestage.co.uk/news/2014/05/75-actors-earn-less-5k-per-year-survey. Accessed on 13 October 2018.

Mihailova, M. (2016) Collaboration without representation: Labor issues in motion and performance capture, *Animation: An Interdisciplinary Journal*, 11: 1, 40–58.

Mirodan, V. (2015) Acting the metaphor: The Laban–Malmgren system of movement psychology and character analysis, *Theatre, Dance and Performance Training*, 6: 1, 30–45.

Mitchell, R. (2013) *The Body Politics of Acting in Contemporary Britain: An Examination of the Role, Agency and Experience of the Actor's Body in the Context of Training and the Business of the Performance Industry*, University of Kent: unpublished PhD dissertation.

Mitchell, R. (2014) Seen but not heard: An embodied account of the (student) actor's aesthetic labour, *Theatre, Dance and Performance Training*, 5: 1, 59–73.

Mitra, R. (2015) *Akram Khan: Dancing New Interculturalism*, Basingstoke: Palgrave Macmillan.

MoCap Vaults (2016) *Interview with Gareth Taylor* [video], London: MoCap Vaults. Available online at: https://youtu.be/UfKOmuAAufA?t=124. Accessed on 13 October 2018.

Murray, S. (2003) *Jacques Lecoq*, London & New York: Routledge.

Murray, S. (2010) 'Jacques Lecoq, Monika Pagneux and Philippe Gaulier: Training for play, lightness and disobedience', in Hodge, A. (ed.) *Actor Training*, London & New York: Routledge, 215–236.

Murray, S. & Keefe, J. (2015) *Physical Theatres: A Critical Introduction*, London & New York: Routledge.

Nascimento, C. (2008) *Crossing Cultural Borders Through the Actor's Work: Foreign Bodies of Knowledge*, London & New York: Routledge.

National Theatre (2014) 'What is a Movement Director?' [video], London: National Theatre. Available online at: www.youtube.com/watch?v=KY-gWqj-FIk. Accessed on 13 October 2018.

Nicol, P. (2016) 'British theatre casts a wider net for talent', Culture magazine, *The Sunday Times*, 31 January 2016, 10–11.

NoFit State Circus (2018) *About*. Available online at: www.nofitstate.org/en/about. Accessed on 13 October 2018.

Novack, C. (1990) *Sharing the Dance: Contact Improvisation and American Culture*, Madison, WI: University of Wisconsin Press.

Ockham's Razor (2014) *Ockham's Razor*. Available online at: www.ockhamsrazor. co.uk. Accessed on 13 October 2018.

Orbach, S. (2010) *Bodies*, London: Profile Books.

Orozco, L. (2013) *Theatre & Animals*, London: Red Globe Press.

Pirelli (2016) 'The future of cinema, according to Steven Spielberg'. Available online at: www.pirelli.com/global/en-ww/life/the-future-of-cinema-according-to-steven-spielberg. Accessed on 13 October 2018.

Pisk, L. (2017) *The Actor and His Body* (4th), London: Methuen Drama.

Pitches, J. & Aquilina, S. (eds) (2017) *Stanislavsky in the World: The System and its Transformations Across Continents*, London & New York: Bloomsbury Methuen.

Radosavljevic, D. (ed.) (2013) *The Contemporary Ensemble: Interviews with Theatre Makers*, London & New York: Routledge.

Rawlins, T. (2014) 'The developing approach to screen acting training at GSA/University of Surrey', unpublished conference paper, Theatre and Performance Research Association annual conference, Royal Holloway University, 18 August 2014.

Rée, J. (1999) *I See A Voice: A Philosophical History of Language, Deafness and the Senses*, London: HarperCollins.

Risner, D. (2009) 'What we know about boys who dance: The limitations of contemporary masculinity and dance education', in Fisher, J. & Shay, A. (eds), *When Men Dance: Choreographing Masculinities across Borders*, New York: Oxford University Press, 57–77.

Roach, J. (1993) *The Player's Passion: Studies in the Science of Acting*, Ann Arbor, MI: University of Michigan Press.

Rogers, A. (2014) Asian mutations: Yellowface from *More Light* to the Royal Shakespeare Company's *The Orphan of Zhao*, *Contemporary Theatre Review*, 24: 4, 452–466.

Rogers, A. & Thorpe, A. (2014) A controversial company: Debating the casting of the RSC's The Orphan of Zhao, *Contemporary Theatre Review*, 24: 4, 428–435.

Rudlin, J. (1994) *Commedia Dell'Arte: An Actor's Handbook*, London & New York: Routledge.

Sandahl, C. & Auslander, P. (eds) (2005) *Bodies in Commotion: Disability and Performance*, Ann Arbor, MI: University of Michigan Press.

Schafer, E. (1997) 'Review of Flesh Fly by Graeae Theatre Company', *RORD*, 36, 113–15. Available online at: www2.warwick.ac.uk/fac/arts/ren/elizabethan_jacobean_drama/ben_jonson/volpone/stage_history/professional/1997graea e?xdoplain=true. Accessed on 29 August 2014.

Schechner, R. & Wolford, L. (eds) (2001) *The Grotowski Sourcebook*, London & New York: Routledge.

Scott, J.-A. (2012) Stories of hyperembodiment: An analysis of personal narratives of and through physically disabled bodies, *Text and Performance Quarterly*, 32: 2, 100–120.

Shepherd, S. (2009) The institution of training, *Performance Research*, 14: 2, 5–15.

Sienaert, E. (1990) Marcel Jousse: The oral style and the anthropology of gesture, *Oral Tradition*, 5: 1, 91–106.

Sierz, A. (2017) 'An introduction to Frantic Assembly', *Digital Theatre Encyclopedia*. Available online at: www.digitaltheatreplus.com/about-us/table-of-contents/theory-criticism/written#encyclopedia. Accessed on 13 October 2018.

Sigal, S. (2013) *The Role of the Writer and Authorship in New Collaborative Performance-Making in the United Kingdom from 2001–2010*, Unpublished PhD thesis: Goldsmiths College, University of London.

Simpson, N. (2016) 'Natalie Simpson: Living as a chameleon', Black History Month blog – Royal Shakespeare Company, *RSC Blogs*. Available online at: www.rsc.org.uk/blogs/black-history-month-blog/natalie-simpson-living-as-a-chameleon. Accessed on 3 November 2016.

Smith, M. (2013) *Processes and Rhetorics of Writing in Contemporary British Devising: Frantic Assembly and Forced Entertainment*. Unpublished PhD thesis, University of York. Available online at: http://etheses.whiterose.ac.uk/8379/1/Processes%20and%20Rhetorics%20of%20Writing%20in%20Contemporary%20British%20Devising%20-%20MARK%20SMITH.pdf. Accessed on 13 October 2018.

Snow, J. (2012) *Movement Training for Actors*, London: Methuen.

Sperb, J. (2012) I'll (Always) Be Back: Virtual performance and post-human labor in the age of digital cinema, *Culture, Theory and Critique*, 53: 3, 383–397.

Stanislavski, K. (2008) *An Actor's Work*, London & New York: Routledge.

Stephens, S. (2002) *Port*, London: Methuen Drama.

Strasberg, L. (1987) *A Dream of Passion*, New York: Plume.

Sulcas, R. (2017) 'Andy Serkis: The War for the Planet of the Apes star on how performance capture is "the end of typecasting"', *The Independent*, 10 July 2017. Available online at: www.independent.co.uk/arts-entertainment/films/features/andy-serkis-war-for-the-planet-of-the-apes-performance-capture-end-of-typecasting-a7833676.html. Accessed on 13 October 2018.

Syssoyeva, K. M. & Proudfit, S. (eds) (2016) *Women, Collective Creation, and Devised Performance*, Basingstoke: Palgrave Macmillan.

Tashkiran, A. (2016) 'British movement directors', in Evans, M. & Kemp, R. (eds), *The Routledge Companion to Jacques Lecoq*, London & New York: Routledge, 227–235.

Tashkiran, A. (2017) 'Introduction', in Pisk, L., *The Actor and His Body* (4th), London: Methuen, iv–xxix.

Taylor, G. (2015) *Interview with Mark Evans*, unpublished. 17 April 2015.

Thorpe, A. (2014) Casting matters: Colour trouble in the RSC's The Orphan of Zhao, *Contemporary Theatre Review*, 24: 4, 436–451.

Trueman, M. 'East Asian actors seek RSC apology over Orphan of Zhao casting', *The Guardian*, 31 October 2012. Available online at: www.theguardian.com/stage/2012/oct/31/east-asian-actors-rsc-apology. Accessed on 13 October 2018.

Tunstall, D. (2012) *Capturing the Moment: The Use of Motion Capture in Actor Training*, Lancaster: PALATINE.

Turner, J. (2004) *Eugenio Barba*, London & New York: Routledge.

Watson, I. (1995) *Towards a Third Theatre: Eugenio Barba and the Odin Teatret*, London & New York: Routledge.

Whyman, R. (2008) *The Stanislavsky System of Acting: Legacy and Influence in Modern Performance*, Cambridge: Cambridge University Press.

Wright, J. (2006) *Why Is That So Funny: A Practical Exploration of Physical Comedy*, London: Nick Hern Books.

Young, I. (1990) *Throwing Like a Girl*, Bloomington, IN: Indiana University Press.

Zaccarini, J.-P. (2009a) 'Languages and codes; how circus meets other arts' (conference paper). La Breche: Le cirque au croisement des frontières *Circus at the crossings*, Conference (April 2009).

Zaccarini, J.-P. (2009b) Fragments of a Circoanalysis, *Den Inre Scenen: Psykoanalys & Teater*, Denmark: stiftelsen för utgivning av teatervetenskapliga studier.

Zaccarini, J.-P. (2012) 'Circus as death writing', available online at: www.academia. edu/8141130/Circus_As_Death_Writing. Accessed on 13 October 2018.

Zaccarini, J.-P. (2013) *Circoanalysis: Circus, Therapy and Psychoanalysis*, Stockholm: University of Dance and Circus.

Zarrilli, P. (ed.) (1995) *Acting (Re)Considered: Theories and Practices*, London & New York: Routledge.

Zarrilli, P. (2008) *Psychophysical Acting: An Intercultural Approach After Stanislavski*, London & New York: Routledge.

Index

Printed by Printforce, the Netherlands